# Celia's Room

Kevin Booth

POBLESECBOOKS

Poble Sec Books

ISBNs: 9788461540976 (Ingram Spark print) / 978-0957655140 (epub) / 9788461553518 (mobi) / 9780993229862 (KDP print)

www.poblesecbooks.com / www.kevinboothart.com

# Contents

# Praise for Celia's Room

**If you like Kerouac or Isherwood you will love *Celia's Room*.**

If you know Barcelona you will find the descriptions and characters complete-ly authentic. I could almost smell the Gothic barrio.

I picked this novel up on a Sunday morning, intending only to read the open-ing salvo ... I didn't put it down until I'd finished it five and a half hours later. It is gripping, intelligent and deeply sensual but also witty and fast-moving. I found it utterly compelling.

... moments of naive joy are cracked open by prejudice, poverty and an under-current of menace. ... packed with shady eccentric characters and sharp poetic im-agery ... passages of almost scholarly historic reference and beautiful expositions of particularly poignant works of art that give the plot a rich cultural context.

It's also funny and very very entertaining ... worth reading. I hope this is an author worth watching out for.


**... successfully captures Barcelona's gay zeitgeist**

Nothing is quite as it seems. This book rejoices in ambiguity and ambivalence, successfully capturing the zeitgeist of Barcelona in the period when the optimism and openness precipitated by the restoration of democracy in Spain was fading as the ETA terrorist campaign continued to take lives, political corruption was exposed by the uncensored media, and the city began to undergo massive redevelopment for the Olympic Games of 1992.

The author's knowledge and love of Barcelona are clear from his vivid descriptions of places, architecture and ambience.

... language so alluring and sensual as to qualify as genuinely erotic, without being pornographic.

As a meditation on sexuality, I found Celia's Room insightful and thought provoking. ... and at times laughed out loud. This intelligent and entertaining book is fun, and definitely well worth reading!

## As far as language goes it's one of the more beautiful books that I've read.

## Quite an unusual book ... it kept me up late

This is an extremely poignant book describing a period in Barcelona's history before it became such a tourist destination as it is now. I was lucky enough to visit the city a couple of years before this book is set (1988) ... and I remember a few wonderfully chaotic nights as take place between Joaquim, Edu, Narcissus and all the other wonderful types who spill out of these pages.

... quite an unusual book but a great read and it kept me up late ... a beautifully compelling read.

## I want to visit Barcelona!

... very descriptive, the main character's relationship with his father was really moving ... quite different to anything I had read, sort of a thriller... the character of Eduardo ... had some great lines! ... Definitely worth reading this one!

To Ria, John and Lesley
and to Evan

# Joaquim I

*"Hire idiots to paint with cold light and hot shade."*

—William Blake

Taking on the house in Barcelona was an idiot's idea. Well, I knew that... as soon as I signed the contract. But there was that thing in me, a kind of niggling, or wilfulness... It was like I wanted to believe in it so strongly, as if taking on a place like that represented exactly who I wished I was...

It's clear now that I'm not... that sort of a person. Or maybe it's simply that the heart stuff, those things that define me... on the journey to the surface, they somehow get changed. See? Already I'm getting lost. Yet I know the only way I can do this is tell it like it happened... My version.

Nineteen-ninety was the year, though it started the November before. We were pruning the vines. It's a time when the mountains, my *serra*—iron hills that flake and rust into the dried blood and dust of the Ebro valley—are godlike—as if I believed in that.

But the vines, I do believe in: twisted veins that crackle and pop, gold and red across hillsides; dead leaves shimmering; it's early Cézanne, Monet's cathedrals in autumn. And in the light, I believe: sky of ice, such a sharp blue it could cut you. I get so... Looking at the mountain range on such a day, it's something in my bones, my veins, which shines out of my body's sweat. If this is confessional, it has to be my own story.

Dad and I, cutting back to the rootstock. I am feeling all this, but he is blind. Doesn't he love the land? When I'm this way, I can't speak, my throat constricts. I hate anyone who could violate this... cathedral calm. But it doesn't seem to affect him. He babbles as if he were frightened, running from the silence with words, any words, stupid words that spill from him and stain the air. Yellow sounds. Corroding into the rusty urine stains on a mattress. Yeah, I used to wet my bed. Till I was around twelve. Confessions. I'm not the son Dad wanted. But I'm the only one.

The words are twisting again. This is not what I want to talk about. My father has nothing to do with this. Nothing at all. He might as well be dead. I'm just trying to explain how, why, I came to Barcelona, how it all happened. Celia, Eduardo, Narcissus... and the house. If Dad is important (which he isn't; every time I see him now, he's smaller, sadder; I find it hard to believe I was so afraid; more and more, he's just an old man). If Dad is important, it's because I wanted to get away, from him, from the village.

Pruning, feeling all kinds of mixed-up things as we work, and that intense, throbbing force of nature around us that's screaming to be expressed, or worshipped. A single bright day in the whole of eternity and that moment is worth more than everything he has ever said in his whole life, or will ever say. We work in parallel. He's on one row. I'm on the next—we're pacing each other. It gets the job done quicker, stops you slacking off. He's talking. I'm trying not to listen, but his words—the statement—sound like they have shot from the ground like a missile, the way a bright-winged bird blasts soaring into the air; or how it gets shot down, falls bloody, thuds to the earth and creates a silence, just like that:

"Joaquim, you need to find yourself a girlfriend. People are starting to talk."

People are starting to talk. People. Who? My father wants me to do what people want. They are more important than my father's son. I would if I could, but I'm not going to do what I can't. This was the problem.

I look at him. He concentrates on his work, unwilling to slack off. I stare at a particular vine, thinking about the old stock, new wood and which runners I want to leave on for next year. The twisted trunk is a puzzle I can't work out. We were pacing each other, but Dad is ahead of me now. He doesn't say anything else, has stopped talking, head down to his work. The air is clear again, fresh, no stains on it yet it tastes like stale nicotine to my lungs. I breathe it in like a smoker, straighten my back, look towards my battered *serra*. The range appears purple, like a bruise.

"Get a move on, or we'll be late for lunch."

And he begins again, blabbering, like before. Yet I know it has all changed. This land is dead. Nature has shut herself in the hills. Early winter. I feel hard sods under my feet, bend myself to the labour.

Narcissus and Álvaro had me clocked from the moment I bought them their first beer. I have that look about me, must do. I look in the mirror—though I hate them, am tired of them rather. I don't care what I look like now. Yet I see this look. It must shine from kilometres away, saying "Going cheap: dumb idiot. Great chance for a swindle. Discount on social retards today."

I don't really look Iberian. Not typical. People think I'm a bit weird. I've always had a thin face, pale though I tan a little in summer. I don't like the beach. Benissola—that's my village—is more inland.

Biggish eyes, kind of googly, slightly Arabic in shape. I'm not saying Arabs have googly eyes; they don't. But I have slightly Arabic eyes, and they look googly on me. I just want to be clear. My hair is black, but my eyes are blue—clear blue, shockingly blue. I'm about sixty-five kilos—not that that's important—and when I came to Barcelona, I was nineteen, in nineteen-nine-ty. One—nine—one—nine—nine—zero. Barcelona was crucial. Think of all the things that happened: Barcelona, nineteen-ninety. Six years after nine-teen-eighty-four. We were cynics. There must be some kind of numerological significance—I don't know—all those ones and nines will work themselves out. They would add up to... One plus nine equals ten, which is one plus zero which is one, like in Tarot... the one is the fool. The idiot's number. Me. If you went and asked one of those Tarot-dealers sitting at her folding table under Plaça Catalunya, that's what she'd say: look me in the eye; large, gold-hoop earrings tangling in her curling hair, her lipstick so threatening, that curvaceous, steaming pink; she'd say, "yes, it's you, Joaquim; it's your number, the fool's number, number one".

So we came in from the vines and sat down. Mum's serving. Chicken, roasted with pine nuts and prunes. She can feel it coming on, always knows. Dad's silent. So am I. I take a drink of water. Only Dad drinks with his dinner. Mum hates him for it. The sentence, when it comes, floats easily out over the table, taking us all by surprise, but me most of all, so many times I've imagined saying it; and here it is :

"Dad, I want to go to Barcelona, to university."

He begins to eat, chewing slowly. We all do, as if I had never said it. But his answer arrives with dessert: egg flan.

"I was down at the Marc de Set with Tomeu. You know what he said?"

"Tomeu's a drunk. If you spent less time with him, we'd all be a lot better off."

Mum is trying her best to avoid it, knows the storm is coming. Can she steer him off course? Dad ignores her. It's an argument they've had out. He won't be drawn, and continues:

"He said he thought the worst tragedy that could befall a man was to have a son who was a faggot."

And if he's your only son... Mum kind of squeals and goes to put the coffee on. I keep eating. It's because I haven't had any girlfriends. Dad used the word faggot, *maricón!* No, I haven't had any girlfriends. I can't talk to them. I can't talk to anyone, boys either. That was what was so special about her: we talked. People say I find it hard to mix. That sounds like my school reports: 'finds it hard to make friends / needs to socialise more'. I don't need to socialise more. I just need to be left alone. I need them to stop trying to make me into something I'm not. I need to get on with what I want to do, make my own life.

"Dad, I want to go to university."

"So you can become one of those poofter intellectuals? Things are bad enough as they are."

"No. I want to study art."

That gets a laugh out of him. He sits there until the coffee comes, eyes creased, tears streaming down his cheeks, laughing… laughing, laughing, laughing. Mum standing at the table with the scalding coffee pot:

"Shut up, Pere."

He dries his eyes.

"Not with my money."

He wants that to be the end of it, but it can't be. He doesn't see that I'm offering him a way out. If I'm so shameful to him, this is a way I can at least get out of his sight. I can't remember if I was thinking that then, or if that was a thought that came later, the bitter solution, a way of camouflaging his anaemic son. But the buzzing is starting, the buzzing is real, when the world seems to hum, to tilt and to sing. My inner me, where things are real, draws in, draws up knees to his chest and wraps his arms tight about himself. The rest of me is floating on this singing rage, like on a magic carpet hovering in the silver air. Words rise up, tumble from my throat: a crystal stream, a vicious cataract. The two of us seem to dance around the dinner table. The words, the words. They glow ruddy, a net of heat ensnaring us, our anger keening, high-pitched around about. Within the whirlwind, he raises an arm, but I am striking out and feel a shuddering clout shake my body. Shadows dim my vision. My flailing arms are trying to reach those two shining points of black, his eyes, dark, that still seem to smirk, laugh at me, and to laugh again.

Then Mum's soft bulk is between us like a bucket of ice water in the face. Her roar douses the fire. I turn and leave the house.

I don't remember where I went. Though I have a memory of the heat of that blow throbbing against my cheek. It wasn't the first, but I remember the tenderness of it. An aching pain extending through my left cheekbone right up to the hinge of my jaw, a ringing in my ears; it hurt to swallow; my skin glowed as if sandpaper had been rubbed across it. I must have walked, as I used to, up and down the hills, among the long tendrils of dry vines, blood throbbing in my cheek. Maybe I swore I would kill him; in fact, I'm sure I did, but doesn't everyone swear some kind of bloodthirsty vengeance on their parents once in a while? It doesn't mean anything, isn't one of the real things.

So what does this have to do with Celia, with what happened? I'm coming to that, coming to Barcelona, the house and everything that happened that year: one—nine—nine—o—Fool's year. My year.

# Eduardo I



*"He who inhabits that bull's hide stretched between the Júcar,*
*Guadalete, Sil and Pisuerga rivers... hears it said with certain fre-*
*quency: 'This has real duende'."*

—Federico García Lorca, "The Duende: Theory and Divertissement", Havana,
Cuba, 1934.

D ad used to say Spain was a woman you had to slap around a little before
she'd give you her best. Those were other times. I prefer "that bull's
hide stretched"—not that I ever knew it. Never knew her real... *duende*. Good
metaphor though. Spain is skin pegged under a harsh sun, bloodying the sand
with gore, stripped from a bull brought to its knees by a quick thrust through
its pumping heart. But Lorca was pushing deeper, for its essence, that "subtle
bridge that links the five senses to that centre of living flesh, of a living cloud, of a
wild sea, of love freed from time"—this is *duende*. Like everything great Spain is,
everything that's diseased in her. I arrived late. Damage done.

I reckon I'm a good person, more or less. Not that I've never done anything
wrong, but I mean I prefer normal to weird, up not down, to be on the right side.
Yet down among the *friquis*—a Spanglish term that's a carry-all for every kind of
hippy, fag or weirdo— down there, going into that mansion in the Barrio Chino
was...

An example: you're looking at a painting, one of those Medieval ones. There're
all sorts of things going on ... it seems innocent, people eating at a banquet,

servants pouring pitchers of mead, dogs squabbling over bones in the rushes underfoot and kids playing at knights outside in the castle courtyard. It all looks normal, romantic even. Villagers washing clothes, cooking, making bread... a perfect school textbook reproduction.

Then you look closer: a worm is squirming out of an apple sitting on the table. More are infecting the pot roast. You realise the servant bringing the food has a goat's tail, or is cloven-hoofed, the people sitting at the banquet have alligator claws, fish-heads, insect bodies... the entire scene is writhing with obscene mutation, as if nature had gone berserk. The dogs are really copulating and are, in fact, human, but bestial at the same time. How could you ever have thought they were animal? And those children... goblin types, are torturing some poor sod on a rack... In the distance, the burning sea of Hell frames the composition. It's all been transformed... Yet it's the same scene, you get me? It's just you, who have changed the way, the intensity with which you're looking at these things.

Is that the right idea? I don't mean before and after, more simultaneous... It always felt weird at the mansion. They had no clue, living as deep within a parody of Spain's essence as kids dressing up in clothes that don't fit. Revelling in degeneration, their parties were like some lost Dante's underworld, divorced from reality outside. I wouldn't have given a rat's arse about them... if it weren't—well, if it weren't for Françoise—but if it weren't that they breathed—that whole pack of politically correct misfits—breathed it in a way I never felt, even the night I heard el Cabrero singing true *cante jondo* in the evening shadow of Granada's cathedral. *Duende*. It makes me want to crush something.

Maybe Barcelona was not where I should have been. Dad was a big flamenco man, Camerón de la Isla always on the tape deck. In Barcelona it's hard to hear good music. Too full of bad garage rock and politically correct, pop-trash wankers floating around. I should have headed *más al sur*, to Granada, Cádiz... I was not in the right place, or arrived too late.

I'm not claiming I'm el Cabrero, but I reckon we all have it. It's what gets you up in the morning, keeps your heart pumping, gives you the urge to fuck. That kind of pulse you can't describe, it just boils up from your balls, the way you're feeling, your soul... that is *duende*.

The whole situation here, the thing I want to get straight, is that I didn't choose to mix with them. They are not my people. I represent a different kind of Spain. And so, what is my excuse? I define myself as a man. But it isn't that simple. All these factors come into it... what you've been drinking, smoking... but other stuff—you know? Like a feeling in the air. The rhythm of the night.

So I was drawn to them. Which makes it sound premeditated... And I hated them.

I had been dating this babe for about a year—Françoise—electric black hair that spat its phosphorescent wake back though your fingers like dancing dolphins. Sensational. But this is not about her. This is the whole story of our nights... the night. An indefinable experience: a black bull endlessly bleeding, stamping and scattering its hot rubies uselessly.

***

In Calafranca, the shimmering day recedes to lilac as the evening *fresca* enters our flat bay. The cool slides past cables, clinking on mastheads, waking you up, taking you back: beach summer evenings of cheap rum and first sex on the sand. But I remember even earlier nights, free from guardians, roaming the rye. We were happy; happy just with beers bought at the supermarket, drunk warm among the ruins of the Roman fort as the sun set behind the hills. Or round the point at Can Isart. Isart had a blind right eye and couldn't see we were underage, just knew we must be adults by the way his old till chuckled as it gulped our parents' hard-earned pocket money, *la paga semanal*.

Sabrina. Ri. Closest thing I have to family here—real family, I mean. How to describe her—indescribable. In your face. In your dreams. Whatever you think first off, you'll be wrong. Because she's quiet. But tough. That's her defining characteristic. And very cool. You have to be cool to know how to do coolness without making a scene. Before you ask, don't go there. She's like my sister. We both ran in the foreign brat pack of Calafranca de l'Empordà village—indifferent parents who let us loose on that not so defenceless seaside town every summer. Ri was the only one who could keep up with me... in loads of ways.

It's summer. Back when we were about nineteen. Two in the morning is not late for Spain. We're sitting on the beach and our debate is on how to fill the next few hours: "We can go round to mine if you want: crash... or just chill out, listen to music."

"But your Mum..."

"They're up in Figueres for the weekend... some arts thing."

Theatre and percussion troupes have commandeered the castle for a charity fundraiser in aid of... Who could give a rat's arse? But my Mum wanted to be there, which was fine by me. We could stay out of each other's hair that way.

"Yeah, I'm actually pretty tired..."

Though I'd prefer to go to Ri's, where there'll be the maid laying on breakfast in the morning (as opposed to my folks who just stuff the freezer and leave extra cash in the commode. The downer is that her parents will be home. My place represents freedom. We're talking about this as we leave the beach. On the esplanade we meet Cal, José and a few others, who have a bottle of Scotch and some hash they need help with. We decide on my place as the best option.

We're heading up the hill from the village, the group of us, and we see this figure wobbling down the street. Swaying in her heels. I assume she's drunk. We get closer, the guys start pissing themselves. It isn't like I'm a saint, but my hackles rise.

"Hey gorgeous! How about a kiss?" and Cal grasps his *paquete*: "Luscious Lips! Come and suck on this!"

"Forget that little *pito*, baby boy. I'll wait till you're out of nappies."

Cal gets angry: "Fucking animal! Freak!"

"Lay off, Cal! Take it easy."

He turns on me: "You like that, do you? What are you?"

I laugh. "Get away!"

"You do!"

There's like this flash in my brain and I feel my knuckles connect with something bony. My hand's on fire, but I can't show it. Cal's on the ground. I've hit him.

"Bastard!"

"Fuck off! You're drunk. Prick!"

I look around for the she-male, not quite sure what I'm going to do. I don't want to have anything to do with it, but it's lurched off—knew what was good for it, is already fifty metres down the street. Then it's gone around a corner. What the fuck was that doing in our village?

Cal's standing, panting, fists clenched. We're squaring off, but it feels weird, like I've been trapped on the wrong side of a civil war.

"What the fuck was that?"

"I don't know. Why'd you stand up for it?"

"I didn't. I didn't know what the fuck it was."

"Okay, let's go look for it, teach it not to hang around this town."

I know Cal's just acting like a kid, that he won't, but I want to see how far he'll go: "Sure then. Come on."

But now we both know we won't. The moment's passed. Sabrina takes my arm as we turn to walk up the hill: "Don't worry. That was cool."

I can't get my thoughts straight. But that thing floats through the haze... and a word. I'm confused. A drunk drag queen has nothing to do with el Cabrero. Yet my guts are all churned up, the striking out at Cal—a good punch though I've never boxed—

adrenalin getting messed up with a throbbing sense of... that's what it is: some Hulk-like force pulled out of primeval slime; a basic, single-cell, grim will to live, a sense of survival—at the least. And that's the chord linking the fag and flamenco, that same base urgency to fuck or to kill. *Duende*. Or a misguided sense of Anglo-Saxon chivalry. Right.

# Joaquim II

*"The beggar said, 'A poet is the soul of his country.'"*

—Graham Greene, The Power and the Glory (1940), Penguin, 1971. p. 113.

There's a painting, I don't know which museum it's in—the Prado, or the MoMA in New York. I saw a print when I was little and the impression it made in that split second expressed me exactly: my mind, the way the cogs go round in there. I see things in a very specific way. It's a view of Toledo, painted about sixteen-something, early on, by Domenico Theotocopuli. The Greek. The amazing thing is the light—liquid, *sub-aqueous*—that buffets the whole scene. It wells from every pore and crevice. The city looks tiny, a drowned graveyard, its silver walls and towers like tombstones on the luminous expanse of an emerald hill. Trees glow vividly, fluid as kelp, while the manmade constructions have that bleached, abandoned quality of bones. A cathedral spikes the skyline bravely, but clouds billow dark in the sky beyond. Nature is gathering this storm. Its swirling heaviness dominates the whole top half of the painting, ready to crash down and sweep all that architectural flotsam into the gully below.

For some reason I always think of this painting when I remember coming to Barcelona, a feeling like impending doom, like night rushing down, even though my emotions were entirely contrary on that journey. Barcelona that year was a city at night. That's how I see it, or maybe a city underwater. We were all swimming through this bubbly, twilit murk, an episode from *Man from Atlantis*. Daylight memories are sparse: chilly, late afternoon sunlight down at the port; the glimpse of a gold-neon sun rising above the Ramblas as I stumble home to bed.

Listening to this, it's saying what I want. Why doesn't this happen when I open my mouth? I was on my way into life, but Dad had won. I was leaving my village yet fulfilling his plans, no longer an embarrassment. Still, I think I was happy. Maybe I would paint. I might find a way.

"Barcelona! They tell me it's some city, eh?" The old man smiles at me as his wife unpacks their lunch on the worn leather seat.

"Don't know, I've never been there before."

"Unbelievable! What an adventure!" She chips in:

"And you're only nineteen! What does your mother think of that?"

"I'm not a kid. I'll be two hours away on the train."

"We went as far as Reus, didn't we, Ignasi? That was plenty big enough for us: on our honeymoon... before the war..."

But we are rolling into Tarragona and they have gone pale and speechless, peering out the window at the size of this metropolis. After that provincial capital, the track closes in to the coast and the Mediterranean is revealed.

"Unbelievable!"

I realise this is a first for them. Their close accents mark them as from Gandesa, a few villages down from mine, where the widest body of water they'll have seen is the Ebro River.

It throws more and more buildings up in your face. That coast makes you wish you could see its whole performance before all the houses were slammed down, wedged in among these rocks; before they blasted away the delicate pinnacles, concreted sand, bulldozed the pines. Each bay is now lashed tight, shackled between two cement arms, the Mediterranean barricaded behind breakwaters. Pre-poured concrete cliffs jostle, huddle around each curving corpse of bare-ribbed beach, ogling the naked sand, shouting it into acquiescence in a coarse babble of mismatching architecture—from the ancient Greeks to Franco's developers and then Pujol's cronies—the flotsam of empires encrusted onto a bleached skeletal coast. You know no-one will gaze on the naked flanks of this shore ever again.

Yet the sea is ecstatic in gold and azure glitter, clattering as happily among rococo promontories as between concrete-block borders. Effeminate. Natural. (Two words that are less opposite than you think.) I stare at the horizon as the tracks click-click me towards Barcelona.

I think of who I am. At what point did I stop being the son my father hoped for? I am—more than ever now—shockingly aware of what makes me different from him (I despise him, would detest to be him) yet I clearly remember my father's love, am unaware of any signpost of transformation within myself. When did I start being the person I am now? When did I stop being the one he loved? When did he see it? Before I did? Was I that unaware? How does such a change take place—so slowly and unnoticeably, not betrayed by any single situation, yet inexorable, real, inescapable—when you awake one morning to discover who you are, that you are an outsider?

The couple leave me at Sitges, where they redeploy with their suitcases onto the platform and into her waiting sister's arms.

"Have fun!"

"We'll have to keep our wits about us here, lots of odd foreigners, they say!"

As the train pulls out, the water loses its lights, dulling to the same sharkskin as El Greco's clouds, shadows condemning land and sky. I think about the ways you could achieve that light: brush or wash, oil or acrylic?

At Bellvitge, I stare at tower blocks thrust up against silver-edged cumulous formations. They are just house-crates stacked in piles against smoky billows, while an air of desolation rolls across the landscape. It's intimidating. Dad and my village are now far behind. We approach Sants, our track joining others, both train and metro, until we become a river of silver rails, channelled into the dark canyon of the station. Then we are in darkness, a manmade catacombs, heavy pillars smirched with soot supporting who knows how many tonnes of concrete above our heads. Platform activity is intense, people climbing aboard while I struggle to heave my heavy suitcase out the door. A strong smell of railway friction burns my nostrils. It is an acrid taste of night that will become this city's signature to me, far more than modernist churches or Mediterranean seascapes will be able.

My first days in the city—January. University proper didn't start till September, but I would be doing a bridging course to prepare for the University Selection Exam. Dad had agreed to pay for Agricultural Engineering, refused to talk about Fine Arts: I had to think of the family. His pathetic dream. I would take over from him, give some meaning to his lifelong toil among the vines, the olive and the almond trees, make something of his concern. But his generosity went as far as paying my fees—a lump sum in an account with my name: Freedom. Still I needed to find some sort of a job fast. I'm not going to describe the mechanics of how I settled, the cousin of ours who put me up that first month. She wanted me gone as soon as humanly possible, which became my priority.

Meeting Narcissus and Álvaro now seems inevitable, but during that first period in freezing, smog-draped Barcelona, I traipsed the streets, exploring its different neighbourhoods, scuffed along curbs, kicked through crowds of pigeons in the plazas and wandered down shadowy alleyways. It didn't seem as if I would ever make any friends in that giant dusty city. In Barcelona you couldn't raise your head because of the dog and pigeon shit covering the cobbles.

Needing to escape one day, I pushed down through the Gothic quarter, crossed the main road—dodging diesel-farting lorries, cars, scooters and desperately wailing ambulances unable to advance—and walked down to Moll de la Fusta. On worn stone steps, I sat looking into the oily water, counted the dead rats floating belly-up. They call it the city with its back to the sea. For me it was the city with no work, no mountains, no place to live.

I was looking for a room, desperate for a job—that was my story. Really I think I was looking for a Life—my own or any—some substitute for my *serra*, which I couldn't identify either in the buttress-like bulk of Montjüic hanging above, imagining defunct canons eerily ready to fire once more on the town, or in that righteous, religious monstrosity that crowned Tibidabo—church and fortress eternally wedded in a pact to press down hard on the struggling souls below. The city lacked the arid, open hillsides spaced with olive and almond trees that I craved.

I was after... hoping to re-establish a private essence I was still unaware of missing. I was searching, so it was logical I should find something, even if Narcissus and Álvaro were not what I was thinking of.

# Eduardo II

*"Everything that has black sounds has duende."*

—Manuel Torres (according to Lorca), on hearing Falla play his own nocturne
"En el Generalife")

We were the elite. Superlative. Post-event I see my childhood like I was a blind kid jay-walking on the A-7. All that moving back and forth—plane trips, changing schools, sorting out languages, falling face-first into unknown peer groups, sussing out the gloating faces in the new class, who to befriend, who's looking for a scrap... Looking back from here though—ripe old age of twenty-three—I can appreciate what I learnt: the diplomacy of a diplomat's son.

Probably because we returned every summer to Calafranca—wherever else we lived that year—my Spanish was fluent from before I can remember. My sister and I—Ri too—we more or less grew up native. Like the rest of the crew who invaded the village from July to September—from different parts of Spain, France, the UK, Zara and I the only Aussies—most of us spoke at least a couple of languages. We knew how to behave—misbehave—almost anywhere. At fourteen I'd learnt what not to say in front of Dad's diplomat mates. You could take us to meet Mum's charity cases, or the publishing execs Ri's parents hung out with; Cal's Dad was a technician with el Español; José's was in politics. By the time we were eighteen, we knew which fork to use plus half a dozen ways to do a line in a hotel bog

***

One day Ri and I are sitting drinking horchata—most refreshing drink in the world, up at Plaza Calvo Sotelo—since renamed by Catalan politicos to Francesc Macià. They've changed everything like that since the *Caudillo* died, but my family still use their true names: Avenida del Generalísimo Francisco Franco and that.

We're on a terrace. Autumn. Eighty-eight? Ri's hair's fluttering in the breeze—she wears it short, but it's fine and blond, loves the wind. Always make me feel I want to grab her scalp between my fingers... I never do. She would freak. Two chicks are sitting nearby. I'd noticed them because they're so obviously lezzos. Not that they're screwing on the table or anything, but you can tell. This kind of indifference, or hardness, you know? I can just tell. I look at Ri. And it was the way she was not looking at those two that made it click: lightning bolt. I realise I'd always known.

"You should get yourself a girlfriend."

She grows incredibly still, pale. Analyses the end of her straw with intensity. I've never seen her so angry. But I still push: "Why not?"

"Sorry?"

She remains absolutely calm, except for a sort of shudder. She looks at me. I think she's about to break my nose: "I'll make my own choices."

"Just a suggestion."

"Fuck off, Edu! Alright?"

There's a pause before she asks: "Where did you get that idea? Doesn't it gross you out?"

"Why should it?"

Then a really long silence.

"Not if I could watch."

"What a dick you are!"

But we've lightened the mood. Like we've saved something. Or have we? I'm feeling like I'm on the wrong side of that civil war again.

"You want something tonight?"

Ri has a solid connection to the purest snow ever to leave Columbia's tropical climes.

"Is that a question?"

Ri counts as family, more than my mother even—though that isn't hard. We can say stuff like that and stay solid. Like the summers spent in Calafranca. A constant.

I was born in Tanzania, Zara in Canberra, because that's where Dad was working, but we grew up in Melbourne. If I feel more Spanish than Australian, it's because of our beach house. Those summers were a ritual. Zara and I would pack everything up and cross the world twice a year. Mum wanted to make sure we wouldn't lose our heritage. She's from Sant Just Desvern, outside Barcelona, though she met Dad in Zaragoza, where he was stationed. He was from Huesca, a town in the Pyrenees; military first, followed by the diplomatic service.

Then there was the black period. I was sent offshore till Mum got her marbles together. High school in Barcelona from fourteen to eighteen years old, living with my aunt Leo, Mum's sister. Mum and I both had to find our way of going on. Anyway, everything's fine now. Mum lives with Paco: he and I had our battles and made our peace a long time ago. It's *aigua al molí*, or grist to the mill as the Catalans say.

I learnt Catalan at high school. No comment. Spain is Spain. I don't have time for those separatist whiners. In Australia, we have different states but we're all Australian—and proud of it. I started Uni in Melbourne, then returned here on an exchange programme. I decided to do my Masters at their business school. Private. Good place. That brings me to Barcelona, nineteen-ninety.

By that time Spain had pretty much lost any pride in herself which—whether you like him or not—the Caudillo had instilled. You talk to the old people: they say things worked better. By nineteen-ninety, the Socialists were giving you a grant to grow a blue pimple on your dick, so the country was getting deeper into debt all the time—their left-wing idea of solidarity with the third-world. F-ing A-place to party though.

"Why don't we check out a lezzo bar?"

"What?"

"Come on, it'll be fun. I love lesbians."

Ri didn't seem keen, but I could tell it was something she really wanted. She didn't know any lesbians and wasn't going to go alone. Cool. This was every guy's fantasy.

***

It was off a side street on another side street off Gran de Gràcia. Discreet. Didn't say "Lezzo Bar" on the door. Even had one of those keyhole shutters to check you out, decide whether you were their stuff, like an American speak-easy. Ri had to thrust her mug in front, bulldog-butch, though I think she's more what they call a lipstick lesbian. They opened up. We'd decided I'd pretend to be gay: I was beyond gay, I was shitting my panties. These were dykes like you only read about in scary movies: heavy women—in more ways than one.

If you want it straight up, it was pretty gut-wrenching. But Ri and I know how to act in any situation, right? So I minced a bit, tried to pout around like that lispy one on *Are you Being Served*? I don't think I got a single smile in the whole place, but then lesbians are not known for their sense of humour. Even the few bona fide gay boys looked at me like I needed a pre-frontal lobotomy for humanitarian reasons.

That's okay, I wasn't there for them. Just keeping Ri company. The things you do for your mates. About a cuba libre and a half later, I was calm enough to look around. The place was packed. You couldn't even raise your cigarette to your lips yet it was thick with smoke. Shithouse DJ, but everybody dancing. It's always the way.

I'm not taking the piss, but once we started talking to those girls... they were okay. Smart and fun. Though a proportion of them... you just didn't want to scratch the surface because it would be scary what you might find. The energy, the aggression, so honed, like one of those old steel clock springs wound too tight, just waiting to be released and lash out with the violence peculiar to hardened steel and shrapnel and those things: blind rage that tears human flesh into slabs of meat. So we had a lot in common.

But it was my first ever experience of... just being the wrong sex... simply wrong.

Ri was in ecstasy. Well, kind of shy—I found out afterwards that was because of me—but she was connecting and getting seriously cruised. I think by closing, she was sorted about the lezzo scene.

"So, your name is Edoo, you are Australian and Spanish; not gay but you come here for your friend?"

It's heading for three and I'm scrunched against the bar with this girl, her Kate-Bush-style hair pinioning me. Only the French wear black night and day from birth to oblivion and get away with it. My bar stool has become an electric chair, but I wouldn't leave it for the world. She's been asking for my deepest confessions on life. One fishnet-clad ankle is twisted around my calf:

"I 'ave a confession."

"Shoot."

"I am not gay, but I am interested."

I'm too drunk to decipher that; just take it to mean what I hope: "Wanna hear my confession?"

"Please, confess."

"I am highly interested."

The rest is history. That's how I met Françoise. In a gay bar, pretending to be a fag, where I only went so my lesbian friend could pick up.

Ri met a girl that night. But it didn't go anywhere. Though she started going back regularly. I wasn't up to going there again. Quite soon after that, she met Marta, this short, kind of jolly chick, who was an artist, had her studio in an *okupa*, or squat house, which is where this story kind of takes off, that year, nineteen-ninety, in Barcelona.

# Joaquim III

*So tall with prophecy:*
*Dreaming of cities*
*Where often clouds shall lean their swan-white neck.*

—Stephen Spender, "The Pylons", 1933.

Narcissus is the one. Álvaro only has any definition in relation to his partner, so that's where I'll start.

His name's pompous and bloated, but says it all. The Caribbean. A different way of using language, of naming your children: Ulysses, Hector, Virgil. History lived and carried along in the hot blood of new sons, along with its violence, aware of not-so-ancient slavery firing every breath, an intuition of casual cruelty—inflicted and suffered—in his gait. He was tall, nappy hair tied tightly back, skin pulled back, tight across his skull. For moments I could call him handsome, but those were like shadows flitting across his face. He had a stare that went beyond confidence—arrogant, insolent, unyielding. Two thick canines erupted like fangs from his mouth when he laughed, his face creasing back behind them, just his eyes visible: liquid crescents that kept a fix on you. Watching and observing. That was Narcissus' way of life. He always wore a suit and tie—I rarely saw him more relaxed—formal wear as a foil to his blackness before police and authority.

"Red wine, a glass."

"Fifty pesetas."

Even the cheap bars are expensive in this city. I take my drink and sit down in a corner. When Narcissus and Álvaro come in, I think they have stepped out of the nineteen-thirties. Narcissus, in front, is dressed in his traditional brown tweed suit, set off by his camelhair overcoat on one arm and a silver-handled cane in his hand. Álvaro is wearing a knee-length leather coat and a wide-brimmed felt hat pulled forward over his eyes. Perhaps I am imagining these details, but this is the sense of them I remember. Narcissus' presence is one I immediately feel. He looks at me and I feel that I, we all, are intensely alive, potent. That's the feeling I get. His eyes kind of capture me, sweep me up in their regard, register and catalogue me while he takes in the whole bar, greets the owners, arranges himself at a table, his cane displayed across the marble top. I crouch a little more on my stool. I suddenly feel more vulnerable, yet special as well. That was the thing: in the few brief moments when he entered the bar, he made me feel special, as if I was the kind of person for whom all my dreams could suddenly become true. That's why taking on the house... wasn't silly, really. It might have been why I suddenly opened up to him, when I never tell anyone anything. With him, I felt like a real painter because he treated me like one.

They notice me, I register out of the corner of my eye. I think they're making comments, but I can't hear what. At one point I creep to the bar, ask for a refill. Then Álvaro is behind me, alongside, leaning casually on the counter, big and physically close. He orders more drinks, looks at me—wide face; pallid, spotted forehead; oval, green eyes.

"Hola," he says.

"Aah, hola!"

I'm always kind of surprised when anyone speaks to me directly. It takes me a while to get over it. I don't quite know what else to say. I look at my drink.

"Do you want to keep drinking alone, or would you prefer company?"

They have picked me out. Narcissus' infallible instinct has told him I could be useful, or fun, I don't know. Maybe I should have focussed less on Narcissus' presence and more on other people's reactions. Whatever. But I nod and come and sit at their table. We introduce ourselves.

At first I am acutely aware of Narcissus' colour. Not that I'm a racist. I don't think. Yet the truth is, I'd never met, or talked with such a *really* black man before. I don't count the odd, monosyllabic exchanges I've had with the *Moros*, the North Africans, who come round every year for the harvest. I feel way out of my depth, dominated by his all-encompassing, fluid, loud, sophisticated, brash—I can't describe it—*exotic* presence so close. I think he picks up something of that, is capable of reading my thoughts almost before I've even conceived them. I can't get my jaw to work, to speak, can't relax. Narcissus makes it worse by putting me immediately on the spot:

"I can see you're from the HINterland, JoaQUIM."

He rolls his words like pastry in his mouth, like chewing something, elaborately stressing HIN-ter-land as if it is some highly significant code word he wants me to pick up.

"Uh-huh. Uh, Benissola, below Reus... How did you know?"

"Because the weather is so CALM."

I look at him, bewildered, and then gulp half a glass of wine. He smiles:

"It is OBVious you stay well aWAY from the sea. For if you went near it, the storms on the Mediterranean would never aBATE. The ocean would be consistently teMPESTuously jealous at not possessing such a miraculous colour as that BLUE in your eyes!"

He howls with laughter, long and triumphant. The whole bar takes notice. For thirty seconds we swelter under a spotlight of public regard. I smile self-consciously. I feel red-faced and stupid. I'm not used to such larger-than-life interaction.

"Didn't you like my piROpo?"

"Uh, yes...um, thanks."

"Aaaaaagggggh!" He expels his breath like a steam train. "These Catalans! These Catalans, you are so self-EFFAcing. The piropo, this witty, flirTAtious COMpliment, was inVENTed here in Spain, yet you have lost all ability to UTILise it in your conversation."

His affirmation makes me boil. I'm not sure what annoys me most: the idea that we can't give piropos, or his assumption that Catalonia and Spain are synonymous.

"Of course we can!" I blurt sharply, responding to the first.

"I don't THINK so. Try me." And he smiles sweetly.

I realise that now I have to come up with one, a piropo grand enough to defend the whole of Catalonia. My brain whirls. All I can focus on, the only element that registers to me at this moment is the colour of Narcissus' skin, but I CAN'T, I think (subconsciously mimicking him). I can't talk about his skin colour. I've got to find something else, but still my mind keeps on, stubbornly building phrases: as black as... as brown as... chocolate, mahogany, copper? Terracotta? Brick? Newly turned ground? I fix on his hands. Long and elegant. The tips, delicate. Not working hands like my own, hardened and scarred from earth and vines.

"Your hands..."

He kind of flutters them up between us, like a butterfly tripping across the table.

"You have the hands of a... you could be a piano-player."

"Well, that will DO, but I think it proves my point about Catalan PIROPOVERTY."

"Hands of a harpist which... for which David could kill a thousand... Turks... or, GOLIATHS."

I feel foolish, can feel heat rushing up my neck into the roots of my hair.

"Ahh, now we are getting SOMEwhere. Thank you very much, YOUNG Joaquim. You have made me feel just like a Greek EPHEBUS in the full flush of his finest conquest!"

Álvaro raises an eyebrow. I have no idea what he is talking about, but know there is a sexual innuendo somewhere in there—the Greeks had a certain reputation... Domenico Theotocopuli, and all that. Narcissus just laughs and changes the subject.

"Do you see that PHOTOgraph?"

The walls of the bar are covered with framed photos, some new, most in sepia tones, fifty or sixty years old, older: street scenes with trams; people formally grouped on café terraces, in saloon-type bars, around upright pianos, and some music-hall scenes. However, the photo Narcissus points to, though black and white, and faded, is strikingly different. The composition holds only two figures, an adolescent boy and a Dalmatian dog. The dog lies on its haunches in the foreground, attentive to somebody above it, outside the left frame. The boy, alabaster skinned, standing to the right and dressed in a dark swimming costume, is drying his dishevelled, blond hair with a towel, looking down at the dog. Light muscle and defined bone structure create dark-bright contrasts up and down his body, counter-pointed by the dog's dappled coat. Above, cloudless sky. Below, a calm bay ringed by sun-scorched hills. The photo breathes that hot midsummer serenity only existing in memory.

"That photographer was a man who KNEW how to give piropos, surprising for a German. They are such a CONSTRAINED people. There are so many contraDICtions."

What I would give to be able to create such a composition... There is a slick, mechanical SCHLUCK.

"I've known some wonderfully unconstrained Germans on occasion."

As Álvaro finishes speaking he slides his camera, a Canon, back under the table. Absorbed by Narcissus' presence, I wasn't aware of him focussing. Narcissus looks annoyed.

"You mean WULF? I wouldn't call him unconstrained, more of a plain slut."

Álvaro smiles.

"He is rather, isn't he?"

"Then perhaps that is something the GERMANS have in common with the MURCIANS."

There is an uncomfortable moment as I knock back more wine. At the same time that I locate Álvaro's accent, I suspect that Narcissus did not want the conversation to head in the direction it has gone. I try to change the subject:

"Who's the photographer?"

"A genius." It is Álvaro. "Herbert List."

Of course. Now I can locate that bay: Baltic Sea, summer of '29, Weimar Republic. That boy, now eighty, must be dead from old age, or killed in the war. Then suddenly I'm off, gushing, wanting to reveal my knowledge, proud that I know SOMEthing about SOMEone. Part of me stands back, shocked that I'm babbling like this in front of people I hardly know. But I can't keep it in; this has always been my passion. The divine decadence: pre-war Berlin; Second Spanish Republic; the English in their universities—hypocritical yet so elegant; Josep Foix, my favourite poet. I notice my thoughts are starting to streak ahead of my words, that my words are failing, but I can't stop because I have to get it out... And the idealism, the politics—fascism, Marxism, anarchism—so clear, so pure in their choices: right or wrong, good and bad, when you could pick a side and fight for it. I can see they're getting edgy, their eyes shiny, but I have to finish... What it would have been like to live through that time—the misery... yet pulsating in a golden light, the epic halo of a single moment... These are my heroes. That look of complicity Narcissus and Álvaro exchange—I'm ignorant of its meaning—is lost on me... almost. Narcissus interrupts:

"WHY are you so interested in PAINTING?"

I stop. But I realise my words had already stopped. It's happened again: inside, so clear yet the thoughts don't make it to the surface. Bigmouth strikes again...

"Uh, It's how... the way I express... what I feel, what I see..."

Narcissus gives a grunt that suggests he is only halfway satisfied by my answer, that there is something there he would like to dig up at a later stage. I don't know whether to be irritated he has dismissed my earlier passion so easily, or thrilled he seems to find me INTERESTING in some small way.

"Our Catalan painter, notre petit Miró, pining for the good old days. RePUBlicans, all three. Álvaro and I are now off to a party. Would you like to acCOMPany us?"

A party. I've been in Barcelona only a few weeks. I'm being invited to a party! Part of me wants to mumble a negative, get up from my chair and escape out the door, avoid contact. Yet the real me inside is bursting with pride. Here I am, in this big city, doing it—I'm doing it! Living! Becoming the kind of person I believe I really am, should be.

When we go to pay, there is a small glitch. Both Narcissus and Álvaro realise they have left their money behind. Apparently, Narcissus thought Álvaro was carrying money and vice versa. I put money on the bar with an assurance I was ignorant of in myself, grateful to be able to show appreciation in some way for the friendship they are offering.

Out in the open air, it's been raining and the cobbles are shiny and dark. I'm aware of us as a group, an impressive image: Caribbean boulevardier, Murcian photographer, Catalan painter (maybe). It's like I see us from afar, the vignette we must cut, as if we embody the cultural icons of some mythical cosmopolis: Isherwood, Spender and List; Lorca, Dalí and Buñuel. Walking three abreast along Nou de la Rambla, Narcissus—camelhair coat flapping out to either side—leads, both walking and in conversation. He sweeps us along, even Álvaro, talking, talking about many things. I am relieved, feel freshly urban, part of a smug group, for the first time, an uplifting feeling that hints at confirmation of indefinable yearnings... to reach out, enact some legendary fiction.

# Eduardo III



*Until the day she tumbled*

*And broke herself in two*

*And her legs and arms were hollow*

*And her yellow head was hollow*

*Behind her eyes of blue.*

—Louis MacNeice, "Christina", July 1939.

Till the thing with Zara and Dad, people used to think our life was a fairy tale. False. We've always had the ready; not rich, but enough. Fame is something else. People think they go together, but that isn't true. Fame sucks. Without money it's like alcohol-free beer—just an attack on your privacy. Zara, my sister, is the only one in our family who even got close. It didn't help her though. Fame doesn't make you immortal.

Though we'd never been famous... that didn't stop my Mum from trying. From about six months old, my pudgy face started to appear on baby food adverts. By the age of three, I was the king of toddler's fashion. There wasn't a lolly, toy, or pom-pom hat down under for which I didn't strut my pre-school stuff.

It all kind of faded away though. Not that I wasn't good, but Zara, she was the best. In a few years, she had pretty much out-haloed my six-year-old expertise. Maybe I was getting a bit long in the tooth, bitter and twisted by the cruel world of fashion, but I remember that when Zara entered the room, it was like this rosewater light washed over everything. She was an absolute cherub, blond and rosy, chuckling, gurgling her way through every casting session. You couldn't be jealous. You knew you were in the presence of a natural. I kept modelling till I was about... fourteen... but it was no longer the priority. She was. I made it my business to look after her. Being her big brother seemed a much more important role than my own life in the limelight.

From the age of three onwards, she didn't stop. She went from doing baby clothes to glossy magazine ads. Her first TV appearance happened at seven, on a talent show called Kidz Bizz. She won it, dressed as a swanky Agnetha, lip-synching to Mamma Mia, which had made Abba's name earlier that year with its airing on the music programme Countdown. Zara covered all the bases in cutesy schmaltz and scored herself a role in the children's show Crackeroo Club, on Channel Nine, as Terry Bawdon's little sister, Sally. It was the kind of bracket hosting show that introduced all the other programmes in the kids' slot. She was great. They started her off with adults all around, organising, but soon she was the one asking the questions and calling the shots:

"I bet all our friends really wanna see ya, Terry, wearing your highland kilt, and doing a real Highland Fling! Don't you, boys and girls?"

In the seventies, men didn't dance. They wore Tom-Selleck moustaches, drove super-heated Holdens and drank beer. But when my eight-year-old sister asked, blond hair frizzing around her like a neon halo, away Terry would go, carousing his way into ridiculousness. It seemed like Zara was a dynamo, generating the light that kept ratings high. The whole of Australia was tuning in to watch, and it was this little blond angel they wanted to see.

***

That was Zara. Who's now gone. And Ri's become a lesbian. I met Françoise in a bollera bar. My women. Things happened in eighty-nine that are relevant. Françoise was like the eye of the hurricane—a dark, très-française, existentialist calm that ignited my passion, but kept me from burning up in the night. The lezzo bar happened in December eighty-eight, after Christmas and before

New Year; the twenty-eighth, I think. I know it was before New Year's because I remember being obsessed by Fra's absent presence the whole night—a party up the coast in Roses—aware of not having her near me and wondering whether I would ever be able to see her again. That life-changing stuff.

By Easter she was with me—me and Ri and Marta—which was the first time I met Ri's future girlfriend. All I remember is that Marta's okupa—her squat—was having some kind of anniversary party. B.Y.O: edibles, drinkables, smokeables, sniffables. It's a cavernous room—a nineteen-forties warehouse shop unused since then—furnished with mattresses, church pews and a long, curving, beautiful-but-cracked marble counter top supported on forty-four gallon drums. I describe it because this was our regular hangout for most of that year.

It felt like when Mum took Zara and I to the zoo as kids: the chimpanzees' tea party; only I have to join in. Yet I couldn't give a toss because I'm entrapped by her hair—the fabulous, electric Françoise—and her scent—slightly bitter, like almonds yet washed with an infantile milkiness; her laugh—as if blood were coagulating in her throat, or fine port kept warm there; and those violet eyes... okay, I'll stop before you choke.

***

"I'm devising an installation that I would love to use you in, Edu."

We're drinking Xibeca beer from one-litre bottles, smoking spliffs—just chilling. The light is sacred—church candles in red plastic tubes—fitting as we approach Christmas. Fra and Ri are dancing (they turn me on). I watch my girlfriend's sensuous and heavy hips—yet so delicate on top—swaying and bucking to the bad Catalan rock spewing from the practice amp. Ri kind of orbits in individualistic spasms of angst around her, a fiery meteor centred by Fra's gravitational pull. I'm having fun watching, so Marta's conversation is a distraction:

"Sure, sounds great. What does it involve?"

That's how I find myself one Saturday evening within the month—January, nineteen-ninety—naked as my birthday, slathering sheep's blood on my genitals, preparing to slip into a two-metre-tall, one-metre-square fish tank with Marta, who has also given herself the afterbirth treatment. We're facing an audience of fifty okupas down at her squat. This somehow connotes the original sin and carnal love, a supposed direct attack on the Catholic church. In the end, we just kind of rub our bodies over each other, getting redder and slimier as the music progresses: kind of Jimi Hendrix playing Star Spangled Banner while he gets electrocuted in the bath.

I end up having quite a good time and I'm getting this real buzz. No drugs. Not sure if it's Marta, or maybe something about playing the exhibitionist in front of all those stoned friquis. That is the night Françoise reckons she fell totally in love with me (which is kind of a backhanded insult: wasn't it love till then?) Ri was looking at me with these small black eyes like CCTV lenses while she did that statue-act of hers. Her comment later:

"If that had lasted a minute longer, your balls would have been history."

I appreciate Ri's frankness. But people loved it so I don't know what she was pissed off about. Her girlfriend's installation was a success. And I'll always treasure that memory: Marta and I writhing blood-stained in that fish tank, both our girlfriends watching.

When we came out, we just wrapped ourselves in these blood-stained towels we'd used to apply the calf placenta—it could be the shower wasn't working, or the power was off—and went out to our public. Blood is great! The smell... the real McCoy.

"That was wild!"

"Right on!"

This fag-friend of Marta's, a Chilean intellectual, kind of latched onto me—I must be some sort of magnet—and launched into this spiel:

"Blood-letting, killing a person or animal, whether you use a ceremonial dagger or meat cleaver, spilling their blood, it is supposed to liberate their aura."

"Yeah, thanks. That's fascinating."

"The ancient Micronesians reached extreme longevity because they drank soy milk mixed with goat's blood. In other cultures too... it is known as a Karmic surge. This is the origin of blood-sacrifice. We see it in bull-fighting, feast rituals... It is even the origins of apparently naïve myths like vampirism..."

The smell gets up your nostrils. Like a drug, it inebriates. I wandered around that party, heady on blood, dick half-mast, feeling like a full-on, fucking minotaur. Fra stayed in tow, keeping me honest. It was a total night, rubbing my bloody torso up against all the babes circulating around that okupa joint.

Then it all turned to custard. One moment we're re-enacting some pseudo-sacred blood ritual, the next people are screaming:

"La pasma! La pasma!"

Marta's pulling us deep into the labyrinth. Looking back, I see a flash of gold braid on brown serge. There's a riot of panicking anarchists. The national police. What a moment to bust up the okupa! Meanwhile, the thin-lipped part of my brain is clicking over: who can I call to bail me out? But discretion's the better part of valour here. So I lift Françoise through a half-bricked-up toilet window into Sabrina's arms and then wriggle my blood-stained torso through after her. That January night was a crisp one: running down Hospital Militar after the girls in my blood-soaked loincloth, my goose bumps are cracking the dried blood on my arms. I seriously hope we won't get nabbed because I'm not sure how many phone calls I'll need to explain this one away.

We end up in a chocolatería off Plaça Lesseps. By this time—though I'm freezing my bollocks off—I'm comfortable with this noble savage persona, feel it gives me presence. The waitress seems to think so too. Exuberant with the adrenalin of our recent escape, I'm tempted to flash her a vista under my towel, but Fra gives me a look.

"All my artwork's back there. I'm never going to get it back."

My apartment key, clothes, wallet and credit cards are all there, but you don't hear me moaning.

"We'll go back in the morning, find a way in. They'll have left one cop on the entrance. If we get in the way we came out, we'll be able to pick up whatever we want, you'll see."

"My canvases won't fit through that toilet window!"

"Don't worry, we'll find a way!"

I'm feeling like I want to vomit now. This smell of blood is getting old.

"I need a shower."

"Let's head back to Edu's. He's got a spare room. There's space for us all. Tomorrow we'll work out what to do."

"What bastards! Why did they have to come in, precisely tonight, the night of the party, of my installation!"

"That's what they're like. Bastards. They've probably been planning this for weeks. It's how they get their kicks."

"Happiness threatens them. The whole point is to try to shut down creativity."

"It's nineteen-eighty-four. This is it. It's happening."

"The point is, you don't have to let them win. They only win if you let them."

"We'll find another squat. This is only the beginning, the revolution is coming!" Listening to them, I'm amazed how fervent their assertions echo. I'm just hoping Juanjo's home to let us in.

But that's how Marta became my flatmate: me, Marta and Juanjo, who's a friend of my cousin's from Zaragoza. It was Juanjo who had the lease, but he desperately needed some inspiration in his life. Steerage, I call it. That was where we came in. Fra and I had been going out together for about a year, Ri and Marta a little less. So it was one of those times when it just seemed right to organise a party.

# Joaquim IV

*"O too lightly he threw down his cap*
*One day when the breeze threw petals from the trees."*

—Stephen Spender, "Ultima Ratio Regum", 1939.

"**A**llow me to introDUCE: *notre petit* MiRÓ."

I grew up kind of political. Dad said we're an occupied nation, have been even since... seventeen fourteen. When I was in school, I started reading everything I could about the thirties, the Second Spanish Republic. The few books in the high school library took me about two minutes, but our history teacher, Mr Benach, was a Republican too. He lent me one on twentieth-century Germany, so I could compare the Weimar Republic to the Spanish one. I ended up doing a project on that for him. Plus he gave me translations of Isherwood and Spender and a book of List's work. That's how I recognised that photo. I suppose I do think it might be, was, like, the last great period of heroes, a kind of golden age.

*Notre petit* MiRÓ: the name Narcissus gave me seemed to stick with everyone we met, made me shiver within the possibilities of my own newly revealed persona. With Narcissus and Álvaro that evening, we entered the Rambla and stopped beside a kiosk. Álvaro had seen two friends who were walking up.

The avenue looked naked. I had seen it as a subtle composition of lead-grey walls, dusty paving and the pigeon-spattered green of kiosk roofs—car exhaust smudging everything soft. But the rain had washed this all away. Now, in the night, brash green and red rays shot from traffic lights, ricocheting off table-tops, shop-fronts and the wet pavement. A glare spilt from kiosks, slashing us with fluorescence.

The squat and swarthy Ludovico—though Álvaro tells me he's a dancer—and his companion, Paul—young, impossibly blond, lithe as a shiny reed—greet us: "Hola, my ebony prince!"

"Ludo! TAKE me in your strong arms, WALTZ me off my feet!"

"Off your feet, again, Narciso? Far too in love with life on your back ... any excuse to get your legs in the air!"

While they tease each other, my eye is pulled by the magazine racks, glossy covers reflecting the cellophane-wrapped flesh of both sexes: red-tinged mounds and curves that are nauseatingly explicit. We have nothing like this in Benissola. I turn at Narcissus's shriek:

"You! It's true, isn't it, they SACKED you after your last Cuban tour because you could no longer dance in any position that wasn't a WIDE fourth, HAVANA style!"

He illustrates the pose, legs spread wide, body thrown forward and the cloth of his trousers stretched tight over the rump he thrusts towards us. Then he goes into a moaning, arse-wagging rendition of the way he assumes Ludo "performed" in Havana.

Paul looks peeved. When I ask him where he is from (dredging non-existent social skills from deep inside me), he seems almost ashamed of his nationality: "From everywhere, de todas partes."

But his fluent Castilian sounds strongly U.S. Is he ashamed of his past, or his past of him? Then they've gone, off to find dinner, saying they'll be along later. People eat at any hour in this city. We continue down the Rambla, turn left into Escudellers. Though the streets smell of dog shit and rubbish is piled at every corner, our eyes are raised toward the heights of artistic promise. The dark metropolis sparkles with stardust—or that's how I feel.

Halfway up the street is the Buen Bocadillo, a shawarma bar. Achmed, a Palestinian exile, leaving his Egyptian helper to prepare our food, comes forward smiling towards Narcissus.

"Eh, my Black Daffodil! How are you, my friend?"

He shakes all our hands energetically. Though sweating freely, his hands are fresh, cool and recently washed. He exudes a perfume of parsley, onion, cumin and paprika.

"How is your book coming along, Achmed?"

"Listen:"

The poem he recites in accented Castilian is long:

"This setting sun, a bleeding rose,

Where straight as stems, tank barrels grow,

Western crusades that moralise man,

Are ardent thorns to crucify our land."

Álvaro whispers to me: "He's been working on this for five years now."

"Wounded, voices denied while keen winds sigh,

A people's breath in this lilac light dies.

The desert breeds tank tracks and families disband

While the sun sheds petals on this red sand."

Felipe, cheerful, Chilean. An eternal student in thick-rimmed, Buddy Holly glasses, applauds:

"Have you read Said's book, *Orientalism*, Achmed?"

"No, I haven't."

"Its thesis is so close to your poem... what the West is... Such a beautiful image! I mean the rose is a Persian symbol, so misconceived by the West, kidnapped by colonial powers as their own... a disenfranchising of the other: An Other is an Other is an Other..."

"Well, I am writing about what is happening to my people, my family..."

The lamb in my sandwich is juicy, hot with spices. The blood of Achmed's rose seems to dribble down my chin. I accept a beer. Its fizzy chill washes the fatty taste of meat from my throat, leaving a bitter, pleasant tang. Narcissus then drowns out Felipe's voice, replying to Achmed, his voice a clear tenor striking out into the street's human rumble:

"...Quand il me prend dans ses bras,

Il me parle tout bas,

Je vois la vie en rose..."

When we roll outside again, Felipe has joined us, as well as Miguel—a shuffling, grinning figure, his sharp profile a kind of scruffy satyr—who drills me with intense, honey-coloured eyes and tells me in slurred Andalusian that he lives down in Barceloneta, by the beach. I can't tell whether he's making conversation or an invitation.

We continue up a narrow side street, cross the Plaça Reial. Before reaching the party, we pause in the bar Quique's, cramped and crowded. Sculpted across one wall, a papier mâché satyr. His phallus thrusts fatly out overhead like an oversized coat peg, a couple of quoits hanging from it. Another beer is placed in my hand and I drink. I'm discovering taste, a taste. As if it gives me confidence. Though I'm not reeling, I trip on the doorstep as we leave.

We locate the party—no-one knows the exact address—from its noise, a confused mist of sound drifting down from the sky. An electric buzzer dangles free on a wire dropped from the roof, clipped to a nail on the doorframe by a clothes peg. Thirty seconds after we press it, the street door creaks open, no sign of a soul, just a rope attached to the latch, jiggling frenetically, disappearing up into the darkness of the stairwell. We enter and climb steeply in single file. Five floors up, we come out onto a terrace lit with red and blue bulbs strung between a television aerial and a clothesline. A row of scraggly cactuses line one parapet. The roof is full of people despite the chill January air. White light blazes from a doorway, beyond which are more people. The scene is anarchic and ebullient.

I'm sitting on a wooden crate, a can of beer in my hand, warm. People press and flow around me, talking, squealing, roaring, whispering, gesticulating. Smoke packs the air in dense layers. My head swims. I suck more beer into my throat to ease the rawness. Françoise who is, could only be, French—all in black: black leggings, a black, hip-hugging tunic, electric black hair that sprays in every direction around her, but violet eyes—suddenly sits in my lap and murmurs into my ear in throaty Spanish:

"'Ullo. Are you a friend of Narcissus? And 'ow did you come to know 'im?"

Her eyes sparkle as if she is suggesting that I could only *'ave come to know 'im* by one route.

"In a bar." I say.

"Ah, yes. Naturally, bien sûr."

She winks, giving the impression she knows of a kind of bar I don't, one where more than just drinking goes on. Her weight crushes my thigh, though she seems so petit. But I don't say anything, drinking more beer instead, finding that tonight, this is the answer to most of the unmanageable situations I'm getting in to.

"He is sexy, don't you find 'im?"

I go blank. I don't know her. I don't feel able to confide in her. How can I say out loud I find another man sexy?

"No." I frown. But I do. I do find him sexy, though I don't like men. I know I don't. Admitting I'm a homosexual would only prove my father right. Is that me? Maybe that is me. This party feels oppressive. Blood beats through my temples in time to the house rhythms. I push Françoise off and shakily stand up. My thigh is killing me where her bones seemed to anaesthetise the muscle. I stagger out of the doorway onto the terrace, searching for fresh air which I consume in great gulps, leaning over the parapet and staring down at the street—tiny—five floors below.

Hands grip my shoulders, push me forward. I tense, rear back. Struggle.

"DON'T JUMP!"

It is Felipe. Laughing his head off through his thick frames.

"It's just it's my turn to clean the stairs tomorrow. I'd be hours washing the blood from the street."

"You live here?"

"At the moment."

Mentally I go through the three people I've met, their three large rooms I have found myself in at different times tonight, and can't place Felipe in any one of them: not with Juanjo, professional slob, his hundred and twenty kilos permanently installed in a sagging armchair beside his gin bottle; or with Edu, Françoise's Australian boyfriend, doing his MBA up in the expensive part of town, who even speaks a bit of grudging Catalan. (This here, for me is a strange country, Foreignland, where Castilian, not Catalan, is the lingua franca); definitely not with Marta, installation artist, whose girlfriend Sabrina, English, *très chic-lez*; girlhood summers spent on the Costa Brava, etcetera, wrenched me to my unsteady feet at one stage and pulled me around the room to The Sacados:

¡Belizzimo! ¡Oh Belizzimo!

¡Vamos! ¡Vamos! ¡Vamos!

¡Venga! ¡Aaii! ¡Venga, chica!

Oh, venga amigo,

Vamos al amor,

Al ritmo, ¡al ritmo de la noche!

Felipe reads my thoughts:

"No. My room is the sofa in the living room." He giggles. "I'm looking for a place."

Felipe has a face that reminds me in some way of Munch's *The Scream*. It starts off strong around his eyes—those chunky glasses—with firm cheek bones, but then seems to eddy down randomly towards his weak chin metres below, finally petering out in a wispy goatee. He is incredibly pale, paler even than I am, a complexion making you think of diluted, blue-blood aristocracy. A few freckles force a small rebellion of colour on the pallid skin. His lips, however, are full and sensuous, almost scarlet. He smiles at me.

"So, Petit Miró, why have you come to Barcelona?"

The alcohol's spinning dance dissipates my concentration.

"I want to paint... I want to study..."

"Aren't you studying?"

"After the summer... I'll be doing Agricultural Engineering. I wanted to study Fine Arts... Dad... He wants me to get my degree, then go back and help him on the land. I hate it."

"Can't you change?"

"He's paying."

"Well, Miró, doing what you want in life isn't about doing the right course at university. You decide what you want and take the first step in that direction. Let fate take care of the rest."

"But he won't let me! I don't know what to do…"

"How can he stop you, Miró? He's down in Tarragona and you're in Barcelona. He doesn't even have to know…"

"But I don't have the money. I need paints, I need a studio…"

I swear that was the first time I thought of Dad's money being used for any other purpose than on farming classes.

"Well you've only got one life. You have to decide how you'll live it. Your Dad's had his chance already. He doesn't own you."

Felipe is looking out over the city rooftops. Close by is the straight, octagonal tower of the Església del Pi, looming so close I think I could reach out and touch it.

"I don't know whether that helps. If you want to paint, you just have to…"

But the tower erupts into bells, deafening, drowning his words. We look at each other, amazed. My fingertips on the wet parapet register vibrations through mortar and brick. A deep double note—*bong-bing*… and again… *bong-bing*… four times—marks the hour; then another, heavier bell strikes out: one… two… three…

Felipe and I continue to stare at each other. His eyes seem huge, appear to expand like whirlpools, molten ripples spreading out. We have given up any attempt to speak over the din. It is as if we are frozen together in a fairy tale world, trapped inside one of those tiny plastic bubble paperweights where snow continually falls onto a painted plastic castle… ten… eleven… twelve… As the booms fade away—before I can react—Felipe leans over and kisses me. His tongue, this frenetic slug, struggles to force its way in between my teeth, and his hands grasp greedily at my body. I pull back, horrified, wiping lips against the back of my hand, trying to rub his saliva from my mouth. He gives a kind of spasm, upset and embarrassed, steps back and smiles, sheepish.

"Sorry. You're very beautiful, you know, Miró."

I don't know what to say, shrug.

"Don't think so. It's okay." Because I can see he is getting really nervous, feels like a fool. "It's just, I don't think I'm into that."

"Are you moLESTing notre petit peintre, Felipe? I saw it ALL."

Felipe's face is instantly, violently awash with blood. He giggles through his blush as Narcissus plants himself between us.

"You can't blame a boy for trying… I want… have to…"

And, haggard, stricken, he is gone, pushing through people, disappearing inside. Narcissus' sharp eyes regard me. I am worried about Felipe, didn't mean to offend him. I sense that Narcissus reads everything going through my mind.

"Don't worry about HIM. He is used to rejection. Or he SHOULD be by now."

His laugh is almost nasty. "Our little Miró, only just arrived here and already you are BREAKING HEARTS."

I don't think this is true, but it does make me feel guilty.

"Can I have some beer?"

He hands me his can and I drink, the cool wash of alcohol blotting out any other consideration. His hard, shiny eyes are studying me. He appears as much in control as ever, unaffected by alcohol or drugs. Álvaro is nowhere in sight.

"I think it is TIME you went. You are looking very IMBIBED. I will walk you home."

I protest that isn't necessary. In fact, I was wanting to stay longer, but my head is ringing and I feel myself lurch as I leave the protection of the parapet. I let him steer me through the people, his firm hands on my shoulders, until we are descending the dark, narrow stairs. I have to hold onto the wall on either side to avoid tumbling headfirst down.

In the street again, we walk away from the Ramblas and the bus that should take me back to my cousin's house. He simply says:

"We will pass by my studio. I want to show you something."

On the way, he gets me to talk about myself, describing everything: my village, my hopes, the fight with my father that finally brought me here, my frustration at having to study farming instead of art. We finally stop at a shopfront roller door. He bends down, unlocks it and screeches the door high enough for us both to duck under. It rattles down again behind us. The space is pitch black. Not even a sliver of light comes in under the door, but I can feel that the space is crowded, dim shapes piled high. I don't move, waiting for him to find a switch. Instead he says:

"Give me your hand."

I raise it and, fumbling, mine connects with his. It is warm and firm, grips my fingers strongly. He pulls me through a labyrinth of bulky obstacles. I duck when he tells me to, and stumble behind him, scraping my shin once on some outcropping object. We come to what feels like a division in the space and he brushes a hand up and down the wall until there is a quiet click. Light from a weak yellow bulb throws tall shadows onto dusty furniture stacked up almost to the ceiling.

"What do you THINK?"

I don't know what I'm supposed to be looking at. I cast my eyes over the tables, chairs, benches, restaurant fridges, dressers and kitchen sinks and give a kind of noncommittal "Mmmm".

"All this is my FUTURE! Look at this—everything I NEED: why here there are the complete furnishings for my enTIRE business."

"Your business?"

"My RESTaurant. WHAT you can see beFORE your EYES, this is worth MILlions of peSEtas. Okay, maybe some of it needs to be cleaned a little... look at this DUST, it is disgusting, but you give all this one thorough once-over and you will find it is as good as if you bought it new from the shop. This is what you call SHARP investment!

His eyes have taken on an almost maniacal gleam. He sounds like a prophet as he preaches the incredible worth of what I can see only as junk. His eyes widen and he brings his face within a few inches of mine. I try to look credibly sober.

"But DO you KNOW the best thing?"

I inhale an almost electric, exciting odour from him. The tiny hairs in his sideburns and scarce goatee seem to crackle with elation. He smiles deep into my eyes. I feel weak.

"The BEST thing is that all this…"

His arm shoots out and planes through space.

"…all THIS, was absolutely FREE. ALL collected from the street. You CAT aLANS… You CATalans are so WASTEful. I have stored a fortune here in the perfectly good objects you have THROWN onto the STREET."

I take a deep breath. My head is spinning wildly and I have the beginnings of a shattering headache. Narcissus' breath enters my nostrils. Does he really smell of cinnamon, or is this some creation of my own mind, a fanciful idea of how Caribbean people should smell? I sway.

Then, for the second time in my life (not counting my father), for the second time that night, a man kisses me. Narcissus' lips, soft and full, invite me to keep pressing my own against them. Our kiss, lasts… a long time.

"AAAHH! I have been wanting to do that ever since I laid EYES on you, Petit Miró."

I am confused. Does this mean I am gay… or is it, could it be a phase… Yet for once, I throw my convoluting mental acrobatics into the air as he walks me through a doorway where I see a bed with a mattress and bedclothes. He turns to me and I feel overwhelmed, grab onto his body to anchor myself with both hands as his arms enclose me tight.

# Eduardo IV

*"'Don't you understand?' said the Queen (still speaking to Digory).
'I was the Queen. They were all my people. What else were they there
for but to do my will?'"*

—C.S. Lewis, The Magician's Nephew (1955), Puffin Books, Penguin Books Ltd,
1976. p. 61.

Our party. The idea started as an exorcism, a cleaning out as much as a celebration. We seemed to need it, sort of to spit out the *mala leche*—that sour taste—of the police raid on Marta's squat, and kind of focus things. From my point of view, lately I'd been hanging with too many *friquis* and wanted to flush them from the woodwork as well, close down the circus. I thought I could use the chance to connect with some of the guys from my Master's course. I'd been at Uni over half a year by this time without having really got into the social thing. But it might have been naïve trying to "straighten things out" because after all, a party is a party and it won't go off without music, or the entertainment.

Living with Juanjo, you realise he's a slob: really, he is a slob, but his family are big money, so he always lives in places with lots of spare rooms and isn't too fussed about who's paying rent and who isn't. He's a lovely guy. A large, three-room place, it worked perfectly for the two of us. Then we had Marta move in, which I liked, because she's ballsy and good for a laugh. That meant Ri was round a lot more too, which made it feel like home.

A recent nasty surprise was that nerdy Chilean from the squat was now sleeping on our couch. It turns out he's a friend of Juanjo's. I was getting ready to give him the boot. It's a pain having someone sleeping in your living room every time you come home drunk, especially if you're with your girl. But I decided to hold off till after the party; it's worth having an extra pair of hands for setting up and cleaning up. Juanjo is not much use in those departments. He's a star when it comes to alcohol supply, but decoration and cleanliness are not his forte.

Fra did loads to help as well. That was great because it meant she was there, though if I'm honest I think we just left Felipe to it on the day itself—so he could earn his keep—and actually spent more time making out in my room.

I'm lying on my back in bed while she rides me, entrapping me in that dark tent of her hair, like making love behind a waterfall. Knock, knock.

"He's such a pain!"

"Don't let him in, I'm nearly..."

"Yeah?"

The look on his face was priceless, worth every millisecond, and would probably fuel his desperate fantasies for the next decade, poor faggot. He stopped knocking on the door after that, just went ahead and got the party ready himself.

And it went off. Felipe had done a prime job decorating and Juanjo had made sure there was a first-class bar. Marta was threatening to set up one of her installations, but actually I don't think she was feeling up to it after losing the squat. The only thing that kind of annoyed me was Felipe inviting a bunch of his *friqui* friends. I mean it's not like it was his party or anything. He was just a guest. So about eleven o'clock this Caribbean guy I know from around the neighbourhood—a total con artist—rolls up dragging his entourage—and I mean drag. Ri and Marta were fine with that—they had their own lezzo friends there anyway. But Françoise just went delirious, turned out to be a total fag hag. That's what comes of meeting your girlfriends in lesbian bars. So in the end, our party could have been a study for a Hieronymus Bosch painting.

And then the clock struck twelve. Things were pumping, more people arriving all the time. Our flat is so close to the Iglesia del Pino—Pine Tree Church, as I call it just to piss off those precious Catalans—that it would make Quasimodo jealous. On the hour those bells do a *clong-cling... clong-cling... clong-cling... clong-cling...* then bash out the time with a *clung... clung... clung...* I was standing in the terrace doorway, looking out at the night. There was a kind of swell of party guests spreading in leaden circles from the direction

of the stairs, like a wake or turbulence as those bells began to sound, drowning the music: one... two... three... Fear no more the heat... I don't know why people weren't freezing their bollocks off on the terrace. Four... five... This apparition like the ice queen of Narnia swirls out of the mêlée... or the furious winter's rages... Two full metres tall, throat to ankle in white fur... eight... nine... I was shell-shocked ... eleven... twelve... And there she was before me: Snow White with this dwarf on her arm. It was carrying a motorcycle helmet. Though it didn't register then, Dopey or Sneezy would be important to me. Well, I did say I wanted things to liven up. Las putas had landed.

It was kind of a changing of the guard. The terrace and flat were dense with people. No idea who. Juanjo and Felipe were engaged in this discussion on the virtues of capitalism, or something:

Juanjo: "How do you define a Communist? It's someone who reads Marx and Lenin."

Felipe: "Obviously. 'The point is not merely to understand the world, but to change it' is what Lenin said."

Juanjo: "'So how do you define an anti-Communist? It's someone who understands Marx and Lenin.' Ha ha! Kissinger said that."

Felipe: "'From each according to his ability; to each according
to his needs' was what Marx aimed for."

Juanjo: "I totally agree. That goes along with what Balzac said: 'For the first half of your life, fuck as much as you can; for the rest of your life, make as much money as you can.'"

I like Juanjo when he's on a roll. He loves to stir the smelly stuff.

Two hands clamped on my shoulders from behind and I was choked by a musky perfume: roses stamped into slush. Strong fingers pushed me forward and sideways while that pale, fake-fur tower swept by. I had just been elbowed aside in my own home! But as she passed, she looked down.

"Hello, Sweetie! What's your name?"

"Edu. I live here."

"Lovely to meet you, Edu. What a fabulous party!"

Felipe pushed his head out from under her wing: "Edu, this is Celia."

"Hi."

I admit I wasn't up to dealing with a guest like that. I left her to Felipe. A home invasion by Hieronymus Bosch was a bit more than I could take. Grabbing Françoise, I kind of flung her into the nearest room, which happened to be mine. Fra's great, knows exactly what to do. Straight on her knees, both hands at my belt. Fingers scrabbled with the buckle, then she had it. Hands messed in her hair, I was already swelling as she pulled down my jeans, daks, took me in her mouth. And we just stayed like that for a while, both of us launched into a sublime nowhere with the sensations, letting it happen. Then I got serious. Fra knows how to follow in the game. Loves it when I'm a bit rough, or forceful, pushing her onto me, making her gag. I pulled her up and kind of manhandled her backwards before me. She falls onto the mattress. Ripping down her leggings and panties, I go in, just wanting to do the business, rooting for my life, loving the feeling of her flesh holding me close, hot, gripping me. God! I love her I love her I love her! I love Françoise. We move together, rough, but in harmony. And I want this to last forever, but the sensations are often just beyond me. Still I hold off, resist, concentrate on the rhythm, examine every beautiful pore in her skin, lick every patch of it, especially under her jaw, where that line of shadow is a trail of vulnerability, do sums in my head—two plus two are four and four and four—continue up behind her ear—are eight and—her eyelids—eight and eight, sixteen—nostrils, the delicate comisura of her lips where they join—and thirty-two... our sweat mingles... sixty-four... I'm panting, breathing, deep into her... a hundred and twenty-eight... drips from my forehead onto her face... I wipe it off, she licks my fingers... two-fifty-six... five-twelve... must be ready to burst... one-thousand-and-twenty-fww... then I can feel Fra starting to come, moaning and bucking; I dig my fingers into her mouth and she's biting down on my hand... hard so I know the marks will be there tomorrow, but she's ready... so I let myself go... and again... my orgasm surges up out of me as the floodgates are thrown open... again... and again... God! I love... you! Till I lie inside her, feeling her holding me tight, so right, locked in each other's arms, like our skin has been heat-sealed into a single piece of rightness.

We lie for ages in the dark, listening to the roar of the party going on outside. I feel... like a little boy lost, a twelve-year-old. Just done something really sneaky and fun with a mate. We laugh together at our own bliss, of just being together in our warm cocoon of reality.

"God, I'm thirsty! I'd kill for a beer."

"Do you want I get you one?"

"In a minute."

I don't want her to move, don't want us to break apart ever from that clinched love-hold we're gripped in. I just want to keep feeling myself a part of Françoise, in her and around her, that the universe is fine, just the way it is. But the door opens, a light clicks on.

"Oh sorry! Didn't know you were there! I'll just get my jacket."

The door closes and we hear words passing from one drunken mouth to another:

"They're having a *quiqui*."

That's broken our mood.

"I go get you a beer, mon chéri."

The party swallows Françoise up. I lie on the bed. What would Zara be doing now if she was alive? Would she have stayed in Oz, or be over here with me? Maybe doing Uni, or who knows where her career might have taken her? If not for the accident, I might not have gone to high school here. Why wouldn't I have chosen a university in London or the States instead? That would have meant not meeting Fra, not having this polvo just now... My mind keeps reeling backwards, down through all the possible 'what-ifs' that can be spun off the accident... What if Zara and my Dad hadn't died. And suddenly I'm so sick of our family euphemism, "the accident". I want to go out there and kill someone.

# Joaquim V



*Unhappy poet, you whose only*
*Real emotion is feeling lonely*
*When suns are setting;*

—WH Auden, "A Communist to Others",1933.

When I'm left alone in the house—evenings I don't have to work, but no money to go out—I sit in the patio, which must have been elegant once. There's a fountain with a statue: a dolphin that winks, its rusty, dried lips sucking on a clogged water pipe. Poseidon heads, horns of plenty, *putti* and palm leaves in bas-relief mould the four bevelled sides of the basin, half an octagon built into the outer retaining wall. This creature—eighteenth, nineteenth century?—its original water source blocked, was later fed, once upon a time, not so long ago, by a brick pipe cemented diagonally down the wall from the rainspout off the kitchen roof. Someone's *chapuza*, a makeshift attempt to bring back its former glory. Yet the nineteen-seventies, prefabricated pipe now seems one age with the *fin de siècle* construction. They have married each other. In the pink and blue Mediterranean twilight, two ages, both old to me, have signed a pact. I watch them as dusk drops—the pipe's thin finger forever yearning towards the dolphin's curving flukes—wondering if I've got it in me to smash their bond, restore the fountain to her youth of elegant singleness, widow her. The cheap, ugly pipe seems to grin, its lascivious finger pointing.

There are also plants on the patio: tough, deep-green, fibrous things, whose terracotta pots are gradually cracking and flaking into the slowly-pulverising floor tiles. Dust to dust. It'll be a job. And what to do about the kitchen? This crumbling outhouse, in theory the most important room in the house—from an immediate survival point of view—is just a rusted mess of split bricks. Its roof beams are termite-hollowed and sag, ready to convert to dust. The wood range is a hulk, disintegrating in flakes, wind from roosting pigeon wings scattering its old iron across the room. There is a shallow marble sink, a bronze tap with a protruding tin-pipe nozzle, but no water. The only water is in the bottom basement. I haul it up in saucepans. No water, no electricity, enough money in bills owed to be able to run my parents' house for a year. It will be a major fight to get the electricity turned back on again.

Instead of dealing with all those things though, on those first nights alone, after the light fades on the patio, I wander through the empty house with just a candle to light my way.

Entering the tall French windows, you find yourself in one of the largest rooms, the ballroom is how I think of it. Its ceiling must be five metres high. Hand-carved beams form a grid-work in... Mudéjar style? Gold-embossed ceiling roses where each beam crosses—like stars gleaming in the firmament, or firelight flickering on a hundred tigers' eyes. Great strips of wallpaper—luxurious silver-leaf and moss-velvet, a design of urns and vines—hang like jungle creepers down the walls. The mildewed plaster glows behind like bones pushing through rotting skin. At shoulder height, a varnished, panelled frieze runs around the room in some noble wood—maybe it's walnut. Then from there to the ground, the walls are tiled in *azulejos*. Peasants and beasts, hand-painted in porcelain white and blue, hunt each other, dance, prowl or growl from the borders of rustic adages, penned illegibly under the glaze. Sometimes a knife-tip, a claw, or a glassy eye has flaked, where the surface has cracked and crazed over time. The floor is a sombre parquet, scratched and worn, still solid, but it's seen better days.

In this room we'll hold—once the others move in—our own banquets, in honour of those lords—industrial textile barons—who might once have held court here. Narcissus presides the long oak table, seated at its head, Álvaro to his right. Celia sits at the other end—it hardly seems I should call it the foot—and I always try to sit next to her, on her left. Yet the night when that is not so is the night she had a special guest.

He takes my place. I move one further along. Opposite him sits Eduardo, and next to Edu, facing me, his girlfriend Françoise. On Françoise's other side, scowled at by Narcissus, yet whose complicity with Álvaro has wheedled him a seat, is Wulf. Wulfgang is a bright-cheeked German boy of twenty-two, sparkling blue eyes that make you laugh just looking at him and whose ash blond hair shoots up in short, rigid tufts. He can't really speak much Spanish, let alone Catalan, but, quick at catching my gaze when I don't think he's looking, winks at me as I drop complete spoonfuls of lentils into my lap. Miguel, from Barceloneta, and R amona, *la Madrileña*, who makes her living as a nightclub photographer, take up the other two places.

We wait and wait for Celia to appear. Finally she makes her entrance, looking almost tomboyish in jeans and a cashmere sweater. The new arrival makes her visibly nervous, and she thoroughly lacks her normal confidence. He has stopped in the city just overnight on his way up to France to visit another of his daughters. A small, thin, bony man with an enormous beaked nose, he must be in his late fifties, or early sixties. His skin is dark and leathery and his eyes small and deep set. Sitting silently to her left without saying a word the entire evening, or even looking up from his plate, he just scowls down at his own reflection in the stew. Celia talks for him, fielding every question aimed his way and, after too brief an answer, throwing the conversation away in another direction. Just once, Françoise tries in French:

"Sir, did you get a chance to visit the magic fountains of Montjuïc?"

"No. I am afraid I am only in Barcelona for just one night. Tomorrow I go."

She insists: "But how is it possible that your daughter gets such poor treatment? Couldn't you stay a little longer, see something of the city with her?"

"Hah! My daughter!"

We sit in silence, shocked at that expression of disgust. For once Celia is mute, stirring her coffee endlessly, around and around. I decide I hate him, that man whose only achievement in the whole world is having fathered her. The dinner finishes in near silence. Celia shows him to a spare room where she's made up a bed. I want to talk to her and wait near the door of the ballroom for her to return. I hear the click of her footsteps leading back, but instead of joining us they stop and then I hear the front door slam. She does not return until very late that night. Her father awakes and leaves early in the morning. I don't know whether they even say goodbye to each other.

I moved into an empty house. Narcissus and Álvaro stayed on for two weeks at the place they were until Felipe finally insisted on reclaiming his apartment. In seconds it seemed the house was full of people. Narcissus drew a continually changing entourage about himself. That's what attracted Celia, that multitudinous whirl. Plus she needed somewhere fast. But at first, I used to wander round the mansion on solitary pilgrimages, entering every space, wondering how that wreck of a mansion could be made liveable.

Sliding open the heavy double doors in the ballroom, panelled and brass-handled, to the left of the patio, leads you through into another salon of the same size. Here the ceiling, the same basic network of beams as the ballroom, is entirely of gold. Intricately carved griffins and peacocks gird the ceiling frieze. Lions' faces stare down out of sunburst manes at the intersection to each joist. The walls are also decorated like the ballroom yet the hanging wallpaper strips are deep crimson and gold. Cedar wood panelling replaces the azulejos from shoulder height to floor level all around and another set of French windows leads out onto the patio.

This room, the way I remember it, contains only one item of furniture: a heavy, carved bedstead—fake, I think—resembling a Louis XV. I know this bed though because it's the same one Narcissus led me to, that night, behind the shopfront roller door. This room became his and Álvaro's bedroom. It is Narcissus who should continue this tour.

The early afternoon sun wakes us, pulling me out of the dark, straight under the lash of my beating temples. I feel like I want to die. The first thing that comes to mind, lying facedown on that mock-Louis XV double bed, is that I am the unfortunate object of that typical school joke: 'If you woke up one morning, with a terrible hangover, saw a man sleeping beside you, a jar of Vaseline open next to the bed and your arse was really, really sore, would you say anything to your girlfriend?' I feel like the butt at that moment, as if I've been constipated for a hundred days, then everything got pushed through at the speed of an express train. I don't see any Vaseline, but two used condoms have been tossed to the dusty floor. Narcissus' heavy warm thigh lies across my own. I wish I could forget, but remember every single detail of the previous night; exactly what I did, from first entering the bar with the List portrait through the party and on until the moment I closed my eyes, willing myself to dive deep into unconsciousness away from that throbbing at my temples. I remember every single thing that we, Narcissus and I, did. He now groans and reaches for me in his sleep, folding me into his arms. I lie there, my body curled into his, feeling the warmth from his chest and legs spreading into my back and thighs, the weight of his sex between my buttocks. The contact is erotic in a dozy, relaxed sort of way. I could stay here like this for the rest of the day, absolutely immobile, trying not to disturb my hangover.

Unexpectedly though, Narcissus sits up, unconcernedly pulling the blanket off us both. All my self-consciousness returns in a flood of confusion, so that I can hardly answer him when he shouts:

"GOOD MORNING, little Miró. Did you sleep WELL?"

I smile guiltily.

"Yeah. Uh... you?"

But I can't hide it: I am happy. So that is what sex is! It is fantastic. Less yet more than everything I have ever imagined. The biggest single mystery in my entire life has been revealed to me fully in one drunken night. My whole being is wrapped in a brand new universe of smells and sensations. My body carries the memory of touches, textures, movements as new to me as if I'd just been born.

"What I LONG for RIGHT now is a COFFEE!"

"I need to have a shower."

That is the prudish part of me, horrified at the thought of carrying all these crude animal smells out onto the street.

"I don't HAVE a shower."

Which makes me kind of glad. I want to luxuriate in this new armour of odours—more like an array of chivalric ribbons, plumes attached to my helm, these new bodily characteristics—for as long as I can. Washing them away would mean shedding and denying the experience. I am proud of what I've done, who I've become. It's like I've discovered a significant part of me. So we dress and squeeze out between the cliffs of Narcissus' 'wealth', and under the roller door, out into the ashen winter sunlight.

At a café table on the corner of the street, we order croissants and coffee. I'm not really hungry. My heart is thrashing about like a bird in my ribcage—more like a butterfly, a *mariposa*—and I have to use all the force of my willpower to keep myself from screaming out my joy. Why do I do that? I am happy, why can't I show it? It is like I'm scared this huge hand will come down out of the clouds and belt me a good wallop for feeling happy. It isn't as if it is a matter even of sex. I get guilty about feeling happy about anything. It makes me angry. There you go: being happy makes me angry. Maybe that's part of why things just don't always come out right.

Narcissus looks at me with gleaming eyes that I find hard to meet. His skin has a kind of deadened quality this morning.

"Little Joaquim, Petit Miró. WHEN are you going to PAINT me?"

I stop with the coffee cup halfway to my lips, then drink. But I can't paint! Is my first reaction, though I'd like to.

"Uh… I need a studio. I haven't even got a flat yet."

"That is soon arranged." He pauses and regards me. "I think I may have the PERFECT place for you."

# Eduardo V

*"His life in this room began a year ago, on the breakwater one fresh autumn day. She had appeared as a distant dash, a dark stroke against the grey sea, like an eyelash balanced on that finger pointing at the deep."*

—Gabriel Sabater, *Conversaciones al otoño*, Ediciones Cáusticas, Barcelona, 1967.

p. 8.

Pumping the pedals along the breakwater is the perfect cure for a hangover. It always puts me in mind of Sabater's *Conversaciones al otoño* since the opening scene is set out here:

> Since they were both walking in the same direction, he found himself following, matching his pace to hers. His contemplation of the Mediterranean seascape came to include the animated flicking of her calves. The gleaming, fake mink coat that reached to below her knees, her crimson scarf and heels of a different hue all strangely suited the dock's oil-stained cement. Under her right arm, she carried a plastic canister.

> Gradually they left the port area and headed out along the breakwater. Huge, precast blocks knocked back the lapping waves. A rough path ran along the top, seaward and breeze-buffeted. Beside

it, a sheer concrete wall hid the cityscape. He allowed distance between them so as not to alarm her, but found himself becoming curious about her purpose. After walking for a long time, passing an occasional fisherman wrapt silently into himself, or accompanied by his wife, on her knees, sawing tiny fish into red and grey pieces of bait, they came to the end.

Under the beacon, she stood for a few minutes. Then unscrewed the cap of the urn and tipped ashes into the sea. The relentless wind blew a stain of brown back across the water towards Barcelona. He felt uncomfortable witnessing that. Then she sat, dropping the container beside her. He was about to turn back, not wanting to intrude, but she looked around, saw him and raised an arm. He came on.

"Do you have a cigarette?"

He did. Words seemed ridiculous, an inadequate bridge, but he tried:

"I'm sorry for your loss."

"My father."

"Sorry."

"We weren't close. The old guy's better off dead."

"I'm sorry."

"Someone had to do it."

Those three sorries stretched his condolence to the limit. They smoked in silence. The sea rose and fell like a retching stomach.

"Would you like a drink?"

She nodded. They walked together back past the anglers.

"Dad used to come out here to fish. It was the only place I could think of to tip him."

At a bar with views out over the waves she asked a waiter to throw away the urn, which he did, looking shocked. She ignored the queasy way he picked it up by his fingertips and carried it from the room at arms' length.

"What am I supposed to do with a used funeral urn? It doesn't exactly have a high resale value."

Then she was melancholic and reflective as they looked at the flat, grey sea.

—Gabriel Sabater, *Conversaciones al otoño*, Ediciones Cáusticas, Barcelona, 1967.

pp. 8–9.

Gabriel Sabater. A great writer, one of my favourites. I don't know what it is that attracts me to that book. It's about a guy who becomes obsessed with a woman. She isn't quite a prostitute, has other jobs too. Over the course of a year, they meet, talk, tell each other stories, like a kind of *Arabian Nights* structure. Yet bit by bit, the power balance tips until she's the one calling the shots. Then one morning, as the dawn comes up, he kills her. That's about all the plot there is. Perhaps it's the casual way he tells the story, almost by accident, without really seeming to make any effort. It isn't that I want to write like that. I prefer action, things to happen. But something about that book got under my skin years ago and I can't shift it.

I was thinking about Sabater's book, which for some reason reminded me of the Ice Queen of Narnia, the one who had "manhandled" me at my party. Françoise made friends with Narcissus, the black guy, which was how she dragged me down into that world—just another version of the *okupas* really. Fun for a while, but I was feeling I needed to move on.

To tell you the truth, things had cooled between Françoise and me. The morning after the night of the party, she woke up seemingly pissed off about something. I couldn't even coax her into a dawn-riser blowjob, which is generally a bit of a ritual. She just seemed so set on poking her nose into weirder and weirder places, which, okay I find interesting for a while, but at the end of the day, I just have to despise them. I mean, those *friquis*, they aren't going anywhere. You're just wasting it, becoming freak-show material.

The other thing was that I needed to get serious about my studies. My Mum was paying to educate me in one of the best universities in Spain and I knew I had to make a go of it. Money counts. You often only get only one run at things. Make your millions first and then you'll have time for all the fun and games you want. "Balzac" was wrong. So was Juanjo; it was Voltaire who said that, but I wasn't in this to educate others—let them pay for their own education.

So I put my head down and started working. The atmosphere at the flat, with Juanjo, Marta, Ri and whoever else felt like dropping in, naturally began to get on my wick. Often it would just be an extended drinking session, including all the bickering and arguing that happens whenever Juanjo has had a few. I started to stay later and later at the university library, or stopped off at the gym on my way home and exercised myself to exhaustion. So I would come home, push through the smoke-filled living room and head straight to my room to crash.

Pretty soon, the others realised that was the cue for the party to break up because if they kept raising a racket while I was trying to sleep, they would know all about it. I don't tolerate people stuffing me around. Does this sound like a different me to the one I've described so far? Well, I've always had two clear sides to my personality. All my family are like that. It's how we get where we want to go. After all, willpower is just putting one foot in front of the other till you reach your destination. I enjoy partying, but at a certain point, I have to haul up the anchor and get back on course, abandon whatever bizarre fauna I've discovered.

This was one of those times. The party had shown me how far off course I had drifted. The *friquis* are like that; they seem like a harmless diversion, but then before you know it, they've got under your skin and are starting to change the way you see things, undermining your determination; they've infiltrated every corner of your existence. Pretty soon you're getting up late, going to bed late, abusing substances, alcohol, achieving nothing, starting to fall into their pathetic habit of blaming the rest of the world for their lack of advancement. As if it were all a capitalist conspiracy. I was going places and I wasn't prepared to be dragged down by a bunch of losers.

I felt like I needed to claim my space back. So as well as knocking the drinking sessions on the head, I also gave Felipe a two-week ultimatum to find a new couch. For his own good. Maybe officially it was Juanjo's flat, but he was always happy to let me take charge. Some people are like that, prefer to have somebody else make the decisions—which is why we have leaders and followers in this world. You have to choose early on which one you want to be. I knew.

***

One night in early February, I was coming back from Uni. I got off the *ferrocarriles* and ran up the steps. I never take escalators; it feels too much like you're part of the mob. Plus, doing a flight of steps three or four times a day keeps you in good nick. In the rotunda under Plaza Cataluña, a band was playing, typical Catalan grunge. They were belting it out. It's freezing and you get the feeling that the crowd gathered around listening are there as much for warmth as any other reason. I joined them, but was only half-listening because a few metres away a Pakistani street merchant had half a dozen alarm clocks set up on a cardboard box. He had them incessantly going off as an advertisement for his products. Even though the band was deafening, having that racket in my ears close by meant I just wanted to turn around and slug him, another illegal immigrant. Eventually I couldn't take it any more. I turned around and headed up towards Café Zurich, managing to kick the box on my way. Alarm clocks went flyi ng:

"Hey! What you do that for? Careful!"

"What you going to do about it? Go to the police? Go on then!"

"There is no right! I am just trying to make a living!"

"Try getting one back in your own country then if you don't like it here!"

Weird thing was that people were looking at me as if I was the one in the wrong yet I hear people complaining about immigrants all the time, how they're taking over the country. Where they're building the Olympic Village, they say you can't get a job if you're Spanish. You have to be Pakistani, English, or German. Café Zurich was packed, people crowding in for warmth. This is one of this city's institutions, with its booming floorboards and rickety mezzanine running around the top. Not only does it have the fastest service in Barcelona, but also the best coffee—an example of the way things used to work before it all went pear-shaped.

I stood at the bar and ordered a *carajillo*. That's an espresso with a shot of brandy. The true *carajillo*, the way they make it in Madrid, should have a coffee bean in it and be set alight, but the Catalans don't like squandering the alcohol. They say it was the staple breakfast of the railway workers back in the old days. It is a bit like having your heart run over by an express train, but it's a good pick-me-up on a cold day.

Looking around, I saw her. She was sitting at a table in the middle of the room, dressed in a fake mink fur with a wig that matched. I watched her. I had come in from the Ramblas side and she was facing towards the Plaza Cataluña door—she either hadn't seen me or was playing it cool.

A full glass of sherry sat on the table and she was smoking, waiting. If she felt people watching her, she didn't let on, but I imagine if you go out dressed like that, you know people will always stare. Then he walked in—the motorcycle dwarf. It was only after the party that I thought: I should know this guy. It was bugging me. I recognised his face, but it was as if I'd never seen him in the flesh, only on TV, or in a photo, or something.

Now here he is again, this well-known face. He kisses her, orders a beer. Waiters, other patrons, seem to arrange themselves around him like ripples after a stone hits the water, so I know he's well known. Not mega-famous, otherwise he wouldn't be in a public spot like this, rather somewhere more secluded, especially with Celia.

They stay just long enough for him to down his beer. She accompanies him with her sherry, but leaves it half-drunk on the table when they get up. They go out through the Ramblas door, passing me close by but giving no sign of recognition. I pay and follow them out, not quite sure why I'm doing this, but intrigued. We wait for the lights, then cross to Las Ramblas. Down by the Canaletas fountain they cross to the right, take Buensuceso. I follow them along the street, she about two metres tall, he about half that, but looking Juanjo-wide in his black leather jacket. They turn to the left and head down towards the market, crossing Pintor Fortuny, then Carmen. Before they reach the market, there's a small square to the right, kind-of "off-Boqueria". They enter a doorway. I wait on the street till I see a third-floor light click on, then I leave.

Why did I do that? I don't know. It's late. I want to get home. I have exams soon and need to put in some study time before bed.

# Joaquim VI

*Here's a knocking indeed! If a man were porter of hellgate,*
*he should have Old turning the key.*

—William Shakespeare, Macbeth, II.3.1.

Álvaro, Françoise, Ludo and Paul are all here for Narcissus's grand tour, Álvaro with a large, church candle under his arm. Fra's boyfriend Eduard is studying tonight.

"He has an exam in a week's time. I never see him ever now." Françoise complains.

We are standing in the street, Carrer Guàrdia, feeling a bit like a United Nations convention—French, Italian, American, Spanish, French-Caribbean—though I, the Catalan, would not be considered a state. Mind you, neither would Narcissus, in the new Europe. He takes a huge iron key from his overcoat pocket—maybe a quarter of a kilo—and brandishes it.

"The KEY to my CASTLE!"

And it actually grinds in the lock, before the heavy oak door squeals as he swings it wide.

"MADEMOISELLE!

He bows to Françoise, who delicately steps across the threshold. We follow like a troupe of tourists, entering a high, roofed patio—a carriage or coach entrance, the porte cochère, that leads towards a low arch, now barred off—the old stable entrance.

"MADEMOISELLE et MESSEURS, le residence des MarQUIS de Dosaguas!"

With a flourish Narcissus turns and leads the way up the marble staircase on the right. He uses a smaller, Yale key to unlock the door on the *Principal* landing. *Duesaigües*, I'm thinking. A Valencian marquis. I never knew they had mansions up in Barcelona.

"You see, this MANSion belongs to the Marquis. He is now eighty years old, can hardly walk; he just SHUFfles along on a short little cane."

Narcissus demonstrates his posture, bent almost double.

"His hair is SILver, completely SILver, but long. It grows down past his shoulders. Oh, he is a wonderful old man, so full of LIFE! He has enTRUSTed us—Álvaro and I—with this project, the refurbishment of his BARCELONA residence. We have so many plans..."

Narcissus leads us into his mansion, through the ballroom, out onto the patio with the fountain.

"I have so MANY plans. This HOUSE... what you are about to see... is the seed of a great DREAM!"

His words float up among the vapour of our breath, silver spirals that disappear into the night. I am truly convinced that dreams can be made real merely by wishing, but the jaded dolphin winks, sly.

We gloss by the kitchen—such practicalities aren't Narcissus' focus—and back to the ballroom, returning through more double doors into the suite of rooms surrounding the front door and main stairwell. These give onto three front salons, each only half the size of the ballroom, yet still spacious. Tall French windows open from each onto its own separate balcony overlooking our street. It is the cold, sunless side of the building and I would not mention it, would keep those windows bolted and shuttered, but this is where... it's one of the important things. The last room of the three was mine, and the first... Celia's. But this comes later. Beyond those three, a cramped, undefined space is lit only by small windows off the stairwell. That completes the planta noble, or main floor.

Narcissus leads us back towards the ballroom, to where a service stair rises to the floor above. This also is our domain. Upstairs it is dark, even in the daytime—a cluster of closets more than rooms, the ceilings so low we have to stoop. Muck litters the floor, a mixture of damp wallpaper, dust and the flotsam of past histories:

"What's that?"

"Oh my God... It's..."

"Dead. Is it?"

"What is it... a dog?"

"A Chihuahua... poor thing."

"How did it get in here?"

"Or who abandoned it?... It doesn't smell..."

Álvaro cautiously prods it with his toe.

"A wig. It's just an old wig. Some old queen left her wig behind."

It lies there, along with a broken plastic ruler, an empty paint tin (lilac—the walls are greasy cream), an almanac of the seasons from 1973, open on a list of Saints' days (today is Saint Timothy's and Saint Titus's day) and three wine glasses, one with a broken stem and another stained with paint (red). Narcissus hands Álvaro and I one each (why me?) and picks up the remaining glass.

"I propose a toast." He assumes the bell-like tones of an evangelist preacher: "LORD, bless this house and may our asPIRAtions and DREAMS come to fruition and SPREAD throughout the land!"

He pretends to toss off the contents in a single gulp and throws the glass over his shoulder with a cry. Françoise ducks. It shatters among the rubbish. Álvaro and I copy his movements—the red paint in my glass touches my lips, tastes bitterly musty, like rust. Álvaro smashes his glass with a giggle. I drop mine onto a pile of newspapers.

"No, no." shrieks Ludo. Grabbing it up, he dashes it against the wall.

"PETIT Miró," Narcissus's eyes bore into mine. "We shall have to find the KEY to UNLOCK that passion withIN you."

I laugh nervously and step back out of the candlelight. Álvaro declares that this suite will become his darkroom.

The rest of the house—its labyrinthine subconscious—is hidden below stairs. Opposite the ballroom is a small door. Its chest-height lintel, with jambs barely a shoulder's width apart, makes it seem more of a closet. Yet the key to this door is as long and heavy as the one for the street, reaching from the tip of my index finger to the ball of my thumb, a heavy weight of iron in my palm. Behind, a narrow stairway—one flight down, a quarter turn to the right, another flight, another turn—twists down to where it broadens into six wide steps in the first basement. We troop down. Here, a broad passage stretches forward, rooms on the left, another stairway ahead. The floor is no longer majolica or parquet, but humble red terracotta. I sit on the lower step, the candle beside me, feeling the wretched atmosphere that fills the empty space. Damp, close air seeps in, seeming to carry the brushing of rugged-up servants' bodies shuffling through the gloom. Only the far room, boasting three high windows along its end wall, and a grimy skylight in the ceiling, lets a little greyness spill in.

"This is where the marquis's ARMY of servants TOILED below stairs for his comfort, washing, drying, pressing the master's clothes. Wouldn't it have been DIVINE to live in those times?"

Paul refuses to be sucked into Narcissus's fantasy:

"Depends on whether you're born a Marquis, or a shirt-presser, like just one of the plebs."

"Or a shirt-lifter," this from Ludo.

"Or," adds Françoise, rolling her eyes dramatically, "a courtesan, having to rely on the favours of men."

"A lady of loose virtue. They had it as hard as the gays."

"Just the way you like it, Ludo," Narcissus suggests. Ludo giggles and backs into Paul's arms.

Looking around, there are no kitchen hearths or chimneys here. Rooms to the left are hinted at by shadowy rectangles. Maybe these weren't kitchens but offices. I imagine a dozen spluttering candles perched on heavy desks, each with its ledger, and black-coated, Dickensian figures curved over, peering at their work—laboriously copying tidy columns of figures in red and black ink. At one of the desks, on his own low podium, the straight-backed chief clerk presides over the others, his spectacles diabolically candle-lit. In my imagination, he has Felipe's features. I ask Narcissus about the history of these basements.

"DunGEONS!" He grins, coming so close I feel his cinnamon breath wash over me. "Even the CHAINS are still here!" His eyes, shining in the candlelight, flick towards the dark doorways. "In fact, this house's most SCANdalous history comes from a more RECent period, during the WAR: this building served as a BROTHel."

"That can't be. The Republicans liberated all brothels."

"Ahh, little MiRÓ, quite the historian, aren't you?. I'm SURE the MarQUIS de Dosaguas KNOWS what went on in his own house!"

Narcissus turns away angry and I feel chastened. I shouldn't have opened my mouth, but Françoise chuckles:

"Ooo, maybe ze Marquis was also ze Madame!"

We go down further. The second basement is darker than the first. Barely any light sifts through grimy skylights built into the floor above. Most enters from the grill closing off the stable arch. Next to this is a cistern with its own continuous spring spilling from a simple copper pipe—the only apparent water supply in the whole building. Stone slabs are arranged for beating out wet clothes. The rooms on this floor are larger, laid out symmetrically, to either side of the central passage. Only this central way is flagged, the other floors just hard-beaten earth. One of them accesses a cavity under the stairs: a plain hole yet equipped with its own locking door and, surprisingly, a single bed—the only piece of furniture in the entire mansion.

"Ahh!" breathes Narcissus. "This is where the PORTER must sleep."

I can't imagine why the smallest, darkest, lowest space (because it really isn't a room) should be the only one still with any furniture. He raps on the door and cackles.

"Here's a knocking inDEED! If a man were porter of HELLGATE, he should have OLD turning the key."

Bent double, rattling the 'keys to the castle' with sinister vehemence, he manages to shake the candle out and we are plunged into darkness. Yet his hackle-raising impersonation continues. I feel something brushing up against me, and gasp. Françoise shrieks playfully. Ludo seems to yell out in earnest. It is a full minute before Paul snaps a lighter on, bringing us back into the real world, all of which time Narcissus doesn't stop his cackling and howling. Now we are all ready to head back up to the main floor.

We place the candle on the floor in the middle of the ballroom and form a circle around it, seated on our jackets. The light scarcely reaches the walls, yet the odd fang flashes from the tiles or a beastly eye gleams. Álvaro opens a 1.5 litre bottle of wine with a plastic stopper which we pass from hand to hand, mouth to mouth. Narcissus begins talking:

"I have so MANY plans. This HOUSE... it will be so grand!" He stands tall in front of our group, eyes shining with abstract prospect, insistent on his dream. "...my plans for this house can include ALL of YOU because I want my FRIENDS to be part of my DREAM." He changes tone: "When I was just a child..."

Álvaro is quiet, but his eyes shine as he follows his friend. It is obvious he is deep in his own private pilgrimage of Narcissus' creation. However Ludo, a baritone, cuts in:

"I asked my mother, what would I be?"

Everyone laughs except Paul, unwilling to participate in this opulent fantasy. Narcissus' tenor takes his cue:

"Would I be pretty? Would I be rich?"

Ludo: "Here's what she said to me:"

They harmonise their way through the chorus:

"Que sera sera

Whatever will be, will be.

The future's not ours to see,

Que sera sera"

Through the applause, Narcissus' laugh is a triumphal roar, but he holds up his hands, silencing us, asking for attention. He flips into a chattier style.

"No, you see as a child..." Suddenly he is Martin Luther King: "I HAD A DREAM!" he becomes a storyteller: "I dreamed that one day I would grow up, travel the world, come to Europe, get myself into all sorts of EXCITING adventures," (he winks at Álvaro)

"Slut!", Ludo bleats.

"Meet WEIRD (eyeballing Ludo) and WONDERFUL (smiling at Françoise) characters, generally DEPORT myself to the best of my abilities!"

A subtly suggestive hip movement invokes my blush in the darkness as his gaze slips across mine. Narcissus and Álvaro smile deeply into each other's eyes.

"But the BEST thing we have in the islands, which surprisingly, you do NOT have here, is that particular, old world ELEGANCE, our COLONIAL heritage. Here in Europe you have all lost it, or are in the PROCESS of LOSING it. What I dream of BEQUEATHING to Europe once again is a REAL institution of OLD WORLD charm!"

"Ah, I see," smirks Ludo. "You've called us here to reopen the brothel."

"Ooooh! I want to be ze Madame!" shrieks Françoise.

"Philistines! My dream is to see this palace reborn in all its former GLORY."

He throws his arms wide, so Paul, looking sceptically at the dusty beams and long, wallpaper creepers, comments:

"The only things to be reborn here for several decades are termites. They've got a complete revival movement going."

"Can you imagine that we tear down this OLD paper? That we clean the walls? That we FLING WIDE all the doors and windows and let in the light? We will paint everything afresh. We will bring in tables, chairs, furniture... here a couple of wingback wicker chairs and a small table... maybe a potted palm. In that recess, my carved mahogany CONSOLE. It will be so... sooo GRAND! Can you THINK, can you PICTURE it? There is enough space for twenty, thirty people to live here comfortably. You could walk through these rooms all day and still not encounter another soul in your path. Álvaro, you need a darkroom—TAKE one! Little Miró, you want a STUDIO, here is one at your disposal. All we have to do is prepare them: A LITTLE work, a little EL-BOW-GREASE."

Now his voice lowers to a whisper. He creeps up towards our circle:

"That is why I have called my FRIENDS here, JUST a select few, tonight. We can make a change, we can redress this place. AND we will ALL share in the PROFITS. THINK! Imagine each of these rooms hired out, for thirty, forty... NO! You could easily ask forty-five thousand pesetas a month when this PALACE is glistening and shipshape. But WE, a small group of FRIENDS will be the PROPRIETORS. Sharing what superficial maintenance must be done AND sharing the PROFITS. WHY, this house could even become quite FAMOUS for its wonderful blend of OLD WORLD CHARM and MODERN CON-VENIENCE. Eventually, we will have cleaners to do the menial work. We will install a proper industrial kitchen. This room will be the restaurant—to seat twenty-five, thirty guests. Not more. We only want a SELECT clientele, none of the RIFF-RAFF. The front rooms—SPECIAL guest suites. Downstairs, we will install various FACILITIES..."

"Downstairs, that will be the brothel?" exclaims Ludo.

"NO! There will be studios, possibly the kitchen, a laundry..."

I shudder at a momentary association of Narcissus with that lost character in Verne's War of the Worlds: a single pathetic survivor ("We'll build a whole new world, underground!") who dreams of tunnelling away from the alien aggressors yet can dig no more than a few metres into soft earth.

Narcissus is standing bright before me again. I drink in his speech: half Harlequin clown, bounding around spritely, arms flung wide; half statesman, chest thrust forward, voice deep, hands expressively punctuating each exclamation. His voice leaps too. It thunders, smiles, seduces, hiccoughs and croons. Every so often a wide laugh—lascivious, joyous, cynical by turns—wells from him, filling his whole being, marking, as it were, the stanzas of his discourse. My heart pours out. I want to believe, create a world from nothing in his company. He smiles down at me. I'm won.

# Eduardo VI

February was a shit month. I fought with Ri, which meant things got quite frigid between Marta and I. Because I'd knocked the party season on the head, Juanjo withdrew into his room where he drank alone. Felipe did move out, back to where he was before—he actually had a flat in his name all this time! That's what they're like, the *friquis*: scavengers. Grab and grab, never give back. If you don't pull them up hard, they'll just take you for everything.

Things weren't going well with Fra. I was so clear that I needed to study. Most of the time when we saw each other, I couldn't shake the feeling that I was wasting precious time. I was so determined to do well in those exams that to sit around for three hours sucking face, or toddle off and drink herbal tea in some cosy couples' café seemed totally like an exercise in inanity.

As well as that, she was hanging around a lot with that Caribbean guy from my party, who I realised basically, I just didn't like. Morbidly fascinated by him, the boyfriend Álvaro, them all. I know about scum like that first glance. I wasn't born yesterday and preferred to keep a distance. Despite that, she dragged me down—once to a dinner they were holding to celebrate Narcissus taking over that huge old mansion down on Calle Guardia—and then later. We'll get to that.

The house. They all went wild over it. I have to say, even I was pretty impressed at first. This nineteenth-century mansion belonging to an important Valencian family, the Marqués de Dosaguas. The night of that dinner, I could see its potential: huge rooms with the original carved wooden ceilings and tile friezes around the walls; a largish patio out the back on the *Principal* floor; a suite of rooms upstairs and two whole basements of smaller rooms which used to be part of a hostel or something. I was impressed, but they were having orgasms. The place was a tip, an absolute dive. No running water and they'd only just got electricity connected the night I saw it. Mould and ancient wallpaper hanging in strips from all the walls. You would need to invest millions to turn it into a liveable space. I couldn't believe they were all so ecstatic.

Narcissus and Álvaro weren't living there yet. They had conned this young bender to take on the contract in his name—all care, *all* responsibility—as well as rent a room in his 'own' house for an exorbitant amount. Plus he was supposed to clean up and paint the rooms ready for their arrival. Fra reckoned he was paying over forty thousand pesetas a month for the privilege! There's one born every day.

***

Barcelona at our feet. An electric city: glittering all the way to the winking runway lights of El Prat; on Montjuïc, the MNAC's Batman beams rake tangerine cloud cover; the Ensanche's gridiron layout glows like an electrified bed base; spotlights shine harsh on the Sagrada Familia towers while strings of headlights etch illuminated cracks through the dark city's armour like strafing fire. Fra's hair flows out towards the window behind her, crackling as if it were drinking power from the electric tapestry. This side of the glass, everything is organic, candle flames lighting pale linen, mahogany chairs and cloth panelling on the walls, flowers in ceramic vases on each table.

And Fra's eyes shine in liquid laughter. She's happy, thank God. We're celebrating. I scored well in my exams, second-highest in the course. Well, I'm not stupid and after the amount of study I put in, I would have been gutted with anything less. First stage of my goal complete. She pours wine, we toast.

"To you, Edu. Genius."

"To you, baby, for putting up with me."

"You're right: to me, for putting up with you."

We drink and the first course arrives.

On the opposite wall are two Goya reproductions, Olimpia, clothed and un-clothed. I don't know much about art, but this painting triggers a memory. Dad took me to visit a theatre museum once. I don't remember almost anything about it, but I have a photo of my face sticking out of a life-size cut-out of one of Velázquez's women, one of the Meninas. I'm about eight years old. I can't remember having that photograph taken, but I remember standing in the hot sun in a car park. That's about all. Fra says something.

"What?"

"We have been invited to dinner."

"Where?"

"Down at the mansion, Narcissus's place."

"Oh."

I really don't want to spoil this night so I'm not going to start anything. I just hope if I can stay noncommittal, I'll be able to find some excuse later. But the *friquis'* mansion is the last place I want to spend an evening. Imagine trapped at the table with the preening Narcissus! Can't we just enjoy the moment we're having together now?

"When?"

"Next Friday."

Enough time to find an excuse?

"What happened between you and Sabrina?"

At least this is a change of subject; one I'm not sure I want to follow up.

"Well, you know what lesbians are like, always wanting to analyse everything down to its smallest component..."

"Not Sabrina, Edu. She is your best friend."

"That doesn't mean she doesn't have her faults, just like any lesbian... like anyone."

"You don't want to talk about this?"

"I don't mind talking about it."

"Ja."

So now it's my problem. Sometimes I hate the way women have of turning things around on you. It looks like we can now kiss goodbye to our celebration. I can see us spiralling down on a narrowing gyre of bickering and psychoanalytical navel-gazing.

"Ri and I just had a difference of opinion. She sees her life in her way and I prefer to live mine how I want. That's all."

"Why don't you ever want to look at issues, Edu, talk about what you are feeling emotionally? Is it because of your sister?"

"Fucking leave it, okay! My sister... or for that matter, Dad, since he's the next one you'll mention... has nothing to do with this! I just had a disagreement with Sabrina, alright?"

I realise people are looking from nearby tables. Well, stuff them. I don't have to explain myself. How to torpedo a fun occasion in two easy steps! Fra is an expert. Now we just eat in silence. I feel a bit ridiculous. This restaurant is costing a bomb, all the other smoochy-smoochy couples are crooning cloyingly at each other and Fra and I choose this place to have a domestic. Do I have to make every emotional nuance I'm feeling explicit? Women are so like this. But I've got to turn it.

"That view is sensational."

"You want to talk about the view?"

"I want to talk... about anything... nice."

"We're just having a discussion, Edu. It's normal for people to talk about their feelings."

"Ya."

Calculating what we're likely to spend tonight, this "discussion" is probably costing me around five hundred pesetas a word. I maintain an economic silence as the second course is brought.

Ri and I go to the same gym, uptown, close to Uni. We met for a drink after the workout—though we work out separately, we often go together or connect afterwards to compare notes on the state of the world economy. This was a normal evening. Did Ri have her period? Had she had a fight with Marta? Fuck knows,

I'm not a clairvoyant. It started off normal. Ri was drinking a TriNa and I was having a Coke.

"How's Fra?"

"Cool. I think she's alright. Marta?"

"Edu!"

"What?"

"I just asked you how your girlfriend was."

"And I told you. So?"

"One word isn't telling. Do you know how she is?"

"Of course I do. She's my girlfriend, isn't she?"

"So how is she?"

"Fine! How's yours?"

"Fuck Edu!"

Now if someone can tell me where I went wrong here, in which murky channel of the labyrinthine delta of femininity I came aground, throw me a cable. So yes, I realised afterwards Ri needed an amoebic analysis of every belch and blow in Fra's spiritual and emotional intestines to feel that I'd answered the question. Okay, so I should have gone into more depth, but I was studying, it was just before exams. To tell you the truth, I didn't have a clue how Fra was. She could have dug up Luis Companys and be dancing the Sardana with him and I wouldn't have known.

What was weird was Ri's reaction. I saw recognition, then a light just seemed to click off as she looked at me. It was a strange feeling of déjà vu and reminded me of the tensed, clock-spring violence of the girls in the bollera bar. Though I know Ri's not like that. It was a pretty full-on battle. When she finally walked out, she didn't say goodbye. I had to pay for her drink. Of course I didn't mention any of that to Fra.

"If you want the truth," I lied, "I think she's having problems with Marta."

# Joaquim VII



*April is the cruellest month, breeding*
*Lilacs out of the dead land, mixing*
*Memory and desire, stirring*
*Dull roots with spring rain.*

—T.S. Eliot, *The Waste Land*, "I. The Burial of the Dead", lines 1–4.

February is the cruellest month. I spend most of it in bed, wrapped in a sleeping bag, thinking about where I can find money to get something to eat.

Downstairs, in the first basement, I've got a studio set up—in the only room with windows—where already a fine layer of dust is settling on those new boxes of oil paint, bought with Dad's "start-up" money: not quite Agrarian and Food Industries classes at the Catalonia Polytechnic. The first painting, sketched out on the easel is of Narcissus: a formal portrait, in suit and tie, standing stiffly beside a pile of leather-bound volumes we found in one of the rooms (*La Vanguardia* newspaper editions, 1978 to 1981, each tome a good twenty-five centimetres thick; he wants me to substitute other titles, like philosophy and religion, as if I were some nineteenth-century portraitist). That scared me from going near the painting again.

Oil paint—though I have hardly experimented—has a kind of aristocratic feel. You uncap it, even squeeze the tube straight onto the canvas if you can afford it—but school fees don't go that far—begin to push that pigment around—it's delirious, sensual—virtually carving it with the spatula. If you don't get it right, go back and do it again. Not like watercolour—which is frustrating: a single brushstroke and you've messed up an entire painting—or sculpture: one false bash and you've turned David's nose into a doorstop. Oil is forgiving. Malleable. Yet arcane in the darkest, oldest sense. Oil painting is the closest human beings have come to alchemy.

The remaining harvest money Dad gave me to help me get on my feet is now in Narcissus's hands: seventy-five thousand pesetas—twenty-five as rent, fifty as a bond. Though I signed the lease, Narcissus convinced me that he should pay the money to the real estate agent. So I pay him. I know I shouldn't have agreed to this. It's too much for a bond, but he managed to make me feel it was worth it, all part of our great investment. I need to make some money fast.

I just kind of got overwhelmed by him—yes, *he* is a total artist, unlike me—and he sucked me into signing my name for that house and taking responsibility for all the debts—past and future—the unpaid bills on four floors of freezing winter palace. The agent looked at me like I only spoke Chinese or something, spelled it out in black and white, scrawled it in large figures on paper the first time we went to his office. I still did it. Later I convinced Dad to put down another block of cash: told him it was standard in Barcelona to pay that for the deposit on a flat. Renting a palace, even in the Barrio Chino, is expensive. He never knew—it was a shock when I found out—how much money was actually owing in bills already. That's how it happened. We even toasted it afterwards. I feel ashamed of everything that went on, but remember, this is 1990, fool's year, my year. Though Celia arriving, made it all worth it.

While I lie under the covers (we hardly ever go out during the day—in the afternoon at the earliest), I imagine returning to my *serra*. I miss the mountains. Life is special down there. You don't get that here—the peace, the calm, when the winter air is like crystal water, when ripples of wind make mountains shudder with chill, yet pale houses glow gold and almost *crackle* in the sunlight. That wind that raises red patches on every exposed spot of your skin,scrapes across you like blunt razorblades. The only thing to take out the chill is a nip of *ratafia*—this steeped-herb liqueur.

My mood—if you want to know the truth—is a copy of Goya's black period—dark, desperate yet exciting, sinful. I must learn more—about art. I don't know enough. There's so much that's been painted and I've seen so little—drawings, pen and wash sketches, sculptures, frescoes, tapestries, even handprints daubed on cave walls that have been turned out since the beginning of time—but the crux, the essence of my crisis is: what will I do? What am I capable of? Do I just want to turn out academic portraits of my friends?

This house—isn't it crazy? What am I doing here, in this echoing mansion? I have no money. I should be downstairs painting. I should be out looking for work. Nothing stands still. No-one will ever leave you alone. I have to escape from this house, am desperate to at times. It presses down on me so. Barcelona is a huge city. It feels like a big black, soot-stained station in which I have to hang around forever. I want to live my life, that's what I came here to do, but I am trapped in this dark labyrinth, still waiting for the right train to come along. Here I am, lying in bed while my studio is being slowly interred under layers of dust.

The buzzer goes. Narcissus and Álvaro are out around town—spending my rent money. I get up and walk through rooms to the front door. Opening, I am confronted by a poster-size representation of Munch's most famous work. Did I say something to him? How did he know? Yet it's how I feel.

"Housewarming present. I thought you needed something to cheer up your décor."

This is the painting to cheer me up? Felipe steps into the hallway.

Still, I thank him. At least Munch's got colour—that expressionist sunset. I show him around the house. Because of the cold, we soon end up sitting on my bed in front of the butane heater I have dragged in here while Narcissus is gone.

"Nice room."

"Minimalist."

My room is a plain box: white walls, white ceiling, grey floor tiles. The door and window frames are also grey. My bed, the only piece of furniture apart from the bedside table and a small desk and chair, is a fake-mahogany, seventies monstrosity we found on the street. It serves a purpose.

"Did you do that?"

The single decoration is a lithograph I made at fifteen of my beloved serra. My art teacher—also my aunt—was experimenting with the technique, and called me and my cousins in one Sunday to try out the process. The mountain range is printed in autumn colours—forest green, rust and lilac—though I think I did the initial sketch during summer. Felipe's framed poster will be the first thing to join it on the wall.

"Experiment."

"Where?"

"The mountain range at home."

"Melancholy... but welcoming."

I feel slightly warmer towards Felipe.

"How are you settling in?"

"Narcissus said we'll be getting the electricity turned on next week. We found a tap by the front door. We've got running water throughout the house now—cold still, but we don't have to bring it up from the bottom basement anymore."

He giggles: "He hasn't changed."

"Have you known him for long?"

"I've known Álvaro longer. We were flatmates together for two years. They met about a year ago. Narcissus had some problem—as he always does—and needed somewhere to stay. Álvaro invited him into the flat and they became lovers. I ended up moving out, a few months ago now, which is how I wound up on Edu's sofa. Them coming here meant I could move back, but there's still three months owing on the other. In my name and I doubt I'll get anything out of Narcissus."

"So you must think they're a couple of scumbags."

"Álvaro's in love with Narcissus, so you can't blame him, can you? And Narcissus... is just himself. I can't really see him changing."

Instead of the required sympathy for Felipe you might imagine, I feel scorn more than anything, a kind of disbelieving disdain for his passive, pathetic inability to stand up for himself.

"Sorry... about that night, Felipe, at the party."

"No, I am. I should learn not to jump on pretty boys the moment I see them."

"Are you gay?"

He giggles. "What do you think? Aren't you?"

"I... I don't know. My father thinks I am, but... I don't know."

"Well, do you like men, or don't you?"

"Some men. It isn't that I like men... Some of the things... I don't think I'm actually gay, Felipe."

"What? Maybe you're bisexual, but bisexual is still..."

"It isn't that simple."

"I saw you leave with Narcissus, you know."

I feel like I'm being led into an admission I am not prepared to offer, into making a false statement. I don't know what I think about Narcissus. Am I in love with him? He wraps me up, sweeps me up in his world like no-one else could possibly do—but does that make me Gay?

It feels ridiculous. You have sex with one guy in your entire life. Does that make you Gay? Does that make you fall in love with him? Come on! But the truth is somehow in between what Felipe thinks and a complete lie. I really hate some of the things that gays are supposed to do with each other; they gross me out. In fact, the act is disgusting. Yet the feelings, the sensations, are an entirely new world.

That night when he went into his big speech, I was sold. I mean, I'm not dumb, I saw that he's a kind of charlatan, that he's fake. I know he makes all these stupid promises—sharing PROFits, and all that—but I just saw him standing there, his eyes shining in the candlelight, and I just wanted to be part of that.

Felipe has moved closer to me on the bed. He puts a hand on my shoulder and eyeballs me intensely through his thick frames.

"Then what you need is to experiment, find out what you like, play around a little..."

I see his lips as the words tumble out drifting relentlessly closer. They look like two slugs orgasming on the slender stalk of his neck. His fingertips are creeping down over my shoulder, fiddling with my chest, tickling the nipple. I can't think how to tell him... Maybe I should just let things happen, but I am not really into this...

The buzzer sounds. There is a God! I spring up from the bed.

"Someone's here. I'll get the door."

"Leave it..."

But I have already skidded out into the passageway and walk briskly to the front door. It is Miguel, standing scruffily in ragged jeans and hair that falls messily into his honeyed eyes. He grins slyly.

"Just passing. Thought I would stop by."

Back in my room, I go to sit at the desk since it would seem a bit crowded on the bed. Miguel is already preparing a joint, with a Bic lighter melting the hash into his palm off a block the size of a marble.

"No, sit here on the bed." Felipe seems a bit unsettled by Miguel. "I was just going."

"Okay." I feel a bit guilty. Maybe I should urge him to stay, but I really can't be bothered. "See you."

"Don't worry. I know my way to the door." And he goes.

"Brrr! It's freezing today." Miguel immediately pulls the sleeping bag up and around both of us and we smoke the joint tightly wrapped together in front of that leaky gas heater. Within seconds, our hands have found the other's body and we are heating each other in a way that would make Felipe wail. Okay, I think, I'll accept I might be bisexual.

***

When Miguel has gone, slapping his casual way down the marble staircase, I get a rare burst of energy and head down to the studio. There might be about an hour and a half of daylight left—a fair amount comes in now the windows are clean. I light a couple of candles, placing them to each side of the canvas. Clipped to one corner, a photo of his smiling face, fangs bared triumphantly, accuses me silently for my weeks of absence. I begin to paint in his shadows.

As I work, I seem to feel his presence looking over my shoulder. He is wearing a critical frown, but I can't stop, not for him, or anyone. Suddenly I FEEL what I should be doing. I have not even finished the dark tones of his face when the brush, almost of its own mind, seems to lash out towards a space hovering behind him on the chalky surface to the left. It is a brown-black smear or tail that streams upward from his shadowed cheek. The brush (not me! This can't be me doing this) begins to scrub at that stain, darkening it, thickening, imbuing form to an amorphous profile that is gathering there back behind his shoulder, slightly to his side. Animal. It crouches. Now I know I'm right, on the right track. Before I smudge everything too blackly in, I hesitate and slash open a bestial eye that from the dark, glares at me while I work. I do not know what this beast is. Now I go back to layering on the foundation of Narcissus's face as that creature watches me, crouched, talons sinking into that stack of books, which appear to tower more, in the stern nature of Bibles, like Babel about to fall.

Then it is too dark to paint and I go out into the streets, wrapped tightly in too thin a jacket. Wasn't thinking. I carry this painting's mood along, find myself running deeper inside myself, following disjointed streets into their narrowest crooks. Barcelona is a city to walk in—stalk, ramble with sightseers, scurry among workers. When you need a rest, you slope between the tables of pseudo-Art Nouveau coffee-shops and coloured-glass bars, where the clientele (strangers) view you with vague disdain over the rims of their glasses, grandly gossiping about Almodóvar, Matirio, Alaska or La Fura.

That is not really my place. I am too self-conscious. You might think I'm a complete psycho. Not true, whether you believe me or not. Maybe I could do that too, but I have my own ideas, my own way of looking at things. Anyway, I don't go into any of those bars—I don't have any money. In the end I just walk around for hours in the cold and then go home to my sleeping bag.

I am sleeping for once—at night. In this house, every part of your body that touches the air, freezes. Late. I hear Narcissus and Álvaro come in—it's them who wake me up, actually. Narcissus is loud and drunk. After about an hour, the house is quiet again. Just the creaks and groans an old house has. My door creaks.

"Miró?"

I turn. It's him. He speaks in a whisper.

"Quiet, little Miró. Álvaro is sleeping. But on such a cold night as this, I wanted to make sure you were warm enough."

He laughs, a throaty, whispering chuckle. I should resist, say no, but at the same time I want to smell, taste, feel his body again. In silence, the act seems to become more erotic, more intimate, more personal, a private act that just the two of us enjoy. Afterwards, he slips away again, back to his sleeping partner, but some of his presence, his odour stays to share my bed and I wrap us closely in my sleeping bag and snuggle down against the cold.

# Eduardo VII



—Anon., "Ojos verdes" [Green Eyes], sung by Concha Piquer.

The dinner party was… *surreal*, Fellini. Françoise and I were the only straight people there except for Ramona, quite a gorgeous blond socialite from Madrid. Her camera didn't stop clicking the entire time, so I guess we all got recorded for posterity. And the old guy. Celia, the Ice Queen, reigned at one end of the table, Narcissus at the other. Álvaro, his boyfriend—the one who had done all the slaving to get the banquet ready—was kind of perched on a tiny stool at Narcissus's right hand. It had become an issue between Françoise and I that I show up. I'd been making excuses, but finally she really spat her dummy:

"You are supposed to be my partner, but you never want to accompany me anywhere! I am…"

"We can go wherever you want! I just don't want to go down *there*, okay? Why is that so hard to understand?"

"Because, Edu, these are my friends, and I want that my boyfriend meet my friends. I am sick of be alone in every social situation!"

"I wouldn't classify those feathered specimens as social, more zoological."

"That is enough! They are my friends! What is your problem, Edu? Are they too different for you? Everybody must be exactly the same as you, is that it?"

"Nobody has to be the same as me; all I ask is that they more or less come from the same planet."

"Ha! Very funny! Well, I will go alone then. Fuck my boyfriend!"

"Okay, I'll come! I didn't realise it was such a big deal."

"You come and you be nice to them."

"Yes, I'll be nice. Of course I'll be nice. I'm nice personified."

"Ja!"

So that was how I ended up seated around a table with the freak gang. I decided to look on it from more of an anthropological perspective. That way I might at least learn something.

They made me sit right beside her. I tried to swap with Françoise, but she was absolutely ignoring me. A statue would have been more sociable. So I dived into the zoological, had no choice but to speak to them. The little faggot with the fishy eyes was sitting almost opposite. Couldn't have planned it better if they'd tried. To top it off, he started on this long ramble about Catalan independence. I was tempted to pick his brains with the corkscrew, grill him (electric or gas?) on his recipes for Molotov cocktails. If Françoise hadn't been there I would have been freer, but I had promised to be nice. I decided monosyllabic was the safe course through the evening, kept my head down and slurped the soup.

The most interesting person there was actually the old bloke, French, who turned out to be the divine one's father. He seemed about as disgusted as myself with the whole company. Unfortunately, my French wasn't good enough to be able to strike up much of a conversation. I had to tag along with what Françoise was saying. It turns out he had lived for years in Argentina though at first he didn't seem capable of, or was uninterested in speaking Spanish. They were talking about the tango. Françoise has been going to classes. That bores me. I'm not a dancer. It's another of Françoise's complaints. Like I said, things hadn't been that hot between us. Then I realised the cashmere princess on my left was watching me.

"See anything interesting?"

"I was wondering what you must think of our small community here."

"What do you mean?"

"Well, I wouldn't have thought this was exactly your social milieu."

"I move in lots of circles."

She had hit the nail on the head though. I found her perfume asphyxiating, like mandarin peel dissolved in bleach, impregnating everything. It clung to the back of my throat in globs, more potent than sniffing glue.

"So what are you studying at university, Eduardo?"

"Business."

"Really? So you'll be a rich executive one day?"

"We'll see. I'm doing okay in my subjects at the moment."

"I'd say you have an excellent aptitude for that career."

What the fuck would she know? The way she said it though, didn't sound like much of a compliment.

"I reckon I will."

"So what attracts you to... business?"

"The same as everyone, making money of course. You can't do much in this world without *pasta*."

"That's so true!"

Like I'd expressed a rare philosophical gem.

"But imagine you had enough money to do anything you wanted, Edu. What would you do then?"

"Why?"

"I'm just interested."

I don't know why I answered her. I don't tell many people my private dream. I wouldn't normally blurt it out to an unknown freak at a party.

"I'd be a writer."

"Really. What genre?"

"Realist fiction... By realist, I don't mean naturalist, or..."

"I know. My degree's in Literature."

That floored me: she had a degree!

"Yes, and a Master's in Film and Television Studies."

"You have a Master's? Then why do you...?"

"The same as you, making money of course. Plus I like the lifestyle."

She laughed and called out to Narcissus:

"Any more wine, honey? This girl's dying of thirst down here!"

The conversation changed, became more general. Françoise commandeered me to get my opinion on something she was talking about with the Frenchman. I was left feeling like I somehow might have slipped, found myself behind enemy lines again in that imaginary civil war. Then the critical moment. Françoise asked the Frenchman about his daughter. If I understood right, it went like:

"Sir, have you had the pleasure of seeing the magical fountains of Montjuïc?"

"No, I'm only in Barcelona for one night."

"Well, your daughter shouldn't accept such poor treatment from her father: having to settle for such a brief time with him. Can't you stay longer?"

He roared: "Hah! Some daughter!"

Silence exploded into the room: I slugged back my wine; the Tarragona kid sawed at the tablecloth with a steak knife; our German friend coughed then hiccoughed; la Madrileña squealed; Álvaro gazed at Narcissus; Narcissus eyeballed Celia. She stirred her coffee for about thirty long seconds, then drank it down in one gulp. She pushed back her chair, stood and walked from the room. The only sound, her staccato heels stabbing the floorboards all the way to her bedroom, then returning as far as the front hall. The main door slammed. We heard her clicking down the marble staircase towards the street.

"Well, she isn't my daughter."

La Madrileña nodded vaguely and started loading a new film into her camera. Françoise and I left soon after. I think everybody did, except the people who lived there.

On the street, Fra and I decided we needed a drink. She took me to La Concha, just down the street, an old-world bar you would think had been lifted from the forties. There isn't a free space on the walls that isn't hung with a photo of Sarah

Montiel in her young Diva days. It was obviously a spot she had collected in the freak gang's company, but it was low-key and intimate.

"Who is Celia?"

"You can see, can't you?"

"Yes, but who is she? I mean her father's French, but she's got an Argentinean accent..."

"She grew up in Buenos Aires. She has been involved with some writer guy... I don't like him. I think she should leave..."

"Why did she come here?"

I don't know. Money..."

"Do people do anything except for money?"

"Adventure maybe."

"Why did... she...?"

"People have to be who are they, Edu. I think Celia is very brave."

"That was one of the weirdest nights of my life!"

"You haven't seen much weird."

"I've seen enough, believe me. ... That was like being kidnapped by the cast of Marat-Sade. Did you see the way that Tarragona kid..."

"Joaquim."

"He was like trying to chop up the table. What a psycho!"

"Stop Edu! They are my friends! Thank you for coming to the dinner, but please don't insult them now."

"No problem. So you see, I was nice personified."

"You were well behaved, Edu. At least I am thankful for that."

"Another drink?"

# Joaquim VIII

The key to the restrictive idolisation of an exaggeratedly feminine and virginal stereotype imposed by the fascist patriarchy on women must be sought in the regime's support for and institutionalisation of Marian Catholicism and in particular, the figure of the Virgin Mary. As the official patron saint of the Armed Forces, in her incarnation as the "Virgin Captain", Mary personified the fascist avenger, the conservative revolutionary, bearing down with drawn sword upon the supposed malaise of the Republic in righteous anger. Virgin but mother, unassailably pure yet treading with the weight and wisdom of maternal responsibility in her role as incubator of new fascist generations, it was an ideal that was impossible for real women to live up to. It forced women into the duplicity of upholding and personifying puritanical ideals while shouldering the reality of a life of un-emancipated, maternal drudgery.

This idealisation of the feminine principle to an impossible height was another way of denying women's essential humanity. It is worthwhile noting that those communities which idealise femininity to the greatest extreme are the same ones where women are granted the least amount of actual power, from entrenched heterosexual patriarchies to female, single-sex communities such as religious orders, and even in certain cross-dressing elements of male homosexual culture.

—Lena Boldfoot, "Fashion to Fascism: Dictating Femininity", in *Mary Mary Quite Contrary: 20th Century Images and Realities of Women*. Oxfordshire, UK: Cotswold UP, 1985, pp. 143–4.

I need you to understand Celia. Have you seen *Le Baiser*? Rodin's statue. It's more alive than most people. She's ... her torso, the statue woman's, is delicate, real flesh under his, the statue man's fingertips, his touch, a caress that's light as a sigh. It traces her marble body, those curves, that hand in a way defines her ... The way their lips meet ... so soft, you can imagine it—a sweet exploration of the other that imprints itself on her mind forever. And she makes him aware of being a man when they're together. He feels his own body rougher and clumsier, but there's male joy in the blunt movement. He hums within that feeling of power restrained, of surrounding and encapsulating her essence while she swoons in his arms, leading him on, inviting him to meld... Like she's a night lake... like he's the metallic moon's shingled road. Braver than ever, bolder, more prepared to bare himself, become vulnerable, there in her room before her. Celia's room. I felt like Rodin, carving her out of clay for the first time. It was as if she had never been and my job was to affirm her existence.

My teachers taught us about *carpe diem*, to seize that moment of living, of intense life. Yet life is not some dragon whose throat you twist to get your maiden. Rather, you have to suck the nectar from each moment, each *epiphany*, a chain of pearls. Celia made me feel like that, seated in her room, enwrapped in her boudoir, within this silken cocoon that was her world, more special than you ever felt anywhere.

People think I'm a psycho, that I'm inadequate, a social retard, too nervous. If I have one saving grace ... it's that I have brains. But not the right kind, not the kind that count. I had to prove to myself I was living, that I was the sort of person I wanted to be. In a way I was. For the first time in my life I was becoming an artist, actually doing it: had a studio, paints, projects. I was having sex too: Narcissus, Miguel… However, with Celia, I aspired to more than I had ever dared.

When I moved in, those three front rooms, the ones opening onto the street—my own, Celia's and the middle one—were uninhabitable: dusty, dirty and shuttered against the city's leaden air. I spent days whitewashing and painting. I'm glad I prepared Celia's—the first, one I painted with love.

Narcissus's bedroom and the ballroom were left as they were, too grandiose to touch. We didn't even tear down those hanging shreds of wallpaper. But elsewhere, white was the colour, like a blank canvas, onto which we could describe our lives.

I toiled for hours on Celia's room, carefully edging the grey trimmed door-frames and French windows in gold leaf. Meanwhile I slept on a mattress in the dead Chihuahua room, kind of out-of-the-way, not part of the grand plan. But that's okay. I knew that one of these three rooms would be mine, thought the first one would be, but am glad it became hers, so different to the Spartan bareness of mine.

We found her bed, this monstrous pre-war monument, in the street. I oiled it, scraped off old paint stains and re-varnished the wood till it looked almost new. It dominated the room, headboard against the right-hand wall. The opposite wall beside the balcony held a dresser with an ornate mirror. Grey age stains sneered through its reflection, but it was usable, still gave you a clear image.

Onto the stage of that house, Celia strutted, a kind of Hollywood star sheathed in white satin. You could have put a long cigarette-holder in one gloved hand à la *Breakfast at Tiffany's*… but now I can't remember whether she smoked. It would be natural that she did—we all did in that house—yet I try to picture her puffing away and can't.

Her arrival in early April was when everything still felt like a dream. My father's money paid our rent for February and March, plus my paints, a bit of food and our nights… but I'll get to that. The crunch came in April—that was the first month when I had real problems—before I finally managed to begin as a telephone operator for a breakdown company. Everything should have been paid up until that point, but I was starting to find that Narcissus's actions—money rather—weren't matching his words.

My first ever vision of her (on the night of Eduardo's party, Narcissus and I had left before she arrived) was in L'Acordeoniste in March. It conjured a memory—key in my own evolution—from when I was eleven. Nineteen-eighty-one. I was just a kid. People still treat me like one, or they did until this happened. With one massive revolution of explosive force I've shown them I no longer am.

I had recently discovered Dad's abandoned dream. It's an area of his life which I know almost nothing about, except for this single flash when I glimpsed what he may have dreamed, maybe when he was my age, maybe later... I saw just its final shreds. What I'm talking about is him as his own person... the man he was while his romance still contained idealism, before it got pruned along the wire of marriage... and offspring... the baggage that tied him down to the drudgery of making ends meet.

So this night I remember. Some friends of my parents—of my father—had come to stay, passing through on their way to Valencia. Mum was distraught throughout the day, ready to lash out at whoever dared cross her:

"Joaquim, get the shopping cart. I need you to help me at the market."

"But you said I could go to the Les Gorgues!"

"Don't argue! We have guests tonight and I've got nothing prepared."

Going to Benissola market was a job I hated. Two hours later, we returned with the trolley groaning with produce. Mum laid siege to her kitchen, scrubbing, peeling, baking and simmering her way through the day. I was allowed to escape. I grabbed my bike—a sturdy contraption I'd bolted together from bits of machines picked up around the village—and raced down the gully that led to the swimming holes and hermit's cave. Les Gorgues was my refuge, a spot in which you could imagine turning your back on the world, living in one of the cave-like *baumas* and surviving on water dripping from its mossy walls. My favourite game there was imagining the whole world had ceased to exist, that I was the last, or the first of the new generation: like Didac, the character in *Typescript of the Second Dawn*, my favourite book, then and now.

When hunger drove me home, Mum was more agitated than ever and all I got was some browning paté on old bread. Dad wasn't there—I only remember him appearing on the scene that evening, with... Her. She was astonishing. The three of them pulled up in this battered, beige Citroën GS. Dad was in the back, a fact that alerted me to these people's importance—I'd never seen his bluff arrogance change that way in front of anybody before. The man drove. She was in the passenger seat. He was squat and balding with the bushiest handlebar moustache I'd seen on anybody. As soon as he pulled up, making the handbrake groan, the stranger was out, bustling, cackling, officiating, organising. A dozen scandalous anecdotes seemed to have frothed between his whiskers even before he got as far as entering our home. The only quality I captured off the lady at that moment, sitting in the dimness of the passenger seat behind a dusty windscreen, was her laugh—ceaseless in her acknowledgement of her partner's quips and asides, tinkling, sophisticated, but with a gurgling undertone that vaguely frightened me. My father got out and actually opened the door for her: nobody did that in my village! When she stepped out, she was tall, wearing a ruby-coloured trouser suit, arranging a cream leather coat around her shoulders. Auburn hair curled and billowed around her pale oval face and she looked a lot younger than my Mum, but that could have been the way she was dressed, or that unplanned, fluid joy she radiated.

Mum had still not come downstairs. I could hear her bumping hurriedly about in her bedroom, above where I stood in the doorway. She had rushed up there as soon as I saw the car turn into our street. Now she banged downstairs in her best dress—lilac with pale flower clumps flounced around the hem—virtually drunk on the perfume she had sprayed on: *White Linen*.

"My son, Joaquim."

Our guests flushed me with the ambrosia of their gaze. I prickled, but felt special, could feel Dad's pride when he said 'son', and felt their respect too. I was one of Dad's achievements. The man cracked a joke that made me laugh though I never ever relax that much with strangers. She laughed too and I found myself smiling into the most intense, green cat's eyes I'd ever seen.

# Eduardo VIII

*If you have not seen the day of Revolution in a small town where
all know all in the town and always have known all, you have seen
nothing.*

—Ernest Hemingway, *For Whom the Bell Tolls*, Scribner Classics, 1996. p. 106.

I am floored: I found out who the motorcycle dwarf is. I mean he's easily recognisable by his physical description. The night I clicked, I was distracted. In between my studies which took up most of my time, I was working on ideas... for a novel. I wanted to set it in Spain, around the time of the Civil War. See, I think there's a lot of false history around now. The reds have taken over the government and paint everything an effeminate shade of pink. Someone needs to publish an account that will level the balance. In a war, both sides commit crimes. Nowadays people seem to think that only Franco's troops ever got out of hand yet the whole cause of the war was the left-wing Republic's mismanagement and inefficiency, its attempts to implement a bunch of weird, leftist fantasies as far divorced from reality as they were from any idea of the country's real problems; and more than anything, the population's desperate hunger. A strong government was needed, one that could unite all institutions, the Church, the army, business. The Republican government just wanted to set up unworkable nature schools for the peasants, free theatre for the masses and so on, stuff that did bugger all to solve Spain's real problems. What really gets me is the endless sycophantic idolising of the supposed courageous Republican defence: the truth is Franco's men were able to walk in and capture Barcelona without firing a single shot.

That's why I want to tell the truth, write a book to redress the balance. I write bits and pieces when I need a break from study. I've got this scrapbook I write in. I'm not too worried about getting a good copy yet, and the chapters are all jumbled up, written over, crossed out and written over again. I'm not totally sure of the plot, but as each chapter gets to a more-or-less polished stage, I type it onto an eight-inch computer floppy disk. The University have some brand new IBM 486s with Windows 3.0—state of the art.

Anyway, it also put the next nail in my coffin with Fra: I was supposed to be meeting her for the opening of this bar behind Plaza Real. She had met up with Narcissus and Álvaro plus a few others beforehand, but I was coming from the university so couldn't get there till later. I went home first since it was nearby, to drop off my bag with all my books and change. Uptown, I wear a collar and tie; it's that kind of place, where people spend a lot of time polishing their executive look. But down where I live, that's not cool.

I was leaving my place—had changed my clothes, put some gel in my hair—just going out of the street door when they roared past on his Harley. She was wearing some kind of satin thing with her hair blowing free—totally seventies, like a Roxy Music album cover. They didn't see me. They cruised down the Calle del Pino and turned up the Ramblas. I just sensed, without knowing it, that they were off to the same opening I was, even though they were heading in the opposite direction. A peculiar pair. I wandered down Calle del Pino to the Ramblas as well, choosing that route instead of the back streets because there's a bar there, one of my favourites, a few doors down from the Café de la Opera. It's a basement bar, long and low with mirrors covering the left wall along which are installed those booths, American soda fountain style—you expect John Travolta and Olivia Newton John to come bouncing out of the back. The bar runs down the right-hand wall, with a row of barstools bolted to the floor in front of it. Paco is a classic, old-style bartender. Always polishing glasses or something, like in *Casablanca*. Keeping him company is one of my best mates here. Rudi, or

Rodolfo to his Mum, is Argentinean. He's been here about five years. Spends his time fighting off Spanish girls with a stick (bit like me really, hehe). Apart from being six-foot, muscular and blond with green eyes, he has that annoying South American habit of wanting to recite poetry to anything in a skirt. They love it, but it's almost been the cause of World War Three between us because sometimes he just doesn't know when to stop.

"Hey Edu! Speak of the devil! We were just reminiscing about you."

"Yeah? Hope it's all good."

"Good for Paco. He was wondering when you'd be in to pay your tab."

"Do I owe you for drinks? Sorry, Paco I didn't realise. Give us a whiskey on the rocks."

One social whiskey wouldn't make me too late for Françoise's opening. I filled in Rudi and Paco on the doings. Paco was understanding:

"Girlfriend commitments. These things totally kill the love. But you've got to do them if you want to keep the home life sweet."

Chatting about one thing or another, I found a second whiskey in my hand, which I had to finish to be sociable. Then I really did have to leave. I sprinted up the steps out of the bar, helping me to discover that I was slightly drunk. Heading along Ferran towards L'Acordeoniste—I think Françoise said it was called—I passed the little Tarragona kid, Joaquim, coming the other way. I nodded, but he had his head down, fists clenched, striding along the pavement like a Palestinian terrorist about to self-destruct. When I reached the bar, everything seemed quite subdued. I wish I'd stayed and had a beer for the road at Paco's. Fra seemed frosty, but I'd told her I was going to be late.

So she turns around—it almost feels like in a spirit of revenge—and says: "Edu, you know Celia, don't you? But I don't think you've met Gabi, Gabriel Sabater?"

My mouth drops open. This is him? My idol? "You're Gabriel Sabater? It's a real pleasure to meet you. *Conversaciones al otoño* is my favourite book."

Even to myself I sound false and sycophantic. But I'm feeling gutted. My idol is revealed as this motorcycle dwarf. Worse: she is on his arm. No justice. I want to spit my dummy and storm from the bar. I choose another escape.

"Who wants a drink? Joana, give me a Cuatro Rosas con hielo."

The dwarf and Snow White go for more of that disgusting pink cava which they've been slugging back at about a glass a minute. I learnt my lesson on that stuff last summer. They'll be chundering off the sidewalks in less than an hour. We toast. Sabater is entertaining: a wit faster than a speeding bullet. Françoise seems happier that I'm cool with her mates, that finally I've found at least one of her friqui *friends* acceptable. I wouldn't go that far, but as long as she's happy...

I'm just trying to stay subdued and decipher a few things through the alcohol vapours: there's the Ice Queen; there's Gimli son of Gloin Sabater. I mean, who he chooses to sleep with is his problem. But then, *Conversaciones al otoño*... What are we talking about here? And I thought Sabater was such a *bourgeois* writer.

Bourgeois. That's actually the quality that I like about him, as un-pc as it might sound. What is he doing down here among all the... He knows Narcissus and Álvaro... He is so obviously a part of Celia's world...

I turn and Celia's watching me: "Poor Edu, it's so confusing, isn't it?"

I look into her eyes, which are brown and very shiny.

"Confusing? Yeah, it's confusing, but I wouldn't call it disappointing."

We touch glasses and drink.

# Joaquim IX

A soldier kills, a carpenter builds, a road-worker makes roads. I am a writer; that is my job. If I do not do it every day for a number of hours, I will not pay the rent. As far as ideology goes, that is another question. It is not a case just of doing; there, one must think, risk and take sides. And your ideological stance is more than an eight-hour working day. You raise your head and you may get shot down.

—Evaristo López, "Los intelectuales y la historia", International Congress of Intellectuals and Artists, Valencia, 16 June 1981.

"Are you working on anything, Pere?"

He asks the question... and it's like the room becomes chilled. All the embarrassment and strain are now concentrated into this one moment. Mum kind of simpers and lunges to pour more coffee. Dad swallows and coughs, preparing his throat to speak, but we all—even I—know it's just a polite question, and that the answer he is finally able to croak out is irrelevant to everyone—even himself.

The man is a successful writer, having written lots of books. She, I'm not quite sure who she is, but she also seems important to everyone there though I sense that Mum would love to drive the paring knife between those ruby-upholstered ribs. They are on their way to Valencia, where an important literary congress is being held, for the first time since before the dictatorship.

Lying in bed that night—Mum's made mine up in the ironing room; They have my bedroom—I can hear Them moving around, his continual murmur, recounting yet another episode, her muted chuckles—tired now—as they prepare for bed. This is the first time I am aware of either of my parents having any kind of past before me. It's strange. I can't imagine Dad belonging to a world as exotic as theirs yet there are mysteries behind what I can immediately see. Frustrating. I strain to catch their words above, like a faint Morse code I need to survive. But the signals are too weak. Soon silence claims the house. I still listen. What if—I know the stuff grown-ups do—What if... they had sex in my bed? The idea is gross yet... also compelling in a way I can't describe. I keep my ears tuned to those well-known springs above, ready to interpret any unusual creak or discreet groan. I capture nothing. Then sleep.

In the morning, after a cup of coffee, They are gone. Mum doesn't get up. Dad is sheepish, blustering and bleary all at once, managing to wish them the best for the conference where the man is going to give a speech. I sit in one corner of the kitchen, not quite bold enough to speak directly to them, but unwilling to withdraw either. She smiles at me, ruffles my hair as if I'm a kid (didn't I tell you?) and I am again swept up through her perfume into an exotic world, somewhere leagues distant from Mum's special smell. Then she searches through her shoulder bag.

"Your Dad tells me you're a bit of a historian."

She puts a small paper envelope before me on the table.

"It's an antique. Forties or fifties, I'm not sure. You'll have a better use for it than me."

Then they are gone, their beige Citroën bouncing away into the dust. I look at the envelope. *Anís Manelic* marks the front. Inside are unevenly shaped paper profiles. It's a puzzle. I piece it together as I slurp chocolate, devour bread and *llonganissa* sausage.

***

There's this moment when Celia and I are alone—a critical event: Sunday, the eighth of April, my birthday—I'm twenty. I want to invite her, but have no money. I'm first feeling the full horror of my responsibilities. I paid the rent—God knows where I found it—but Celia still hasn't given me her share, neither have Narcissus or Álvaro. Celia says she'll pay for lunch (I can take it off that month's rent) and we go out, down to Barceloneta beach. We go for lunch down among the *chiringuitos*, the dozen or so semi-makeshift paella restaurants that leach out onto the sand. People say they'll pull them down before the Olympic Games, but nobody really believes they could destroy an icon like these.

The beach faces more or less south-east and at two o'clock on a clear April Sunday, you feel summer is just making its first showing. The sun hits forcefully and kids are beginning to populate the sand. This is one of the few memories I have of full daylight, where this city is not a city at night. We sit at a shaded table, its feet deep in sand and stare out at the glittering Mediterranean. I sense Celia's distance, her absence. I wish I could reach out yet I can't read her eyes through the shades she is wearing. Maybe something occurred last night—out and about. Instead I watch a swarm of teenagers arguing over the rules of beach volley, it must be the first game of the summer. They look thin and opalescent, skins of golden oyster translucence; pale, deep-sea creatures that have slithered out of the indigo depths to play on the sand. Yet two of them are at a standoff. The group's squat, curly-headed leader, volleyball balanced casually between thrust hip and wrist, jabs his dominance into a taller, bleach-headed boy. Rhythmic and earnest, the gang's captain, or whoever he is, prods the other's sternum using a muscular arm, taut index finger, stabbing him backwards across the beach. The group ebbs and flows around them animatedly.

We order a *paella a la marinera*, a bottle of Monopole. Leagues out of my price range but *un día es un día*. Why not? If it will cheer Celia up?

*Apoyá en el quicio de la mancebía*
*Miraba encenderse la noche de Mayo.*

The gypsy-cowboy guitarist with the beak nose is regaling a group of tourists at an inner table: *Ojos verdes*, green eyes.


*Pasaban los hombres y yo sonreía*
*Hasta que a mi puerta paraste el caballo.*


I get a double memory: The night Celia's father stayed—Pah! Ma fille!—comes back to me along with an older recollection. I shrink into myself. It is as if I am simultaneously in three places: his screwed-up face in the candlelight, that look of disgust; the white-gold boys, frenetic and puppy-deadly on the sand before us; while in another sunlit scene, my hand is clamped in my father's. He is lifting me above breakers which flash white like toothpaste ads in the sun yet foam as vicious as sharks, seem about to rip out my innards. I am only aware of my terror which surges through every vein and artery of my being, and of Dad's laughter, aggressive, hearty, just hoisting me at the last minute above the treacherous ocean from which I can't escape.


*Serrana, ¿me das candela? y yo te dije: gaché*
*Ven y tómala en mis labios.*


Then the paella comes, its prawns lipstick-red, greasy and desirable on their wide bed of saffron rice. We begin to eat.

That might have been when I began to hate Dad, when he became that shadow in my life. An innocent memory really, compared to others.


*Que yo fuego te dare*
*Dejaste el caballo*
*Y lumbre te dí*
*Y fueron dos verdes luceros de mayo tus ojos pa' mí.*

Maybe when I began to stop being the son he loved.

*Ojos verdes,*
*Verdes como la albahaca.*

***

It was some time after that visit—when I was eleven, or twelve—I came across some of Dad's writings. An old notebook, but elegantly bound in leather and marbled covers. The first date inside is April 23rd, 1968, a dedication from my mother on St George's Day:

To my darling Pere,
Let's tear down the walls, ford the rivers, explore new lands, together, forever!
Here describe our Brave New World.
With all my love,
Celia.

That's Mum's name, Mum's handwriting. The first poem is within a week of that date, a love poem—what else?

Tumbling streams these sun-silver tresses,
Like whorling water-worn wells
Amid the mountain torrent
Those secret hollows beside your throat.
And rounded bones of limestone,
Whittled by life into delicate form,
Your tired happiness is a river boulder

I hold embraced in my arms.

Be my land; I shall
Lay out this dusky parchment
That we may scribe the world's reaches,
Bravely, together.

There are two or three other poems, pretty much in the same vein of naive ardour, turning Mum into boulder-strewn wildernesses, dark continents, sunny meadows, even a city at night. Later on the formality loosens: poems become drafts, complete with crossings-out; even the odd page ripped out; then things descend almost to jottings. There are lots of undated entries, lists of things to be done or bought, the odd diary-like account of a dinner party or some social event yet not enough detail given to create any interest:

Miguel v. drunk by dessert. Facetious comments about E's legs.
??? What was the line??? About the nature of Swedes??? Swedish??
Use this!!!

The final entry is about a quarter of the way into the book, dated impressively 19th March, 1970—less than a month before I was born—as if this was an important date yet all there is, scribbled across the middle of the page is:

Call Ricard!!!

Maybe I was at that age when every kid wishes their father has some hidden genius, or at least the odd grace to save him from being the mediocre entity he quite clearly appears. If that's what I was looking for, I was savagely disappointed.

***

*Ojos verdes,*
*Verdes como la albahaca.*
*Verdes como el trigo verde*
*Y el verde, verde limón.*

Celia raises her glass.

"Happy birthday, Joaquim."

The boys on the beach finish their game and slowly scatter towards bikes and skateboards, passing close as they go. A few of them do stare, but I'm feeling too happy in Celia's company to care.

# Eduardo IX

**HORROR IN ZARAGOZA: 7 DEAD, 3 CHILDREN**

*A SAVAGE TERRORIST ATTACK ON THE ZARAGOZA CIVIL GUARD BARRACKS YESTERDAY BY BASQUE TERRORIST GROUP ETA LEFT SEVEN DEAD, INCLUDING THREE YOUNG GIRLS, AND 18 PEOPLE INJURED, SIX HOSPITALISED.*

At six o'clock yesterday evening, a van loaded with Goma-2 explosive rolled down the street and exploded in the entrance to the quarters of the Spanish ...

—*La Vanguardia*. Saturday edition, 15 June 1981, p. 1.

It was April before I saw Celia again. I had been working on this project at Uni with a couple of mates, Dani and José. I should say at this time I wasn't seeing much of Ri. Not that we'd drifted apart—I don't think, but after I hammered our party season to an end, she and Marta were spending more time at Ri's place and, you know, those girls and their mates must have had plenty on because they were always way too busy to hang out with me anymore. I wasn't going to admit that our argument was the cause; that should have had nothing to do with anything.

At twenty-five, Dani looks like a two-metre-tall fifteen-year-old. He never quite seems to have grown up though he's got an incredibly sharp brain. His specialisation's Human Resources and I've never seen anyone so quick to solve human logistics problems in the most efficient manner: sack them all. But he's a hell of a nice guy and should do well once he leaves school.

José is a kind of Sancho Panza of Computer Science—sort of plods around after everyone, picking up dropped pieces of hardware and half-finished programming projects, which he'll then meld together into an ingenuous suit of cast-off armour all of his own design, submit it as a project and score an A. He has his head screwed on.

So these two and I—I'm on the management side, more the wide view of things—had to get a project together: introducing mechanised processes into a hypothetical car factory—we based it on TEAS—for our mid-course assessment. We were spending late nights at Uni and often, after achieving a certain milestone along our road, we would reach a consensus:

"¿Qué, unas birras o qué?"

Down we'd head to the local bar, talking animatedly about the project—how many plebs we could knock off and still keep it legal—but other subjects would start to wend their way into the discourse. Beer. Girls. Beer. Sex. Girls. Beer. More beer… The girls and sex would get a bit bleary. The other two were single and I might as well have been, the way Fra was giving out.

José has an old, rust-eaten Citroën of which he's intensely proud—I don't know why. But at a certain point after a few beers, we found ourselves cruising the streets up around Camp Nou—just for a laugh—which Dani calls the *campo enemigo*, enemy territory. He's an Español fan. José's more of a computer geek than a football lout and I, probably because I've moved around so much, I've never really felt any pull towards national sports—either Australian Rules, or European football. Not that this tangent has the slightest bit to do with anything.

So anyway, we're cruising around the "girls" up there around the football ground, screaming drunk stuff out of the windows as you do. I mean it's all just for fun, isn't it? Then José slows because there are a couple of cop cars ahead—the *nacionales*. We sort of pull our heads in a bit. There are always cops around here, I mean it's a hooker zone. Of course. They want to relieve the night's tedium as well. We grind to a halt because all the traffic has stopped in both directions.

Then I see her. And I blame all this on the slight connection we made at that dinner. I mean normally, I wouldn't care and definitely wouldn't want to get involved... not in that situation, not in front of my Uni mates; it's enough to have my girlfriend fag-hagging around the mansion, making friends with them; the last thing I need is to establish any social links to the friquis. She's sitting on a curb in one of her satiny things, holding a man's handkerchief to her eyes. Without quite registering what I'm doing, I'm out of the car and over there. Why am I such a mental knight in shining armour? Mental being the operative adjective.

"Hi Celia."

"Edu! Hello."

"Are you okay?"

"Some bastard just tried to kidnap me! Pepper-sprayed me the moment I got in the car. I knew he would be a problem when I first laid eyes him!"

"But you got out?"

"Why don't I ever just trust my girl power! Javier, one of our men in brown over there..."

She nodded towards the nacionales:

"The young blond—cute, isn't he?—a friend of mine—says he's in love with me... But aren't they all, sweets? I've never been so thankful to hear the Cavalry's bugle call: *Santiago y Arriba España!*"

I laugh. I mean she isn't exactly the damsel-in-need-of-rescuing type.

"Oh thank you for your sympathy! Eduardo the charmer!"

"He arrested him?"

"Sirens wailing, street blockaded and everything. It was quite the American movie..."

But this is getting chatty and I'm not planning to become her best friend, or anything.

"What about your eyes?"

Then I run out of words, unusual for me. I'm aware of Dani and José watching from the car.

"Help me up. You'll have to walk me home. Do you mind? I'm blinder than a geriatric with a wank addiction."

"Right."

I decide not to run the gauntlet of Dani and José, so I wave vaguely to them and direct Celia down the road towards the taxi rank. They look at each other, mystified. Then José accelerates. The traffic's cleared.

"Fuck my eyes! I won't be able to work tomorrow at this rate."

It's the first time I've been alone with Celia. As we're walking down the street I'm aware of her height and her heels. She has me in the traditional courting grip, gloved fingers vicelike around my bicep.

"So Edu? I've noticed you're always slightly on the defensive. What does it take to make you loosen up?"

"I wouldn't call myself defensive. I thought I was quite relaxed."

"You're always making smart cracks, but that's a defence, you know it is."

"Yeah, right."

"Tell me about your family."

But I wasn't going to go into that. I had my reasons.

"What? Well, I don't have much. Not for about nine years now..."

"Why?"

And then—surprising myself—I did:

"Zaragoza. Nineteen eighty-one. Dad and my sister got blown up."

"Oh my God!"

That sort of reaction is why it isn't worth telling people.

"I'm so sorry. How old were you? Tell me what happened."

"Fourteen, I think. We were staying on the Costa Brava—we used to come over most summers. We've got an apartment there at Calafranca. Dad had gone into

Zaragoza to see some of his old buddies. He used to be *Benemérita*, the Civil Guard, before he got into the diplomatic corps. He was retired... retired early. Because he could. He loved politics. He used to say Australia had no politics, except for Malcolm Fraser who was keeping the Reds from the door... that it was a frontier town. I didn't understand him really, didn't follow Aussie politics, but then that was him."

I stopped speaking. The flow of words had felt somehow acted. I stood separate from them the way a spectator watches premixed concrete on a building site come oozing out of its long pipe to slop into its prepared mould, covering all the mess of steel and clay in the foundation trenches.

"He had taken Zara, my sister..."

I was back in the words then. It became real:

"She had made friends with the daughter of one of his mates and they had arranged... the girls, three of them, were off to see a movie together. Dad and Zara arrived a bit late. Everyone was standing around in the courtyard outside the barracks. Dad and his mates—a couple of their wives—were planning to head out to a restaurant to chew over old times. A van rolled down the street. It hit the archway of the Civil Guard barracks. Exploded. Packed with fuck-knows-how-many kilos of Goma-2, ETA's favourite. Seven people died. All the girls. Zara. My sister. Dad died... Two of his mates... one of the women... That summer half my family was gone... almost nine years ago now. One of ETA's crack performances."

"I'm sorry, Edu."

"I don't tell people this. Don't go screaming it around, alright?"

"Of course not... I wouldn't... I'm really sorry. Were you... How did your mother and you...?"

I was aware she had just said "sorry" three times, like in Sabater's book.

"Well, my Mum is... she's different. Not a typical mother. She survived. But you're always close to your family, especially when they're dead. Zara though... Zara... She was... had nothing to do with ETA's fucking crimes, had never even heard of them; there was no fucking reason for her to die... I still don't get it, how any fucker could do that? Bunch of animals!"

"Well, yeah. Terrorism in any form... sucks..."

"Terrorism doesn't just suck. Those bastards deserve to be skewered up their anuses with a rusty metal spike! I will do it, you know... I'll fucking do it...!"

I thought she was going to say sorry again, but thank God she was silent. I realised it was a mistake to tell her. We weren't far from Avenida Generalísimo now. Maybe I could chuck her in a taxi.

"My first boyfriend... Juan... he was murdered too."

"What?"

Was this about to become a competition about who's suffered the most? I shouldn't have told her.

"I was in love with him... he was the most important thing in my life..."

"Yeah, look. I'm not... I mean your boyfriend was hardly family..."

That sure got her back up:

"He was *my* family! Didn't you meet my sweet father? ... You lost half your family. I lost all of mine when I hit adolescence. Juan was... Juan was my new family... everything... You said there was no reason for your family to die. In his case, there was a reason the terrorists killed him... He was doing something, fighting..."

"You had terrorists in Argentina?"

"We had a government of terrorists. Juan was involved with a printing press... They took him away one night and he never returned. That was when I decided to get out and come to Europe. I still have no idea what happened to him. I probably never will. No body. No cross. Nothing."

"But... hadn't he been causing trouble? Breaking the law? You said he was printing stuff..."

"Pro-democracy leaflets. It was a dictatorship, Edu. You got killed for thinking your own thoughts, trying to change the system."

I didn't see the connection. Celia was associating the death of my family—nothing but delirious bloodlust—with the activities of some subversives acting against the government of the time, dictatorship or not. What did the system of government have to do with it anyway? It was the crime itself that mattered!

"Here you go."

I opened the door of the taxi and stood back. Celia got in and I shut it.

"Have you got money?"

"Edu…"

"See you around."

I started walking down the Generalísimo's Avenue in the direction of Calvo Sotelo. I felt like an idiot for the situation I had just got into.

# Joaquim X

"We have to populate the Earth! Do you realise how much we have ahead, how much work, still?"

"Of course; we're only just beginning!"

—Manuel de Pedrolo, *Mecanoscrit del segon origen* [*Typescript of the Second Dawn*], Edicions 62, Barcelona, 1974, pp. 178-9.

"S hhh!"

That's him, in my room again. But this is not about him; it's about her. Umber. Ochre. Sienna. Burnt and raw. Titanium White. Red for her warmth and green in her shadows. When painting Narcissus I used Red Rust, Verdigris and Zinc Yellow. His personality demanded contrasts that were primary... industrial. Celia was earthen. These colour schemes are simplistic. Yes, I finally painted her, but this is getting mixed up. I have to start with meeting, back in March. Yet Narcissus intrudes:

"Shhh!"

He is lying on top of me in the dark. We listen to his bedroom door close distantly, and to Álvaro's footsteps striking the tiles. Then the front door slams and his feet clatter away down the staircase into the *porte cochère*. Finally, the heavy oak door to the street gives a tired creak and boom. Then we can't hear him anymore. For a long moment Narcissus doesn't move, nor do I. We lie immobile, his weight pinioning me to the bed.

"Shit!"

Now he does, rolls off me and the magic—both our own, and Álvaro's spell for immobility—has vanished. Narcissus, perched on the edge of the mattress, peering down into his hands as if they would reveal his destiny, appears shrunken. I feel suddenly revolted by him, by myself. Is this what we glorified in, wallowing exultantly as we inflicted such pain? Stooped and shambling—the contrast imprints itself on my brain like a flash of blue lightening—he collects his clothes and returns to his empty room. I switch on the bedside light, stare at the greens and rusts of my serra in the lithograph. Ten minutes later I hear Narcissus leave too.

***

The first time I saw Celia, she entered the bar we were at like a painful memory from the past. That evening was like a waltz, it seems so elegant, as if it were lit by chandeliers. It's Joana's barwarming: L'Accordéoniste, off Carrer Ferran—black lacquer tops, checked tile floor, Piaf's sawn voice raging over the sound system:

> *Mais plus rien de la moto et plus rien de ce démon*
> *Qui semait la terreur dans toute la région ...*

And a black-leather-upholstered bike—leather tassels and raised handlebars—pulls up outside the door, a woman riding pillion. She appears, satin-clad with windblown hair still curling, flung around her powdered face—a personification of her—with him. Of course, it wasn't who I remembered, my green-eyed goddess, but it was definitely him, the Writer. The shock makes me realise, because it's so much clearer now from a few years ago—have I grown up so much, so quickly?—why they had made the breath stop in my chest, and in Mum's.

> *Jamais il ne se coiffait, jamais il ne se lavait*

He's a few years older, greyer in the temples, heavier.

*Les ongles pleins de cambouis mais sur les biceps il avait*

His moustache even fuller if possible yet neatly trimmed and waxed.

*Un tatouage avec un coeur bleu sur la peau blême*

But a sagging paunch that fashionable pullovers can't quite hide any longer.

*Et juste à l'intérieur, on lisait : "Maman je t'aime"*

He still bounces in the door, kissing Joana on both cheeks, launching into a report of a Marilyn Horne recital they've heard at the Liceu Opera House earlier that evening. Yet I'm transfixed by her. Her presence next to this man from Dad's past reveals so much more about my father. Though only later would I make the connection.

*Il avait une petite amie du nom de Marie-Lou*
*On la prenait en pitié, une enfant de son âge*

Since he has left her while he greets friends, she stands at the bar alone, smoking a cigarette. She is stunning; he, deflated, quite jaded.

*Car tout le monde savait bien qu'il aimait entre tout*
*Sa chienne de moto bien davantage ...*

We had arrived as a group—Narcissus, Álvaro, Françoise, me and others—I think Juanjo is here—didn't come with us, but is in a corner spitting gin at the evils of the Catalan Republican Left—he and I have never seen eye to eye. Joana's passing around trays of little white-bread squares spread with tuna pâté and may-onnaise—a kind of *Barrio Chino hors d'oeuvre*. She's also serving complimentary cava, the cheap pink bubbles you can get at the bodega down by Set Portes. I have already suffered a couple of hangovers from this label, but free is free on any night of the week. Narcissus is also eyeing her.

"Now THERE is a Lady with a story."

But before Álvaro can make his move, the Writer has surged across the room and washed up among our group, swamping us all in his swell—well, Narcissus, really:

"Are you a friend of Tomàs?"

"ToMÀS! You know ToMÀS?"

"He owes me money."

"*Ahh!* Not such a good friend, no. How is Tomàs?"

"I hope he's well enough to pay me the money he owes me soon."

"I haven't seen Tomàs for... oh SIX, SEVen months, at least."

"I always thought you two were thick as thieves."

Narcissus almost snarls: "I HEAR you're WORKing on something at the moment?"

"I'll invite you to the launch!" And he's washed his way on towards Joana, towards the cava, towards another group of more accessible groupies.

"Nothing as SAD as a HAS-been arTISTE..." His eyes swivel towards me. "Except maybe a never-WILL-be one. WHEN are you ever going to show us your MASterpiece, Petit Miró?"

It's been over a month. "Uh... soon."

"SOON? I thought we had an aGREEment?"

"Soon."

But I have already left, refuse to let myself see what I am doing, cannot believe it, until suddenly I have crossed the room and stand before her.

"Would you like a drink?" I have two glasses of champagne in my hands I am not aware of having picked up.

"Thank you. You're very sweet."

"Uhh, I'm Joaquim"

"Thank you, Joaquim. Celia."

"Ah. My Mum's name."

"Thanks." Sardonic. The wrong thing to say.

"But... you're beautiful! I mean... more than her."

And my social repertoire has dried up. I stand half a metre from her, bathed in her ravishing aura, breathless, wordless, marooned by my social impetuosity.

"I'm sure that isn't the case... if it was her gave you those cute baby-blues."

"Could I paint you?"

"Are you a painter, Joaquim? My, that is so flattering!"

I don't, can't look at her directly, but stare at her shoulder—my height; she is taller than me—where a pearl-coloured bra strap peeks from beneath the satin collar of her dress, transforming the hollow above her collar bone into a place of erotic reverie.

"I can paint you, I could... I'm just starting out, but I'm good... I would do you as a classical goddess, like Olympia, like Manet, but contemporary. It would be great. You'd have to come round the house... that's where I've got my studio."

She laughs. I blush, feel stupid. We're speaking Spanish. Of course. She has just a slight Argentinean accent. Spanish is a kind of lingua franca of the night because so many people we meet are foreigners.

Then the Writer is upon us. I'm about to introduce myself. I want to ask him about Dad, but he pre-empts me:

"Are you one of Narcissus's boys?"

"Oh, Gabi, where're your manners? People aren't always just the sum of their friends. Joaquim here has offered to paint my portrait."

He looks at me properly for the first time that night.

"Are you a painter?"

"You were a friend of my Dad's, Pere...? You stayed at our house one night, on your way to a writers' conference in Valencia... Nine years ago? You were travelling with a... woman..."

"Her? God! How could I forget her! God! God, yes! So you're Pere's son? Ugh! Am I that old already?"

"Gabi, behave!" Celia interjects. He takes a gulp of his drink and surveys the room.

"Was Dad... Was... What was Dad like when he was young?"

"*We* were all so... so active... Those days were intense..."

Then he chuckles:

"Your Dad was one of us... in the early days anyway. We were fighting for fre edom... democracy... there was so much to do, the fight demanded everything... He could have done more... should have maybe... but then... the old bastard went and died on us... And suddenly, there was no fight left. It was like we had it all. We were so happy... Why write? Why fight? And so many people did stop... writing, creating... settled down just to be happy. Maybe they were the wise ones, but we all make our choices... live with them."

He seems to have become hypnotised by the sound of his own voice. A few people have stopped their conversations and are listening respectfully. I decide not to press for more information, am feeling too much in the spotlight. I shouldn't have told him who I was... We just do things sometimes that don't get us anywhere. Then Françoise and Álvaro are upon us. I manage to stutter out introductions.

Françoise whispers: "You don't know who this is?"

"Sort of... He knew my Dad."

Her eyes widen, giggling around the rims: "Your Dad and He were friends? Wheeoo, Joaquim, you do have some secrets from me still!"

That is not what this is about! I frown—I think I hate more not knowing what this is about... and the kind of unpleasant stories my own mind weaves feels like treason... though I won't let Dad off the hook that easily, won't suddenly become loyal to him just because tonight in this seedy bar in the Barrio Chino I'm discovering—no, too strong—suspecting a different history about my father to the one I've grown up under, felt *threatened* by throughout my entire life.

"I don't know how close they were."

But the Writer has overheard me: "Your Daddy was what we called a *camp-fol-lower* back in those days, Blue-Eyes. Had the most gorgeous butt I ever saw, but... you'll have to ask the others for details... I never visited that Mecca personally!"

I'm ready to hit him. I feel that wind rising inside me so I can't hear anything else. Álvaro puts an arm around my shoulders:

"Relax, Joaquim. He's just taking the piss, can't you see?"

But Álvaro is not the one to tell me anything and no, I can't see and that buzzing, floating feeling is starting, where the air seems to be singing, keening and everything's glowing hot. I shrug off Álvaro's arm.

"I couldn't imagine anyone would want to... to get close to you... a fucking ugly fat bastard and a... crap writer as well!"

I storm out, I always storm out. The whole bar has gone silent—my outburst coincides with a pause in the music. All I register is a ring of frozen pale faces around me, then I'm scrabbling at the glass doors. I finally get them open and leave, stalking through the night, where everyone around me seems to be giggling, smirking, screaming, screeching with glee, having fun, enjoying the night and it's all like this huge conspiracy against *ME!* Like everyone on the streets who glances my way could suddenly read my head, look into me and see the real *ME* that is glaring around, roaring to get out. I hate it, hate the fact there are so many people—it's Saturday night—and I just can't get away. People seem to throng Carrer Ferran and the Rambles in droves—all hilariously, hideously happy. I turn up one street and down another and just come across more and more people, I can't find a space! I want to kill them all!

Finally I head along Carrer Unió—a dark, quiet street, cut up past the hookers to Carrer Pau—want to hit them to shut them up, silence their wheedling advances:

"Ooo my man, have fun with me? Fucky fucky?"

—along Pau to Paral·lel, stalking up Fontrodona, walking off my rage. Then before long I'm on the back of the mountain, Montjuïc, where it's cold, dark and empty... soothingly empty of people... of laughing... of gleeful insinuations.

I walk up among the pines and holm oaks... Now I'm feeling the consequences of how I acted... the familiar pressure, the stress of being me... Joaquim the Fool... I feel like an idiot, my destiny. My imaginary tarot lady seems to be confirming just what a fool I am, Joaquim, King of Fools, having made a complete idiot of myself before the cream of the party crowd.

I sit down on some steps and look out at the lights of the city. If only I wasn't me! If only I could do something really special, superlative, be someone or something. But I am inescapably Joaquim the Fool. I will never be anyone, never do anything great. My father was mediocre and I'll be mediocre too. I want to leave, but for the first time I don't want to go home, not down to my *serra*, I just want to leave, go, go away, forever.

# Eduardo X

*... angelheaded hipsters burning for the ancient*
*heavenly connection to the starry dynamo*
*in the machinery of the night ...*

—Allen Ginsberg, "Howl".

Sometimes I wonder if the life I'm living is the one I should be. Things had been going well up until that point—studies, flat, girlfriend—yet maybe I hadn't been paying close enough attention. I mean, how can things go from perfect to Hell in such a short time, with no advance warning of the change? There must have been some tear, like a stitch or two missing, some tiny rupture that had existed way before, which I hadn't noticed, gradually widening into a huge rent in my marvellous existence until there, suddenly the entire flood was pouring in through the portholes; before you knew it my life had gone pear-shaped. Maybe it was that gap—like a piece that had always been absent (I'd never paid it much importance)—as if one span of the bridge were never built, had crumbled the moment the cement was dry—or were blasted into nothing by a tonne or so of Goma-2—which took away the reason for the whole construction.

My secret was out. I realised walking down the street afterwards that my story would do the rounds of Freaksville. Very few people around me knew nowadays: my Mum and the rest of the family obviously; Ri, Juanjo and a few of the Calafranca gang... When half your family gets vaporised by terrorists, it's difficult to hide it from the world. But time passes. People forget. I let them forget. That's why hardly any friends around me now knew. Not my Uni friends. All Fra knew was that Zara and Dad had died when I was young. I left it at that. People have different ways of dealing with death. It's uncomfortable to mention, most people prefer to creep around the edges. For months after the funerals I used to see people's nervousness, wanting to pry, commiserate, but not knowing whether to open their mouths. Finally I got sick of it, made sure that new people in my life wouldn't be likely to find out.

Of everybody I could have told, I don't know why I spilled my guts to Celia. Well, I do. She and I connected. However different she might be in terms of, you know, her stuff, we did connect. I felt seriously pissed off with her, didn't feel she had the right to relate our two stories—as if they had some kind of chord in common, a shared history. People are unbelievable! I really couldn't stand seeing her for a good while after that and I made sure I didn't. When Françoise wanted to boogie with the weirdos, she went alone.

I stayed uptown—where just the prices kept the *friquis* away. My favourite club, on Avenida Tibidabo, was Cielito. Dani, José and I would do two or three bars, a few get-yourself-in-the-mood white lines and then head up.

We met up a few nights after my rescue mission of Celia and did just that. I told them she was a friend of Fra's—which she was, I wasn't lying—though I knew they thought it was a bit odd. What was I doing associating with—even knowing second-hand—a creature like that? My attitude is I couldn't give a rat's arse. I talk to who I want and nobody will tell me who I'm not supposed to socialise with. But the truth is, you break some social rules and people are pretty unforgiving. Neither of them asked me about her when we met, so my first mistake was offering any explanation. José just kind of looked at me and nodded, sipped his beer. He's known me all my life; it would be difficult to rock him. Dani seemed annoyed, uncomfortable and upset all at the same time, wouldn't meet my eyes. I realised I had crossed a line.

Cielito is a four-level building crouched on the mountainside—all glass frontage with views over the city—much cooler than the low, sweaty halls where the *friquis* hung out. It's divided into seven sections, each with a different colour—I think the idea is it's supposed to represent the seven levels of heaven—but the reality is there are only three different music spaces.

That night all I needed was a whiskey *cubata* and a space to chill for a while. I sat above the stairs, where there's a kind of upholstered swing chair hung on chains. You look out over the lights of the city—more in the direction of L'Hospitalet. A lot of the clubland shitheads can't get at you there to destroy your night. I was still pissed with Celia, but couldn't shake her from my night. In my imagination, I could feel her cool eyes on me, like she wanted something. What I told Celia was not half of the truth. How could I explain what I felt? Zara was twelve. One of the longest-running faces on *Kidz Bizz*, a real pro. Sometimes she used to get on my wick, but I still adored her. Amazingly, the Australian press weren't too interested in a child star getting blown to shreds in Europe. Wasn't she famous enough? Or maybe it was too difficult a topic for them to slot into their format, wouldn't sit quite comfortably next to Chichi Zefire's third divorce or Cindy Reinhardt's tit operation.

I was fourteen. I didn't quite understand what was going on, or just a little too much. I wasn't a kid, but I was a long way from being grown-up. We were at the beach that afternoon, had been there exactly fifty minutes after having a late pizza for lunch at one of the beachfront restaurants. I was lying on my towel, ticking off the minutes. Mum wouldn't let me go in the water till at least an hour had passed after lunch. She was reading *Hola* magazine. I could see Cal and José sunbathing on the raft moored out in the bay, where I wanted to be. Rolling over to check my watch, which was stashed in my backpack—it was four-forty—I saw a Civil Guard sergeant step down off the esplanade and start plodding

across the sand. I knew he was looking for us—don't ask me how.

"Mum."

I nudged her arm and nodded towards the sergeant. Mum looked around, saw him and rose to meet him. She knew as well. I will never forget that image: my Mum standing there, sun-brown and tiny in her pale blue bikini, the Hola forgotten on the sand at her feet, while that green-uniformed, sweating sergeant came clumping like a curse between the limp bodies across the hot sand.

"Señora, may I have a word?"

I collected our stuff and followed the two adults back up onto the esplanade, into the pizzeria. Mum and that sergeant sat at a table in the sun-darkened space—lunch was long over, the tables deserted—while I was told to wait on the terrace, given an horchata to sip.

Then she wouldn't tell me. I knew something was wrong, but she wouldn't say a thing. The sergeant walked us back up to our apartment, with another of the greens—a corporal. He was the one who phoned Mum's sister, my aunt Eleonora, who came straight up from Barcelona. Mum just went into her room and locked the door.

"Edu."

I was sitting in my room. I kind of didn't have the guts to ask anyone what was going on, so I was sitting in my room looking through this *Mortadelo y Filemón* comic. Eleonora—Leo—was in the doorway. She came and sat on my bed.

"Edu, there's been an accident."

Even then she never used real words: "accident"; this stupid euphemism for a bloody terrorist attack, for some cowardly bastards who were afraid to show their faces and fight like honest men, who had killed my sister. She never ever called it anything but an "accident". Then Ri came around and I asked Leo if I could go out and she said yes, so Ri and I went out and walked right out to the point past Cal Ramon where we just kind of sat on the rocks and let the Mediterranean spray cool us.

The next time I saw my Mum was at the funeral, looking totally Jackie Onassis. I had been living with Auntie Leo since the accident. For whatever reason—should have known my Mum better—I expected that after the funeral, I would go back home to Australia with her, we'd pick up our lives again.

We were in Zaragoza, standing in the reception that followed the funeral, in this huge, echoing, military hall, vomit-coloured paint peeling from the walls. It was obvious the government was paying for it all—spare no expense. Ri was beside me. The whole place was full of uniforms. Ri and I knew how to misbehave anywhere, but this was challenging. I didn't understand why Zara had to be buried in a military barracks. Mum came up, Leo on one arm, and some guy on the other.

"Darling, this is all too much. Emilio's taking me back to the hotel. Alright? Be good and we'll see each other soon."

She kissed me on the forehead. Leo kind of hugged me around the arm that Ri wasn't holding.

"Your Mum and I were chatting, Edu. We were thinking it would be a nice idea if you could stay on with us down in Barcelona for a while."

I watched Mum leave the hall with Emilio. That was the last time I saw her for three years.

"Your Mum needs a bit of a rest to get over all this. Maybe Sabrina could come down and stay too. Would you like that Sabrina?"

So I returned to Sarrià with Auntie Leo. That's the real reason I spent four years in high school in Barcelona. My Mum was swinging from the chandeliers—a total basket case—though still getting a lot of acrobatic sex in, from what I heard.

Then the summer I turned seventeen, Mum and Paco—her new beau—decided to come up and spend the summer in the Costa Brava apartment. Up till then, it had been our free domain: Leo's, her husband Javi's and mine. It was a weird meeting. Once Mum and Paco had settled in, I was to go up and spend the weekend. I didn't want to, didn't want anything to do with either of them, but Leo insisted. That was the start of the Paco-Edu Wars, which lasted about two years, before we both just seemed to get tired. I think I realised that life was not going to unwind, or go backwards to where I was before. Dad and Zara were gone, but basically so was Mum, as if she'd ever been there. At a certain point, you've just got to toughen up and say "Fuck them!" Get on with life. Ri became my family.

***

"Hello?"

"Ri? Come up. I'm at Cielito. It's hot."

"Edu?"

"Are you coming up or not?"

I hear her puff melodramatically.

"Okay, in half an hour."

"See you."

I'm back in the swing when Ri comes in, Marta in tow. Ri's in her basic lesbian black—jeans, sleeveless tee, studded belt—against the contrast of her spiked, blond hair, carrying about half a jar of gel, which is already starting to flatten. It's too fine for the look she wants. Marta is sent off to get drinks and she leans against the window, silhouetted by L'Hospitalet's lights.

I should admit I left out certain nuances when I mentioned our fight earlier. The truth is we got into some fairly bloody territory. The tiff about our girlfriends was just the detonator. I went ballistic. She went ballistic. We stood in the gym cafeteria for five minutes screaming our heads off at each other.

"Last time we saw each other, you told me to fuck off."

"Come on, you said the same." While I was waiting for her, I calculated this was coming. "You know that means fuck all."

"You did mean it, Edu. You fucking well know you did."

"Okay, yeah. Sorry. I was a bit strong."

Marta arrives with drinks for Ri and her, giving me a kind of tired greeting. The paradise of our living situation has been pretty strained for almost a month now. I wish she'd move out and leave Juanjo and I to ourselves. That way I could concentrate on recovering my friendship with Ri, instead of having this three-way communication fuck-up. It's perfectly possible Marta is at the bottom of all Ri's and my hassles.

"Hi Marta."

I hope she's going to take a hint and bugger off and dance so Ri and I can talk, but she goes and leans against the glass like Ri, but on her far side, a little way off. She looks down at me.

"How are you, Edu?"

"*What?*"

*"I said how are you?"*

*"Fine!"*

Great. It's like she's positioned herself purposely, so she and Ri can chat without raising their voices, but anything her and I say to each other, we'll be competing over the music. Fuck this. I stand up.

"Let's go and dance."

We head down to the lower dance floor, which is the best one. José is leaning against the bar. He and Ri kiss on both cheeks. They aren't that close, but know each other from Calafranca. He nods to Marta. I head for the dance floor, acknowledging that my great peace treaty attempt has been vetoed for the moment. I see Dani on the other edge of the dance floor, shouting into a girl's ear. I wave, but he doesn't see me, or pretends not to see me, so I let myself go to the music. Dancing is a way to deal with shit, the passion, the aggression you can't release by hitting people when you want to. It's what I need now. I lose myself for about fifteen minutes, until opening my eyes, I see Ri is gesturing me from the bar. I go over.

"What is it?"

"Do you want a blowjob?"

"Okay."

After that, I say:

"How about a rail?"

The ice has cracked. When we come out of the bogs—we ended up having to use the marble top of the washbasin because the cubicles were all busy—we get another three blowjobs—Bailey's, Kahlua and cream—lined up on the bar, down them and hit the dance floor. What a night! The best way to lose any sense of responsibility or moral order you might be grasping onto.

I'm dancing. Happy. Never so happy as when I'm on the dance floor, shaking my tits off. At some point we're piling into a taxi: José, Ri, Marta and I. Dani's disappeared. San Francisco. Downtown. By the end of the night, it deserved the name Alaska for the amount of snow blowing around. I've been boogying away with her for about ten minutes before I register that the chick bobbing her tits up and down next to me is the Satin Queen herself. She's sweating and I can actually glimpse her face through the makeup. Not pretty. But the dance of her big boobs is mesmerising. Maybe I'm just wanting to tease, but the game gets hornier the longer we dance. At one point we're almost touching. Her dress is silk or rayon. The physical contact charges static energy into my body. But next thing I'm jolted and that Tarragona fag is pushing between us, his fanatical madman's eyes trained on Celia like some puppy wanting to root its Mistress's shin. She just smiles down at him.

"Joaquim, sweetie! I'm parched. You couldn't get us a drink? Do you want a drink, Edu?"

I nod.

"Get us both a drink, cari. You know the one."

Joaquim disappears towards the bar and I push my sweaty torso back towards Celia's silky, inflated tits. Everybody is high as a fucking kite that evening. We had no idea what we were doing. The night's a game you play—like billiards: it needs less strategy, but more balls.

# Joaquim XI

*Oh Fool! You, who are everyman, zero ground, that space on which I stand before I take the first step – an odyssey in ignorance, in blissful faith ... Oh Fool, my teacher.*

–Rodemon, Cielo, *Veinte-dos pasos: desvelando los misterios de la Gran Arcana*, Publicaciones del Arco Iris, Barcelona, 1964.

That was our first meeting. And then she moved in. She needed a room fast. So she took the almost finished one which I was working on, the one that would be hers—bone-white walls, pearl-gray frames, gold-leaf edging. I continued sleeping in the dead Chihuahua room and began to paint another of those three, which would become mine. Just the space between us remained empty.

Those initial weeks she lived with us were bliss, like a continuation of that first elegance, at L'Accordéoniste. Yet now, when we emerged for the night, we shone. Narcissus and Celia together were like the King and Queen of a fantastic realm. We all... Álvaro, Françoise, Miguel, Luigi, Paul, Wulf, even Felipe... were citizens of that landless State. Night. Our realm was a magical isle, winked into being by the sinking of the sun and cut off by its rising.

Ready for the evening, we would issue forth from our mansion, Narcissus, Álvaro, Celia and I, bedecked in knightly glamour: loud silk shirts, studded or engraved belts, spikey hair; Narcissus with his sweeping jackets or brash, silk scarves; Celia in pale satin or sequins. We would congregate at the bar where

Wulf worked—that first one where I had met Narcissus and Álvaro—or else at L'Accordéoniste. Other nocturnal creatures appeared: Marta and Sabrina, the squabbling lesbians; Adele, a voluminous Belgian opera diva; hairy Roberto from Extremadura who had just opened a gallery con Carrer Unió; olive-skinned Giovanni, his pixie-like Andalusian boyfriend; Pedro Paramour, the one Álvaro calls the boy in the black dress though he only uses drag to perform political street theatre with Nico and Nicola, two drama school mates; Sunyar (originally Xavi), a small shaved Buddhist from Vic; Morden, a lanky, black blues singer from Detroit; Jürgen, a DJ and Bavarian separatist; Nasir, who had a shop in our street with his seven brothers; Jorge, a boy with the beguiling eyes of old Castile; Sansón, an Argentinean acrobat; Kyoko and Toshi, two students of Spanish; Jim, a black, Irish architect; Ragnar, a writer from Iceland and his Portuguese girlfriend Elzira, a dancer.

It was in that dark realm where Celia and I picked out the steps of an intimate dance, moving slowly closer. It began like a tango—slow, elegant—before its passion rose as it whirled gently faster. Finally—beautiful as the metaphor of a crystal goblet dashed to splinters in the fireplace—we got to the panting centre of our passionate, private gyre. Our courting happened amidst this entire crowd—we hardly ever managed to be alone, but in a weird way, that was right; that was the context in which we both had meaning, where we both operated best.

The night would unroll: after a few drinks at that first bar, a group of us would leave for a restaurant, possibly La Fragua, Romesco's or Mesón David, where two courses, wine, dessert and coffee cost under six hundred pesetas.

Rolling out of that restaurant at around midnight, we headed on to Quique's, or Guinea on Avinguda Diagonal (someone always paid the taxi) for Cuba libres, to dance to Ritmo, ritmo de la noche—my favourite song that summer—and then after two, hit San Francisco on Consell de Cent.

San Francisco forms the apex of our night. Even if we end up later at Martin's, Velvet or Distrito Marítimo, San Francisco signifies the most intense epiphany of our existence. Entering the low-ceilinged space, it feels like you pass through several "husks" before reaching the night's inner heart. First, there is an outer bar area strewn with café tables; then closed off behind a chain mesh partition, an arcade of pinball machines. Guys—mainly guys—are hitting, smashing, shaking and tilting the machines at all hours. This frenetic activity acts like a buffer of violence between bar and club—a testosterone-fuelled whirlpool. Passing through, you are in, really in: a wide low space with an L-shaped bar to the right. This is the real San Francisco, the inner kernel, the setting for Celia's and my secret romance.

Though our connection is also just a single link in the wide mesh of relationships the space condones. I'm dancing with Morden in the darkness, his teeth flashing a smile, long limbs enwrapping me fully while barely touching. I'm with Jürgen in the box one night, arms raised, rocking as he mixes. Leaning against the wall, I'm talking to Nasir—far too timid to dance. I'm in the toilets sandwiched between Jorge and Jim, snorting up a line of coke then kissing—everywhere my lips touch their bodies, exhilarating in the thrust and energy of being young. I'm feeling guilty about Celia, but the night sweeps you up, carries you away, dissolving responsibility. One night is a night is a night. What happens after, none of us control.

But San Francisco is really about Celia, *la Reina de la Noche*. She stands at the bar, tall and silver—the Writer has long since been dissolved into her past. We never saw him again once she became one of us. Watching her, surrounded by a chorus of adoring guys, I'm not jealous. What her and I have is special, can't be encroached on by these others. I won't crowd, prefer to watch from a distance, knowing there is this special link, which nobody really knows anything about... which will pull us together at the end of the night.

...Except one person. Problems come creeping into our paradise. People are so envious of happiness. Though... maybe I deserve it.

Narcissus and Celia, black king and white queen, they never stand together. Like twin peaks with the entire valley of the club between them, they live together, arrive together yet each has their own entourage. I am probably the only one who is truly part of both groups. Miguel, Pedro, Elzira and Jürgen make up Celia's train; Álvaro, Françoise, Luigi and Felipe are part of Narcissus's. I am like the messenger between both camps—the one that gets killed.

"You must be feeling rich tonight!"

He's right. Cava in this club costs an arm, even the baby bottles Celia prefers. Álvaro has this unsettling way of materialising beside you at the bar like that. He is always speaking a double language: you don't know quite what he's getting at; it's like there's another layer of meaning below his words.

"I need to find a job."

Actually I've still got some of Dad's money left, but I'm starting to get the idea that you can't be too open with Álvaro and Narcissus. Barely a month since I've been living there, only a week or two since Celia has moved in.

"Well, you must think she's worth it. Spending your precious cash."

And he's gone, back towards his side of the room, back towards his lord. I never knew how Narcissus and Álvaro resolved their breach. Nothing outwardly really changed in their behaviour, except Narcissus stopped coming to see me in the night. I don't think I felt that upset... really. But I had been so knocked off my feet by him—still was. Though by now Celia was another strong presence in my life, a countering gravitational pull—the moon against the sun. Even with Celia—because Celia was there—I kind of felt I needed to protect her, provide her with a safe haven. Why did I sign for all Narcissus and Álvaro's debts really? Was it just that I was living, felt I could finally live? I could do anything! This was the first time ever that I had been sucked up in this whirl of Life. I was so absolutely enjoying myself, I didn't want to think. Responsibility was for old people, people like Dad, who had smothered any creative urge he might have had in favour of security, a safe haven. A Safe Haven. Even these words seem to be screaming at me, accusing me of lying, being false. I don't know then, I just did it. I did it because I wanted to. Because I wanted to and because I could.

But on that night, when Álvaro made that comment, I should have been more aware, aware that he was watching. The things you do have consequences. You have to be ready to accept those consequences. That's the hardest lesson life can teach you.

I've blanked out a whole lot of those consequences here, I think. If I was happy I was also wretched... because when Narcissus stopped sneaking to my bed, I thought it was also unfair, unfair because I felt I was so much better for him than Álvaro was—though I knew so little about them then, about myself. The nights we didn't go out, the nights when there was no San Francisco, when we, or I, didn't have the money even for a single beer at our local on Nou de la Rambla, I would lie in my cold room—it remained chilly well into May—wrapped in my sleeping bag and miss him so intensely! It was unfair! When I knew I fulfilled him far more than Álvaro could (yet I didn't know them then and I was wrong), nothing could replace that vacuum I felt like an iron hollow in my gut—not even Miguel, who used to come around every now and again; not even Celia, who was like a powerful goddess who had just alighted in my life yet still distant as if perched on a mountain peak towards whom I squinted up from out of my valley's shadow.

# Eduardo XI

And then, in that low sun, Mr Hand cast three shadows; two helped him aside, and he struggled until a sound came, the sound John Paul had made in town with his ice pick, like ice being chipped, or bone struck, and the hatless man cried out—plea, promise, threat, all at once—and staggered to the wagon and shouted at the water dripping into the dust. The ice was no larger than a man, and bleeding in the same way.

—Paul Theroux, "The Imperial Icehouse" in *The Collected Stories*, Penguin Books, London, 1997. p. 32.

Confessions as hefty as my hangover felt the following morning failed to materialise. Drifting on the fringes of consciousness, I pushed down my nausea. Was it guilt at letting things get so out of hand, or sickness at the sort of person I had glimpsed in myself the night before? I wasn't about to deal with it. At the end of the day, a night's a night. Pun intended.

Françoise lay curled into me, asleep, her beautiful hair splaying out over both our torsos, thighs interlocked warm with mine, hot breath tickling the hairs on my forearm. After San Francisco I had taken a taxi to her flat in Calle Princesa and high as I was, she had let me in. Cocooned with her in this intimate space, the artificial possessiveness of Celia's tits seemed far away.

Yet Celia's presence did not. Since our conversation on the street, as much as it sickened me, some chord seemed to link us. Why was I unable to let it go?

What did I want? I had no idea. But the moment the vague idea of talking to her entered my head, I became obsessed. I realised I had to talk it out more. This compulsion had little to do with sex—I have a girlfriend I love screwing, I'm no pervert needing to act out his filthy fetishes—rather, it was more about reaching a resolution with myself. If I was feeling curiosity on the sexual side, that's all it was: superficial.

I had to think then how I would arrange it. A morning would be perfect because I knew the Tarragona kid worked then. Narcissus and Álvaro were night owls, never up that early, if I could avoid waking them. Yet Celia worked nights too, so she'd also be sleeping. I might end up hanging on that doorbell for a good hour before anyone rose. And I didn't want anyone else in the mansion to answer. Chances were slim I'd catch her that way.

So I returned to Camp Nou, which I didn't like. Too many people, too many chances to be seen and remarked on, remembered. Not that I was doing anything wrong, I just wanted anonymity. Choosing a Friday when I thought the friquis would be out and about, I found Celia and paid for a night. Never thought I would do that. We went back to her room. I thought after our talk I could creep out without any of them seeing—hoping they would be out partying. In theory I don't care what they see, but they would think... and I'm not like that. I'm not. I just needed to talk. The thing is, whatever recriminations, accusations, you make against me, we were there to talk, not have sex.

The problem is, since I was fourteen... when Zara and Dad got vaporised... there's been NOBODY who has understood. Even Ri... She's like family, but even Ri doesn't know how to listen because IT'S NEVER HAPPENED TO HER!

One of the major problems with this world—which is why I think it was better under the old *Caudillo*—is that people have become more detached. It's like the world doesn't matter anymore... And I want the world to matter! I want the world to be a proud project I can be a part of! The things that have happened, they have DAMN WELL HAPPENED and they should be scribed, etched into our history so that we grow up knowing and respecting them from the first moment of our birth. Otherwise, what do things matter? How does one thing become more important than another? There's no criteria. So anything I do can be forgotten tomorrow... Unless there's a system that can record our glories, our past, who we are... I wanted Zara to be remembered and I was facing a world that had no idea she had ever lived. Zara was no more important than the *friquis* with their fatuous projects for improving humanity and creating a world of love. And they were like cockroaches scrabbling in the rubbish. I wanted more for Zara than that.

So I needed to know from Celia what she thought. Was this a terrorist-victim thing? I didn't think so, but the fact her beau had been topped by a hit squad gave us something in common. My basic question: was this just psychobabble, or a project I could be proud of, commit to? If all I'm doing with these feelings is acting out some psycho-dramatic urging prompted from the loss of my family to terrorists, then I would forget it right now, go to a shrink and sort it. In that case life really is meaningless. And all we do is eat, drink, sleep, fuck and die. Or... is there something else? Is it worth committing yourself to the creation of... civilisation—for lack of a better word. In that case, I would be right and the *friquis*—wrong.

We entered the House, the mansion, and walked around the front to her room. The smell in Celia's Room was like being hit with a floral sledgehammer, enough perfume, powder (and stale sweat) to stock a perfume shop for a month. She went away and came back with a couple of small glasses, pulled a bottle of *manzanilla* sherry from her wardrobe.

"Sorry, it's all I've got."

I waved my acceptance. "As long as it's alcohol."

"Bottled sunshine."

She sat at her dressing table, began doing stuff with her makeup. I don't think she was actually doing anything, just trying to take the focus off our situation. I sat in a small, imitation Louis XIV armchair in a corner, tried to organise my thoughts.

"Tell me about the guy, your bloke, who died."

"Edu, you pay me, you can have sex or conversation. But we don't talk about me, we talk about you, unless you want me to make it up."

"I didn't come for sex…"

"Talk then? Shoot. I've got clients who love talking…"

"You lost that guy… I need to know…"

She frowned into the mirror, adjusted a hairclip: "Damn you, Eduardo. That's all past!"

"Hey, I told you, about Dad and… and my sister."

"This is not…"

"Who was he?"

"I was nineteen. He was a month off his twenty-fifth birthday when I met him. We were… it was all new, we had only been together about eight months."

"Uh-huh. So… what happened?"

"I don't know what you know about Argentina, but we had a military junta. A dictatorship. They banned everything, including maths, it was all suspect, even children's books…"

"Maybe they were bad books…"

Eduardo, they banned *The Little Prince*!"

"So what was your bloke's name?"

"Juan. Juan Bautista Fuenlabrada. A graphic designer."

"Sounds cool."

"He'd been helping… designing posters for actions against the junta… demonstrations, pamphlets… He… Then one night he didn't come home. That was it, he was gone, *desaparecido*."

"What did you do?"

"I waited all night. Phoned every friend we had who might know anything. In the morning I went to the police… stupid maybe, but I had to do it."

"Well, you would, wouldn't you?"

"No, Eduardo. Not if you didn't want more problems."

"But what was your emotional take, like how did it feel? What did you feel like you had to do? Where did it leave you?"

I got up and walked towards her dressing table, stood beside her, started playing with the perfume bottles while she continued doing stuff in the mirror.

"Feel? How do you think it felt? You lose the most precious person in your existence... you know how it feels. Do anything? It felt hopeless, like a numbness deep in every bone in my body... We fought against those bastards... we had to... and we eventually won... But when Juan went, I felt like I couldn't do anything. I just had to get out of there...

"And friends... I wasn't living the life I am now, but still I was... Friends warned me that I should leave... not because of who I was, or what I was doing—not part of the fight like Juan—but because of *what I was*. So I left."

She looked up at me. There was an instant, like a pause. Then she half-turned in her chair and pushed me so I kind of stumbled, fell back onto the bed. Before I knew it she was on top.

"Hey...!"

But her stinking lipstick-and-talc mask was shoved right into my face. She was strong. I was shocked. I just kind of lay there for a moment while she kissed me, disgusted by her greasy lips, not knowing what to do. Then suddenly I realised what was happening, where I was...

"Get off me! Fucking... !"

I went ballistic, shoved her upwards, squirmed to the side and pushed her again so she slipped to the floor.

"Eduardo...!"

But I was out the door.

"Fuck you! I didn't want that alright? I'm not like that, get it?"

I stormed out of their flat. What a dumb idea, to come down and fraternise with the *friquis*! I took the marble steps of the main staircase five at a time. It wasn't till I heard the street door slam and was walking up the shit-stained Calle Guardia, feeling free, safe, cold... that I realised I'd left my jacket up there. Damn! Because it was a chilly night. But I'd be buggered if I was going back... pun intended. I had other jackets at home—I'd call that one a donation to the *friquis*.

I walked home. Juanjo was watching some seedy documentary on TVE-2 when I got in.

"Fancy a whiskey? I'm just having one—Single Malt Scotch. A delicate dream of spring water perfumed with Scotland's native peat... Ah, Scotland the Brave... Delicious!"

Juanjo could have been an ad-man, but his whiskey sold itself. We sat together on the sofa and laughed our way through this late-night interview with Carmen do Manresa—Barcelona's famous silicon-lipped sex freak—best antidote ever for a straight guy's curiosity.

"So what did you get up to?"

"Just around."

"Françoise called for you."

"I'll call her tomorrow."

"Three times."

"I'll call her."

"The last time she sounded seriously irritated."

"Tomorrow."

# Joaquim XII

In the dark room she is brightly lit, garish almost, in contrast to the two dark figures accompanying her: black maid; black cat. The servant, dressed in pale crinoline, holds a bright bouquet, gazing in astonishment at her mistress, wondering, perhaps, why any respectable white woman would choose to shed her clothes so lightly, sacrifice her decorum, for this disreputable painter. She has no idea of the seductive power of artistic immortality.

—Eugeni Devineé, "The Art of Massacre in Manet's Olympia" in *Cultura y gente*, Autumn 1989, vol. 16.3, p. 35.

One broad, bright brushstroke defines the light on her thigh. So much sensual pleasure in one fat ribbon of pigment. I have finally got her down here. I want her to stretch out the way I'd imagined.

"Joaquim, I'm not going near that disgusting thing. You could release a whole pest bomb in here and that mattress would still run out giggling."

"I'll... I'll wrap it... here's some cloths. Try and get... you've got to see the different colours—It's supposed to look like a chaise longue."

"What are those, your paint rags? Joaquim, this looks like... and is... an old pestilent, rubber mattress wrapped in greasy rags. That's the only reality there is."

"I know, but try. Look, this is her." I show her the picture I have taped to my easel: "Olympia. It has to look like that... more or less... I'll do it differently... my version."

It's too late. Celia has left the room, heading back upstairs. I want to have a fit. It's taken me so long just to coerce her down to my studio. All because of a stupid chaise longue... I return to my easel.

Olympia. Goddess of love who lived on a mountain. High up, aloof from the lowland people in her snowy world—people who had rejected her... because they thought she was a witch... Another outsider... but more woman than any woman could ever be because she's the essence... all femininity distilled into a single form. If only Celia would relax, trust me.

***

Celia and I. It's evening. At home. I'm sitting on her bed, pad on knee, using charcoal. She's at her dressing table, preparing for work. The powders, bottles, tubes and sprays arrayed there help her in a complex ritual I feel privileged to watch. Step by careful step she builds herself, from the deep cleansing, moisturising and the closing of pores with several astringent lotions. Then the foundation, applied layer by thorough layer, the colour and blush, the painstaking detail of lips and eyes. Finally, setting and protecting her creation with powder, spray and gel. She exudes this powerful presence, essence of... woman. I wish I could drown in this... *L'eau de Célia.*

"When can I come and do you at work."

"Never. You'd just get me flustered."

She waitresses in a bar somewhere over near Les Corts, some cocktail lounge. None of her friends are allowed to visit her at work. That's her biggest taboo. I wish I could go. I wish I knew everything about her. I fantasise with following her one night, but I know I would never betray that trust.

"Hold that for a sec."

"I'm pushed for time, Sweetie."

"Just one second more... how your hand has got the lipstick... That's it. Go on."

"Thank you, dearest."

Every evening, she has an early dinner, does her makeup and is gone from the house by nine. It's after three, most nights, when she returns.

I want to do this painting in the old way, sitting by sitting. I know people who paint from photographs, but I don't think that would be fair to Celia, not if I want to really get her essence. And I see her relaxing session by session, learning to give in to me. I can be incredibly tenacious when I want.

"Open the top of your blouse further. I want the light to fall on the curve..."

"Of my breast?"

"Ah... uh-huh."

"Is that enough?"

"Ah... yeah... No... Open it further... In fact, unbutton it fully."

I surprise myself, getting off the bed, unbuttoning her blouse, pulling back the gauzy material until her breasts are quite apparent.

This painting... doing my version... the problem is there are so many versions... Ingres' odalisques, Goya, Manet... Olympia the outsider, Olympia the witch... It's a painting that... Well, I know what you are thinking—if you know it—whether I'm going to make a real copy. But it's a painting that always shocks, breaks with the old... It's got to scream at you, demand life, suck your jugular. Manet's version has got a maid, a hefty black woman dressed in pink calico, holding a huge bouquet of flowers, gazing into Olympia's eyes with a slightly bemused look, like unsure why her mistress has decided to strip, display herself so obscenely to the painter. Who or what can I use for the maid? My thoughts flick to my half-finished portrait of Narcissus leaning in the shadows, but he would be furious and it would be just totally the wrong look. In the end, I decide to paint myself in. There is no-one else I can trust to come down and endure a sitting and keep our confidence.

You're also asking—because the same thing is starting to bug me—when, where, to who are we going to show this piece if we're being so secretive about creating it? I didn't start it with the idea of showing it. I just wanted to paint Celia for her own sake because I found her captivating, still do, because I loved her, I think. But there's something about creation—no matter how private you may think you want to keep it, in the end you become proud, you truly feel like the creator. So it's inevitable you want to show people. People have to see how magnificent is the humble thing you've done... because creating something is the humblest process there is, but observing your created work brings up the strongest feelings of pride you can ever feel. People say it's like having a baby. Not that I've ever had a baby, but I bet it is. So I put myself in the painting, as Celia's manservant. I'm worried about what we'll do when it's finished. One painting doesn't make an exhibition and I'm not sure I want to show it just to anybody, but I do want to show it to *somebody*, whoever that is.

There's also a cat. Black. I actually identify more with the cat, but I'm not sure whether to paint that in. Because I'm not superstitious. Or maybe because I am. That gypsy woman at her folding table under Plaça Catalunya would look me in the eye and tell me what to do.

I don't want to mix things in here that don't go because I'm talking about painting, but these days I'm getting seriously worried about money. And the pressure of it is getting to the point where I can't even face painting. I keep asking Narcissus and Álvaro for their share of the rent. Since *that* night, when Álvaro left, when Narcissus left looking for him, though outwardly nothing changed, things have not been very warm between them, nor has Álvaro been very friendly towards me—no surprise. But Celia claims she's broke too. Everyone is promising me it next week. We're only behind one month so far, apart from the standing debt that we've said we'll pay a little bit on each month. Then everyone—well, Narcissus really—is starting to talk about outrageous expenses—sorry, investments—we'll have to outlay for the party, which we'll get back plus more, he reckons. But I don't know how much longer I can cope with all this, the unknowing.

***

There's a few pages in that notebook of Dad's that I didn't pay much attention to, but later, as I got to know Celia, I remembered them one day, went and read them over again. At first I thought they were notes for a story he was working on. But it was too "unliterary", like he hadn't thought about what he was writing, just kind of scribbled it down. He's talking about a person called C. At first I thought it might be Mum: C for Celia, but I know it isn't. It just doesn't sound like it. Partly because they were already going out. She had given him the diary. It couldn't be. Dad writes that he went and talked to this person, trying to reason with them:

Went round and saw C. Is very remorseful. Thankfully stone cold sober. The reality of the situation has sunk in. Has cleared the flat of all the bottles. That won't get J out of hospital, but it shows C is thinking, wanting to make changes. Not sure what to do—Police? I'm not a traitor, but don't want to do nothing. C must act! Have a conscience! I now have my doubts about that, but can't believe will not act in some way to rectify the situation. Swears to me things will be different now. Can I believe? Do I want to believe, hoping the problem will go away? I could not sleep last night, thinking about this.

***

"Celia, the guy you were with, you know, the writer, what's he like?"

It's unusual, this evening, Felipe is with us. We're planning, after Celia goes to work, to head out for a curry at El Gallo Kikirikiki.

"Huh! Him!"

"Uhh... he was a friend of my Dad's..."

"Your poor Dad!"

"But what's he like?"

"*Him*? I don't really want to talk about *him*, Joaquim."

"...Right."

Then Felipe speaks:

"A victim of the fight."

"What?"

"A victim."

"Hardly!" From Celia.

But Felipe is off:

"A lot of people in this country put their whole lives into the fight for democracy, Joaquim. It was an all-or-nothing kind of time. You know... right up to seventy-five and beyond. The fascists had cut off the 'intellectual head' of this country... they did it as a conscious policy... annihilated an entire generation of thinkers... assassinated university people, school teachers... a whole tier of knowledge-holders... especially in regions like Galicia... anybody who might remember, record, reason or contradict. For forty years Spain was a headless automaton, controlled by the dictator's regime, arm-in-arm with the Church... lumbering back towards an unreal, idolised feudalism—one in which that nepotistic alliance of Church and State had outlawed freedom and knowledge. Any resilient cultures of resistance here, or in exile, formed this country's sole, intellectual hope.

"But lots of those who kept up the fight, from inside the country and out, who formed Spain's lifeline to some kind of thinking future... when Democracy arrived, they were euphoric... But there wasn't much setting to rights... only a kind of blanketing amnesia that the politicians had negotiated in order to ensure peace. The murderers, the executioners, those who had wielded the axe, who had done the cutting, were never tried, but often rewarded and allowed to continue smug in their hegemony... as politicians, as the president of an autonomous region, or in some other capacity, simply reinventing themselves as belated democrats.

"For many people in the struggle, democracy turned out to be a huge anti-climax. They'd been fighting for it for so long, but when it came it was a watered down compromise... A lot of the criminals ended up being confirmed in their place...

"Then also, things began to change so fast... some of the real heroes of that period hardly had the chance to enjoy that negotiated freedom before they were left behind, had become anachronistic... That's good.. That's how life should work, but nobody was used to that speed of change here... It's wearying as well."

He looks at Celia who is staring woodenly at a mascara stick in her hand.

"He..." Felipe continues, "I sense that he just feels tired nowadays... slightly out of step. He used to be the Man, with his finger on the pulse... Now he's less and less relevant..."

"You studied all this in Chile?"

"No, I went to University here. This is one of the bases for my Doctorate."

"Wow, I've never heard it put like that before."

Celia speaks:

"Well Felipe, here's something they don't teach you in University: what happens when your Great Left-Wing Hero beats you unconscious with a chair leg because you talked to somebody at a party? Is he still such a hero?"

Felipe goes pale, silent. Celia's hand is shaking as she tries to apply her mascara. I try to clarify what she's just said:

"You mean you... he...?"

"Would I have mentioned it if it wasn't the case? There are two sides to every equation, Mr Intellectual. A rose may be a rose may be a rose, but a man is still a man is still a man."

She abandons the mascara, flings a Spanish shawl around her shoulders, checks her look one final time in the mirror and strides from her room, stilettos clicking down the hallway. Felipe and I look at each other and I don't know what to say. At that moment I remember Dad's diary, realise the C was actually a G.

# Eduardo XII

I wonder where I'm going in life, what I'm going to be. Write? Or end up as some kind of sad, middle-management fuckup in an insurance firm. Okay, I know I'll never settle for that. I'm exaggerating. Slightly. Yet something stops me finding a nice girl like Françoise—is she a "nice" girl? She's a sensationally hot girl... her smell, that vibrancy... even her furious temper sends me off this planet—I mean a girl to go steady with, concentrate on my exams, finish my Master's, score a profitable job as a cutthroat exec, raking in the claw-backs, just having a fab time—doing coke on weekends and not worrying too much about other, intangible things. I seem to get halfway along the gangplank, then pull out my pistol and shoot myself in the foot. Is it lack of guts, or of *duende*?

What in the name of the hooker-of-the-seven-veils made me think of going round to talk with Celia? I even paid the trashy prostitute! Waking up the next morning—the hangover must have been all that peat in Juanjo's whiskey—I wanted to drive a meat cleaver between my frontal lobes. What if anyone finds out, if Celia decides to blab? I left my jacket there! Pillock! Nothing happened, really. Right. Fra would cut my balls off—with good reason! It was definitely one of those acts in life you wish you could tear from the newsprint of your sordid existence and flush down the bog. I lay in bed for over an hour, knowing I was going to be late for class, but totally incapable of stirring a limb to hit the shower.

Every time I started to come awake, I just thought "What a frigging moron!" and then I'd kind of push myself down under the duvet again, hoping when I woke a second, third, fourth time, it would have gone, *desaparecido*.

Finally I crawled from the covers and went and stood under the shower till the water went cold. Juanjo wouldn't be up for another couple of hours and if he did decide to stir, a cold shower would be good for him. I left home and headed down to my local bar. Paco was still in slumberland. His sidekick José Antonio serves in the mornings—good because Paco can read your state of mind like a crystal ball, not pretty before the caffeine fix. J.A. is kind of tall and craggy—around twenty-two—scraggly bumfluff and acne crawling all over his face. Nice guy, but simple.

*Un café con leche super cargado de café*—meaning enough caffeine to make my eyelids peel—and I'm starting to feel my hangover in all its epic proportions. As well as realising the extent of my problem. I have seriously departed from my game plan, 'fucked up' if you want the technical term. My jacket is at the *friquis'* mansion. Where's it going to go from there? She's obviously not going to wear it, it's a guy's jacket. Will she just leave it in her wardrobe, waiting for me to come back for it? I doubt it. Give it to one of the others—Narcissus, Álvaro, Joaquim? They might not recognise it, but if they wear it out... There's one person who surely will recognise it, who's around that mansion a lot, too much: Fra.

The coffee's not doing it for my hangover. I head out and along to the pharmacy where I get a box of aspirin. Walking up the Ramblas I swallow four without water, Yum, hoping it will do the trick. Somehow I need to get back into the mansion and get my jacket. I'm fairly sure Celia will keep her mouth shut, but any of the others... I can imagine their gleeful exultation when they realise that Edu—Fra's regular boyfriend—has been visiting the Satin Hooker on the sly.

On the other hand, she knows it's my jacket. She knows where I live. She could just bring it round. I cringe. If Juanjo answers the door, or worse, Marta, or even if Françoise is around... I desperately hope Celia doesn't get any ideas. Descending the steps of the *ferrocarril* feels like sinking into Hell, or Purgatory. It isn't till I'm sitting on the train that will take me up to Reina Elisenda that I think: I'll have to go back up and see her at Camp Nou.

That thought is like alpine spring water splashed onto my face. It stings but it's clear and cold. That's it, of course. The easiest way. I go up, meet her, and if she hasn't got it on her, I tell her to bring it the next night and no-one has to know. I relax my neck muscles back onto the velvet headrest—at least Catalans know how to do one thing: build bloody comfortable trains—and feel with relief those Aspirin start to kick in.

Coming out at Reina Elisenda, I head along the road towards school. There's a phone box halfway, below the Jesuits College. I'm late anyway, no point going to my first lecture, so I stop and call Françoise at her work.

"*Buenos días*. Nouvelle Monde Insurance. How can I help you?"

"Give me Extension 523, please."

"Nouvelle Monde. May I be of assistance?"

"Fra?"

"*Merde!*"

"Juanjo said you rang. I was… out. It was late when I got back… too late to…"

"Where did you go out?"

"Just out… With Dani. We just started drinking, crapping on, you know? I didn't think it got so late! Man, baby! I'm so hung over this morning! My head, it's just…"

"Edu, I called your flat three times! Don't bullshit me, Edu! I know when you are bullshitting me, alright?"

"I'm not bullshitting you! I was out with Dani. Ask him! Fra, why would I lie to you? You know I like to go out and have a few the odd school night! What's the problem?"

Those aspirin are shyte! My frontal lobes whine as they press in agony against the phone booth's cool panes.

"I have to go. I have a call waiting. This is not over, Edu, you hear?"

"I hear. But I dunno what you're making a big fuss about, Fra. I'll call you tonight, okay?"

"I've got to go. We'll talk later."

She left me with the comfort of the dial tone.

Needless to say, this day doesn't exist in any practical or pedagogical sense. The worst thing is Dani is not at school and I desperately need to do some straightening of stories with him. I call his place a couple of times, but either there's no answer, or the flatmates I talk to (six of them share the apartment) haven't seen anything of him for a couple of days. Finally I retreat to the library, open *Procedimientos judiciales analizados en defensa del plagio de los derechos pretendidos de personas jurídicas constituidos bajo la legislación española y las protecciones posibles a sus derechohabientes y consecuencias y causas en el ámbito del derecho internacional—Tomo III, 1976 al 1985*. It has the softest pages of any I know. Resting my head, I try to prepare a plan of attack for that evening.

"It doesn't go in by osmosis, you know."

"Dani! Where the fuck have you been?"

"Thanks, Edu, yeah cool. Everything's great. Thanks for asking."

"Whatever. Listen, I need your help. This is important..."

"Don't start, please. I'm not in the mood to deal..."

"I told you I need your help..."

"Fuck, Edu! I'm not interested, okay?"

"What?"

This is a university library. It isn't the place to have a mental fit. People are looking. Doesn't do my headache too much good either.

"Since you don't want to ask, my Dad collapsed yesterday. I've been at the hospital for the last thirty-six hours."

"Oh look, I'm really sorry, Dani. What a bastard I am. Yeah, you're right. What was it, some kind of ahh... collapse, ah a...?"

"No, more like heart palpitations, but not a heart attack. It turns out he's got like water in his lungs which they've had to pump out. Difficulty breathing and stuff."

"I am really sorry, Dani. I am so sorry."

Headaches, girlfriends, palpitating progenitors... Today is highly *Fellini* and it isn't even eleven yet. Dani sits down and starts to tell me all about the family crisis. I'm a good listener when I want to be. I know what questions to ask, when not to say anything.

"Listen, all of this is a real strain. It's really good what you're doing for your family, that you're rallying around at a time like this. Don't forget your own needs though, your primal needs. Give yourself downtime. Take some time out, grab a beer."

"Yeah, maybe you're right. It's all pretty intense."

"You need your own chilling time. Me too. Man, Fra's been giving me an intense time lately."

"Yeah? Yeah, she called me."

"What? When?"

"Yesterday. I'd just stopped home for a shower, shave and change of clothes before heading back to the hospital when she rang."

Shit!

"Rang?"

My arse is cooked.

"Yeah. Don't worry, I said I hadn't seen you."

How to explain...

"So you want to get together this evening for those beers?"

"I don't know... It'd be good, but I'm having to check up fairly regularly with the hospital."

"If you can't, no problem."

No, I need my jacket. To get rid of the evidence. Then I can sort Françoise out.

"Dani boy, we should do that, have some chill-out time and get you back at the hospital in an hour. We'll have a couple of beers, go for a drive, what do you say? Maybe head up and give the whores round Camp Nou a bit of a look-over? What do you reckon?"

He looks at me: "Edu, I'm not surprised Françoise is on your case if you spend all your time cruising round Camp Nou!"

How is that supposed to make me feel? When I've been totally faithful! But he knows what he needs. We arrange to meet about ten.

# Joaquim XIII

*You could say that I have no inspiration, that I only need to paint.*

—Francis Bacon.

**M**ontjuïc. The quality of the air here above the city is gilded. If I could only take this atmosphere, trim the gold and melt it down to pay the rent... I amble down the silent paths towards Poble Sec, still with no answers to the house situation... even my food situation. I follow Carrer Salvà down, past the house where the singer Serrat was born. Montjuïc is always the place I go to think, where I can stick my head in the clouds and get out of myself for a little while. It's furniture collection day for Sants and Montjuïc, so broken sofas, tables, chairs and beds form low mountains of junk on street corners, fencing in the rubbish containers.

Then I see it. It's perfect. Upholstered in red velvet, worn in a few places, but still basically good. Gilded feet curve down, slender and carved like griffins, their wings beating up into the velvet plush. Gold cord beading runs along the join between cloth and wood and there is a gold cord fringe that is only coming away in a couple of places. I could easily pin it back up. I can't wait to show her. It's so absolutely Celia!

***

I step forward and swing back the heavy knocker. The old house seems to shudder and shake. *Here's a knocking indeed.* I have to bang three times, bringing neighbour's heads popping from windows. Finally it's Álvaro who sticks his head out of the middle room balcony. He stares down, blank: "Why don't you use the electric bell, Miró?" There's one screwed to the doorframe, but it didn't feel right. "What happened to you?"

I realise I must look like I've run a marathon. My chest is still heaving—got to stop smoking!—and my clothes are as soaking as if I had thrown myself into the Llobregat. I'm literally wet with sweat. But my new acquisition sits in the street beside me.

"It's a... a chaise longue."

He looks dumb.

"I need it for my painting... Can you help me?"

"Just a minute." He disappears. A minute or so later, he opens the street door. "Why didn't you use the buzzer? We thought it was kids, being stupid."

"Didn't feel like it."

Together we take an end each. "Where are we taking it? This would look good in the ball..."

"It's going in my studio. I need it for my painting."

He tries to argue. It's the predator, conman instinct both he and Narcissus have so finely honed.

"You can have it in the ballroom later. For the party. I need it for my painting first."

"Well, make sure you don't spill paint on it. It'll totally ruin it."

As if it were his! But I need his help. We open the downstairs stable door and carry it into the first basement, then up to my studio. It's obvious he wants to come in.

"Thanks. I'll take it from here."

"Don't be a dick, Joaquim. I'm not going to rob your artwork. I promise I'll keep my eyes closed."

But I can't take the chance. The Narcissus portrait is uncovered and I'm not that ready.

"It's fine. I'll take it."

Once Álvaro's headed back up to his eyrie, I unlock my studio and drag in the chaise longue. Yeah, I know I'm a dick, but there are some areas I can't go; they're kind of sacred. I think about Celia's reaction.

***

"**I** WISH to see my PORtrait, JoaQUIM. I beLIEVE we had an aGREEment."

Morning. Our mansion's all out of coffee. We're standing in our local bar, the one with the List photo. So there's no immediate threat that Narcissus will collar me and drag me screaming down to my studio.

"It's... coming... along... but you should wait. I've got problems. I... I need to work them out..."

"PROBlems? What PROBlems are there? Painting problems? Are you saying you can't paint ME?"

"Yes... I can. They're just working... difficulties... It's normal. But you won't appreciate it till it's finished."

"TWO weeks, MiRÓ. I give you two MORE weeks. Then we will finally SEE whether you are half the fabulous PAINter you claim to be!"

He lets it go at that. But before I head for work, his ultimatum grabs me by the scruff of the neck, forces me back... down... into the studio, to uncover his canvas. (The only one I could ever afford to buy: Celia and everyone else is painted on board, stuff I've just picked up off the street, primed and used like that.) He is set up at the opposite end of the narrow room from her. The paintings confront each other across the space as if they were commanding a time-frozen San Francisco. His portrait is okay, the face clear—I think I've got it. Maybe his expression's a bit sharper than he would have liked, a bit more arrogant or something, but you can see it's him and his personality is right there, striking. It's all the rest that's the problem: an inescapably accurate rendition of my own muddy indecision. So much for my fabulous intuition. The idea that's been driving it... I still like it, but I can't see that he... or others will. The Beast. He looks like a brown blob. Crouching in a corner, peering over Narcissus's shoulder. Decision. Tonight I'll paint over him and do something else. After all, everyone will be looking at the face, not the rest. Yet he already seems to exist with a strength that is greater than mine. It's like he's tricked me onto this canvas and now squats in his space with a niggling wilfulness, holding to existence through his livid grip on the pigment... And some perverse inner nature of mine has also dug its heels in, absolutely refusing to renege. I LIKE THE BEAST! But... I have to resolve this: it's a composition, not a psychodrama session. I won't make modifications, not for anyone, not even if I lose all the friends I have so far gained in this city of night.

A realisation: I seem to have friends. Down in Benissola, I couldn't speak to anyone. Everyone thought I was a psycho. Like, I had friends at school, but I never confided in them the way I can with Celia, Françoise, or even Felipe. Now it's like, more adult. I can say I've actually got friends of a sort: Narcissus, Álvaro, Françoise. Miguel, Felipe, Celia: they are friends. I think I could rely on them... if I had to. I can talk to them as much as... well, more all the time.

So I have to resolve the composition. Why didn't I sort this out before I started, do sketches and that? Because it's the first painting I've attempted up here in Barcelona, because my passion for Narcissus was driving me and it just felt like, this amazing masterpiece would *have* to flow out of me... Okay, I got his face right. But now the Beast is staring out at me, mocking. He won't go. He knows I know he won't go. I stare and he stares, baleful. It's late. I'm late. I start at eleven and it must be almost that. The morning sun hits the skylight above as it tops the tall bulk of the building behind our patio. Light flows onto and around the easel. Then the Beast smiles, his bristling form smoothing and beautifying in the golden air. His is a friendly face. And I know who he is.

***

"We desire a selECT clienTELE."

"From experience, Honey, you want people who can pay the bills.

"I DON't think you TRUly understand the CONcept I am trying to conCEIVE."

Celia lights a cigarette.

"Narcissus, I understand clients. I understand business... the foundation of all the business on this entire planet."

"THAT is to put it rather poETiCALly..."

"Or realistically. But suit yourself. I thought you needed help to pay the bills on this mansion."

"My PLANS are deVELoping suPERbly!"

"Little Joaquim here tells me you're now three months behind on the rent. You know what that means, don't you? E-VIC-TION..."

***

It's time to talk about Álvaro. I realise I've been leaving him out, but he's important to this, to the whole thing, to what happened. Their relationship was fundamental. He did install his darkroom at the top of the house, in the Chihuahua room once I'd moved into mine. Sometimes when all the others are out, it will just be me—working down in my studio—and Álvaro, developing pictures under a red bulb on the top floor. Though I don't have good enough light; I'm wondering whether Narcissus will let me move my studio to the room between Celia's and my own. When people come in, they go up to Álvaro's studio, not down to mine. It's crazy: he seals off the light that is rampant up there while, down in the basement, only the dustiest, dimmest light leaches down to me at the brightest hour of day, aided by both electricity and candles. Yet they all, Narcissus and Celia, Ludo and Paul, Françoise and Edu, troop up the stairs to check out what Álvaro's doing. Except for Felipe and Miguel. They are becoming my special friends, but they come to my bedroom. That's as social as I get. I don't let anyone in my studio.

So Narcissus's portrait stares me down from the easel, resilient, like a concrete bulkhead, or breakwater; it will gather slime, seaweed, history... but it will not be worn away. I look at the other face also taped to the easel now: from a black and white series; a discarded proof—that wide forehead luminous under a vertical spot, eyes glowing incandescent in the brightness. Really—and this is what I should have realised before, where my intuition has corrected me—it is impossible to paint Narcissus alone; they are a pair. I can't do a portrait just of Narcissus, but must acknowledge their symbiotic relationship. A double portrait: Narcissus and Álvaro on the same canvas, the infamous couple.

# Eduardo XIII

*My fault, my failure, is not in the passions I have, but in my lack of control of them.*

—Jack Kerouac.

That evening there wasn't much action up in Whoresville. But the girls were still out working. Thank God Dani decided to come out. Without his car this would have been impossible. It isn't like I could go traipsing around on foot, or in a taxi. We're cruising up and down, but I can't see her anywhere. Dani's getting bored, I can tell, and I don't know how much longer I can string him along. I think he feels he's being used.

"Listen, Edu, I've got to phone the hospital. Look out for a call box."

"They'll be fine at the hospital. Stop worrying so much. We can phone them in a minute. God! Look at her! There's one for you, Dano-boy!"

She's a short, really wide mulatto princess, plastered with pink and blue eye shadow.

"So are you into one of these 'girls', Edu? Just tell me so we can get this over with."

We've been drinking fairly heavily. Otherwise it wouldn't be much fun cruising these pseudo-chicks. We started with a quarter bottle of whiskey I grabbed from home—no, it wasn't Juanjo's peat-laden spring water, which the suspicious sod had hidden—and continued with a six-pack we grabbed from a local shop. So when Dani asked me for a confession like that, I didn't get as riled as I should have:

"Well, sort of, but it isn't what you think."

"Hey I'm not going to judge you for whatever thing you're into, just be honest and stop fucking around."

I almost slug him then, except he's driving. Besides, at this point, one of these girls would be preferable to the fiery dragon Françoise, who I had to walk out on to let her cool off. I still say:

"I'm not into this shit okay? Don't give me that. There's another reason. Just cut me some slack."

The situation was I got home from Uni about seven. I was exhausted from trying to do a full day while staving off a hangover.

I had a hot shower then dived into bed and went straight to sleep. Or would have. After about half an hour, the phone rings:

"Edu!" shouts Marta, "Françoise."

I groan into consciousness. Now how am I going to play this?

"Hi Baby."

"So... tell me, Edu. What happened last night?"

"Darling, why are we having this conversation? I just went out for a few drinks."

"Except I ring Dani's place. I spoke to him. He was just going back to the hospital and not seen you."

"Yes, I know." (I think: 1. How does Fra have Dani's number? 2. That's more information than his flatmates would give me, and 3. Thank God I ran into Dani this morning, otherwise I'd be really toasted.) "His Dad collapsed, some kind of palpitations. He's been at the hospital. We met to talk about it. Then had a few drinks. Time got away on us. End of story."

"Then why did he say he hadn't seen you?"

"He did see me, but *after* he spoke to you. He really needed to unwind. I was doing a mate a favour..."

"Is that all?"

"Of course it's all. I came home, had a couple of whiskies with Juanjo. He told me you'd rung, but it was too late to ring you back. I went to bed. Hangover this morning. What else do you want to know?"

"You better not be lying to me, Edu."

At that point I feel a bit of righteous anger is called for, which gives me a lever and partial excuse not to meet tonight—she's talking about dinner around at her place—but candles and sweet nothings are not what I need at the moment. I can't say things are good between us when we hang up. At least it's given me a day or two to try and sort out this frigging mess I've created for myself. I went back to bed at that point.

But about nine-thirty, there's a knock on my bedroom door and Françoise slips in. She sits on my bed, takes advantage of the fact I'm half-asleep, and eyeballs me:

"Swear to me, you didn't do anything last night. Tell me what happened."

I swear she's got witch blood.

"Fra, I'm tired. This has been a shitty day..."

"Swear!"

"I swear... that I didn't get off with any other woman, man or beast of burden when I went out last night! Satisfied?"

But she wasn't. Secretly, I'm not sure which category Celia would fit into anyway. When Fra wants a domestic, she won't stop until her frenzy is satiated. But I was too short on neurons to take it that night. I jumped out of bed, stormed out to the kitchen, grabbed a hair of the dog—beer might do the trick. As I passed back through the living room, Marta and Ri stopped smooching on the sofa. Marta looked shocked. Ri spat her dummy:

"Edu! We don't want to look at that! Put some underpants on!"

"Envy's an ugly emotion, girls."

I returned to the battle zone. But it was more of a slaughter. I didn't have the stamina that evening. Half an hour later I walked out. By ten-thirty, I was waiting under the Umbrella House on the Ramblas, whiskey under my jacket, for Dani to cruise by and pick me up.

We now must have covered the whole zone three or four times. Nothing. No Celia. We're both getting pretty plastered. No clue how he can still even drive. Then I see her. Getting out of a Mercedes at the corner.

"Wait two seconds."

I'm out of the car, walking fast towards her. She doesn't see me until I'm almost on her.

"Celia."

"Hello Edu. Just a minute, Sweetie."

She turns smiling back towards the Mercedes driver.

"I'm not waiting a minute. I want to talk."

"In one minute, alright? I am talking with my friend."

This is too much. I go to pull her away, to face me.

"What the..! Let go of me!"

Then things start to happen fast. Suddenly that fat mulatto is between us, pushing me.

"You got a problem, Sunshine? Step back from the Lady, alright?"

"Fuck you, get out of my way. I need to talk with her!"

The Mercedes drives off. Celia turns on me.

"Bugger you, Eduardo! That was a client, an important one!"

"And I told you I wanted to talk to you! What's your problem, you fucking whore?"

Then the lights seem to go out. I'm on the ground, realise the mulatto "chick" has slugged me. I go to get up, see a pair of brown serge trousers in front of me. Thank Christ!

"This guy bothering you, Celia?"

"Bothering her? Officer, this bitch just hit me!"

"Okay, on your way Pal. You've got three seconds before I take you in."

"What the fuck?"

"Celia, do you want to lay charges against him?"

"She fucking hit me!"

"Just get him the fuck out of here! You want to lay real low, Edu baby, I could bring your world tumbling down around you."

"That's a threat! That's a fucking threat! Didn't you hear that, Officer?"

"Whatever. You're drunk, mate. And you need to go home and calm down, or you'll have some serious problems."

"Edu! Come on, get in."

It's Dani, who's seen the whole bloody film, credits included.

"I haven't finished with you, Bitch!"

But I stumble into the car and Dani floors it before the cop can think to arrest me for that last statement, which damn well was a threat... and she deserved it.

"What the fuck were you thinking of, Edu? You don't fucking go around threatening the whores. Of course they've got protection. What planet have you come down from?"

I grab another beer off the floor, pop it open and down virtually the whole can in one.

"It's not what you think, Dani. I haven't fucked her, okay? I'm not into that. The other day I just needed to talk, but she's got something of mine and I want it back."

"Whatever. You don't have to justify yourself to me."

"I'm NOT FUCKING JUSTIFYING! Where do I have to dot the frigging 'i's for you to get it?"

The car skids to a stop. The burke almost causes an accident on the Avenida Generalísimo.

"Okay, this is your stop, Edu. Get the fuck out of my car."

I grab the last remaining beer and get out.

"Suit yourself, Dani. Get in a strop then, you loser. But don't come whining to me in the future."

"Believe me, I won't."

He floors it and roars off.

# Joaquim XIV

*What sphinx of cement and aluminium bashed open their skulls*
*and ate up their brains and imagination?*

—Allen Ginsberg, "Howl", II.1, 1956.

"Have you any idea how much money I have coughed up already? Of course you don't... too busy playing the artist... Now you want more? We could have paid the village's food bill for a year... Forget about the harvest: let them all sit there fondling their eggs. Well you can cut that act right now! No son of mine is going to spend my cash like that... or prance around as a fag either!"

"Just because you failed as one... as a writer!.... Because your work was boring and mediocre that no-one would want to read... I know..."

I didn't tell him I'd read his diaries, didn't state the other thing, the fact I hadn't really stopped wondering about since L'Accordéoniste. It was the perfect moment to strike back, but I don't think I'd even realised it myself at that point. Then Mum is framed in the doorway, a bouquet of knives clutched at her breast, the steel dripping suds. Again she comes between us. Always keeping the peace, I think. Why? I feel my fists balling. Because this time Dad and I will kill each other. And I don't care. Then things turn black for two seconds and my head is buzzing from the blow. I open my eyes as the polished pine of our dining table top is veering away from my cheek. But it is Mum's palm that has sent me flying:

"Don't speak to your father like that! Get out of my house until you learn some respect!"

Again I leave. Though I don't go walking among the vines. I walk out, down the street, around the town square and back again towards my parents' house. I make no effort to keep quiet. There is silence from the living room, but I don't go in there. Instead I go straight to my room, take a large sports bag—another of their wasted purchases—throw in clothes, photos, books, anything portable I see. When it is finally full, I can hardly lift it from my bed. Yet I manage to drag it downstairs. I pause at the bottom, listening. Nothing, not silence but a lack of noise. They are sitting up there listening too. I open the front door, drag my bag onto the front step, remember a pair of boots in the laundry that I want, go back for them. Still no sound from above. I step out the door holding those boots, next to my bag. No sound. I close the door. I have left. Dragging my bag down the street towards the station I refuse to look back, don't know whether they're watching from the window, refuse to care.

***

A Rubens afternoon. This is another exception, another afternoon—not the city at night. Piles of cumulus clouds stacked in pink and gold on an aquamarine sky. I've never liked him, but he knew how to paint those skies. The wind is blowing crisp behind me as I climb up towards the palace, pulling gulls and pigeons into the air and flinging and whirling them around my head.

Montjuïc is a mass of construction work—preparation for the Olympic Games in full swing—twenty-eight months away. Narcissus has made his demand of me. My efforts have to be dragged from the dark cave of my studio before all those people—and they will see just how mad I've become. I squeeze between the partitions of the workmen's barrier and trudge up the old steps beside where they're installing outdoor escalators. Bright mud and fresh concrete are splashed all over the weathered stone. New quarry-cut pavers stand in random stacks on the terraces. The lupines have been slashed back from the site.

I put a padlock on my studio.

"What is this for, JoaQUIM? We have no secrets from each other in THIS house."

I mumble something. Even I don't quite know what I'm trying to articulate.

"What?"

"You'll see when it's finished."

"*Ahhh!*" His eyes gleam. "The closeted arTISTE!"

He seems proud, imagines perhaps I'm working on a masterpiece, wouldn't be so smug if he'd actually seen it. Celia's portrait is nearly finished though I know I'll never show it. Narcissus's—it needs so much more time—I work and work, but what I'm trying to do is just too much. And I know that I'll have to show this one. His pride demands it. Of me. Yet I don't think I can. It's just getting too personal.

Cold air covers the city like liquid glass, has a kind of magnifying effect, so that as I get higher, every point that my eye rests on slowly zooms into focus in the most minute detail. It's like I can look into the back patio of every single Barcelona home; pick out every bit of laundry flapping on every balcony across the whole of Sants; tell pigeon droppings from lichen patches on the Església del Pi tower; even see the Japanese and American tourists trooping up the stairs of the Sagrada Família spires, the flash of their well-conditioned heads as they bob past those miniscule windows: blond, dark, blond, blond, dark...

Narcissus made an announcement before I went back home. I had hoped to get some money to tide me over until I could get paid from my job, but Dad finally turned the key in the lock, stingy bastard. Who knows where we'll find the money we owe on the house. I didn't think it was so much already. Narcissus says that is a small matter, tells me I can raise that easily, just have to stop thinking small, begin to think corporate, creative...

***

Whardropcap When I come home from my job—when I'm on morning shift—I get in mid-afternoon. I generally stop in Celia's room. I sit on her bed and talk to her, sketch her, tell her about my day as she powders, perfumes, lipsticks, frizzes her hair, ready for work. Yet lately, it seems like Celia is impatient with me. Our relationship has lost some of its intimacy. She is offhand, stays out later... Does her bar really demand she work such long hours? She doesn't seem to value me as before. A twinge of resentment has entered the relationship. I let her off last month's rent because she claimed to have no money yet still she goes out every night, has money for drinks, but no longer invites me like she used to. This is a torturous Spring. So it's in Celia's room where Narcissus finds us. He kind of bursts in, shiny-eyed—a thing she hates. Her room is her boudoir, an impregnable space. She hates anyone to enter without knocking.

"I have an anNOUNcement!"

Celia doesn't bat an eyelid—her hand is steady, concentrating on the application of mascara, a delicate operation. But I am drawn in—as always.

"I beLIEVE the time is ripe... for the grand inauguREItion... of this house! The date... Álvaro and I, have it fixed... the twenty-third of June, *verbena de San Juan*."

St John's Eve, the summer solstice.

"There will be FIREworks on the terRACE, DANcing in the ballroom!"

Celia and Narcissus—white queen and black king—they live in the same house, go out to the same bars... yet they are so distinct. There has always been a lack of connection between them, but they aren't hostile. I think Narcissus finds her attractive—that is, I think he finds the idea of her attractive, her concept, what Celia represents. Yet they are somehow opposites; not antagonistic, just opposed—facing each other across their wide valley. Narcissus moves, conceives a single step at a time. Celia travels, crosses the board in clean sweeps, can blast anyone she wants before her. At the end of the game though, it's who's still left on the board who wins.

The party, the party; Narcissus is so sold on the party and I still haven't paid the rent yet—last month's—I wouldn't mind if it was just this month's.

"We will make so much MONEY!"

As if he's drunk. How can he be so blasé, so unconcerned? We have to pay the rent! But he goes on:

"This will be the BEST investment any of us will make this year... me... you, Joaquim... you... Celia... We are going to be RICH!"

The eyeballs are glazed yet I feel myself drawn... if it will just bring in enough for the rent... to rid ourselves of that pressure, the throb of cash needed... why do we need a world where we are so dependent on dirty money? I think of the life we've got, of Celia, her and my... what we've got... that that kind of purity can be smirched by money... Yet it's what we need: money, money, money.

"Forty THOUsand pesetas."

"Forty thousand pesetas?"

The price. Our down payment to enter Paradise. It might as well be four hundred thousand. After the fight with my folks, that's wealth beyond my means—we owe a hundred and twenty thousand for last month alone. Celia is the first to speak:

"Of course, honey. Forty mil? No probs. I'll just pop out tonight and milk one of my clients."

I look at her, a little confused. Doesn't she get paid a wage?

"Tips, baby, tips."

But she looks at Narcissus:

"So what are you planning to spend that pitiful amount on, for this party of yours?"

His eyes widen:

"There are COSTS! When you set up a PRIME quality eVENT, there are inVESTments! Are you DOUBTing my inTEGrity?"

Celia just starts delving into her jewellery box like she's trying to bury something. But I see the sarcastic expression on her face. I'm not so sure either. I simply don't have the money to pay if I wanted, So it almost isn't a problem for me.

"We will transFORM this house! It will be a PARagon to its bygone days!"

I have a dizzying sense of déjà vu.

"I see CANdles lighting the stairwell, the PORTE cochère... chandeLIERs in the BALLroom..."

Celia puffs powder onto her face. Narcissus coughs.

"...A COStume party! A masquerade in the old style!"

I ask:

"Won't that be dangerous for Sant Joan... What if people burn themselves, or their costumes?"

He frowns with scorn.

"The fireworks will be confined to the terrace! We will have a humble charcoal brazier in the *porte cochère*... I do not think the MarQUIS de DOSaguas would be very PLEASED if we RAZED his mansion."

He winks and I am caught again.

"...Then... at TWELVE o'clock..." his voice grows solemn, "... our guests shall desCEND the stairs... to the gallery!"

My heart skips. His eyes shine.

"Yes, Petit Miró, you and Álvaro shall EACH unveil... your MASterpiece!"

Masterpiece... I know nothing about a masterpiece, or about creative either. I go down into my studio because it is one place where I will be left alone, can forget it all for awhile. It's like Narcissus has just signed my death warrant.

# Eduardo XIV

I have this uncomfortable sense of déjà vu tramping down the Avenida Generalísimo towards Calvo Sotelo. Totally blown it. What started as a simple deviation from the game plan rapidly seems to have become a major breach in my identity. In under twenty-four hours I've antagonised the Satin Hooker, fought with my girlfriend and seriously pissed off one of my best friends—who now also thinks I'm some kind of weird sexual deviant into the bargain. I scrunch the last beer can and throw it at a rubbish bin. It bounces off and skids out into the road. A car brakes and honks so I give it a *butifarra*, or "up yours". For a wavering moment I suspect the driver is going to make something of it, but then he screams something unintelligible and zooms off.

What I really feel like is screwing. This always happens when I'm in a tight spot. Things turn to custard and I get hot for pussy. And I don't want to pay for it. Will Françoise be sitting at home waiting for me? I doubt it, but she might. I can't believe she'll be giving out in the present state of affairs though. So my place is out of the question. I think Karma. That's the old standby, always something—or someone—happening there. At least I'll be able to get another drink. I flag down a taxi.

Down in Plaza Real the night is just getting going. It's early, before one. Karma will be empty so I head next door to the Rey de Copas for a couple. Leaning at the bar are the last two degenerates I think I ever want to meet: Narcissus and Álvaro. Then I change my mind.

"How's it going?"

"Everything is a WHIRL!"

"A whirl?"

"Of preparation... for the eVENT! Hasn't Françoise told you?"

"You guys having an event, what—a party?"

"More than a PARty, SO much more!"

Álvaro clarifies before I get irreversibly bored with the Caribbean conman's flowery bullshit.

"We're organising a masque ball for Saint John's Eve, Midsummer Night. Are you interested?"

"I'll see. I'll have to talk with Fra."

"There are LIMited tickets. Don't leave it TOO late."

So they're going to make people pay to go to their party? I order a beer. Out of the corner of my eye, I can sense the pair are kind of waiting for me to offer them a drink, but I know these two. I wasn't born yesterday. Besides, they're the last couple of drinking buddies I could ask for. Even if I wanted something... So we stand at the bar. I drink and the pair of them pretend they just aren't thirsty while they elaborate on their plans for this mega-fiesta with which they want to inaugurate the house—and scrabble back towards solvency.

"You guys want a beer?"

I can be slow sometimes to realise what's good for me. They accept as I knew they would. Letting them drink and fantasise their way on into the night, I let my mind wander over the details of my problem's solution.

"Into some hash, guys?"

Of course they are! Look a gift horse those two? Never! I'm happy to score a *pedra de chocolate*, but make clear that I won't do any rolling or smoking in the street (which I've done hundreds of times, but there's some advantage to having the reputation for being a pijo, or rich kid: nobody questions me when I make a dumb demand like that.

We roll out of the Rey de Copas and over to the corner of Plaza Real and the Ramblas, one of the worst places to score if you're talking value for money, but I'm in a hurry. From there we take Nueva de las Ramblas and then Guardia. Second time in twenty-four hours I'm back in this mansion. We settle back in that big ballroom-cum-dining room where Fra and I came for dinner. The wallpaper is still hanging in strips from the walls, but there's more evidence of habitation: the kitchen looks like it's been cleaned; there's a fridge chugging away in one corner. An electric heater is going full blast in the cool, cavernous space—despite there being no need for it at this time of year—so I assume they've created a puente, bypassing the meter to access free power. We settle down around it. The first part of my plan is basically to get them stoned. That shouldn't be hard. I doubt that Celia will be home for a good while—probably needs to spend a few more hours on her back—but I still freeze when the buzzer goes. It isn't her but Felipe, the gay guy who spent a few months sleeping on our sofa.

"Hey, Felipe, how's it going? What's up?"

"Hi Eduardo! What a surprise! Where's Françoise?"

"Oh you know, she's sleeping. We're just having a joint before we head for Karma. Want some?"

It probably seems a little odd that I'm here, the one straight guy with these three fags, getting stoned, but who cares? I'm not prejudiced. Some of my best friends are fags. We're just hanging out.

"I don't do hash. It makes me too paranoid. I'll have a sip of that though."

He indicates the bottle of some blackberry sweet stuff that Álvaro has grudgingly produced. We're drinking it out of the tiniest glasses, which I suppose is a ploy to conserve resources. They don't know old Edu well enough though. If I'm going to get these guys stoned, I'm going to have my fair share of their alcohol. I've already refilled my own glass twice.

Narcissus has been telling us of his plans for the party. He now recaps for Felipe's benefit, but I suspect from the polite way the Chilean is nodding, he's heard it all before. Maybe he knows Narcissus too well. The hash is not as strong as I was hoping—I want them stoned. Maybe it'll react with the alcohol to get them off their tits. Then I decide I might as well act. Things are starting to rearrange themselves in my own brain too. What if Celia comes home? What if I can't find my jacket?

"I'm off for a slash."

I get up, stagger. Felipe laughs.

"I'll help you!"

"Fuck off! I don't need anyone to hold my willy!"

My reputation—unearned, I reckon—for being a homophobe might save me that. I get out of the ballroom, closing the door behind me, but then find everything is pitch black. I have to grope my way right around to the other side of the stairwell through all those rooms—trying not to crash into anything—to reach the bog. Celia's room is en route. Pleasant coincidence. Not hard to find. That face-slapping perfume hits you before you get within five metres. The whole of this side of the mansion is dark. I push at her door. It's ajar. I enter. The smell rolls up like a heavy, green-black wave on a polluted coastline, so strong it feels like she's standing there, pushing her breasts up against me. Should I turn on a light or not? After standing there thinking about it for several moments—I'm actually spinning something chronic! How did I get this way? All the alcohol and dope are turning in my head. In the dark, flashes of colour swirl and pop against my retinas like some kind of epileptic representation of the life and death of Ocaña. Finally I decide the light will be too dangerous. I can open a shutter. Streetlight should be enough to navigate by. Shuffling in the direction of where I think the window is, I bash into something—a chair?—which overbalances something else. There's a crash; glass shatters. And something convulses on the other side of the room:

"Who's there?"

The voice is high-pitched, edgy, but threatening. Jesus! Someone's in the room with me! It isn't her, nothing like her voice. My head is turning cartwheels in the darkness—I couldn't even locate the door at this rate. My body feels chilled.

"No-one, I... aahh, the toilet?"

A light clicks on beside the bed, rose-tinted, soft. The first thing I notice around my feet is a chair fallen on its side among the shards of a mirror. I remember it—a tall, narrow, unframed sheet of glass that leant against the wall next to Celia's dressing table. History now. Worse, lying on Celia's bed, his clothes kind of loose about him—I think his pants might even be unbuttoned, but can't tell in that first flash of recognition—is the Tarragona kid, Joaquim. He's staring at me from the bed, kind of pale and petrified.

"What do you want?"

"Ahh... looking for the toilet."

"The toilet isn't here. It's along the hall further, on the left."

"Uh, yeah, I know, I think. I must have lost my way." I laugh.

"Pretty stoned. Sorry."

He just looks at me. I shuffle towards the door, hardly having the presence of mind to look around the room as I go. Can't see my jacket.

"Sorry about the mess."

I leave, remember to head up to the toilet, stand there with my brain swirling for a couple of minutes before I pull the chain and leave. When I pass by Celia's room, the light is out again, but I don't know whether he's in there or not. I can't risk it.

"Okay, I'm off, guys. Thanks for the... the drink."

"You're not coming to Karma?"

"Too stoned. Another night."

I clatter down the marble steps towards the street and I'm thinking: "Fuck! Loser! You fucking dipstick! Why couldn't you pull off a simple plan like that? Instead you've given the friquis a free night of booze and smoke, like a retard."

I've got no idea how all this is going to turn out, but I can't think straight now. I need to sleep. I head home.

# Joaquim XV

"This recipe", Mrs Altafulla now said, "is ancient, almost prehistoric. A Catalan dish, the roots of which have been lost to memory. It's a little like our country: poetic and prosaic. Capable of flying without its feet ever leaving the ground. You see, my queen-bee, there's no land like this one. It is... like a cabbage, which sprouts underground and flourishes into a fat plant, shut into itself, but at the same time open... That's Catalonia, girl. Like a cabbage".

—Montserrat Roig, *L'opera quotidiana*, Edicions 62, Barcelona, 1991. p. 82.

Before I show her, I want to create the space so it's all just right, a gift to her. Celia. Olympia. What am I trying to create? The goddess of love? I'll start a new painting, treat the other as a study.

I wish I could paint on canvas, but it just isn't possible. At least there is collection night, which provides me with free panels instead. Because if you can't get canvas, hardboard, properly primed is next best. I've got two perfect surfaces I've been saving. People throw out a lot of furniture, especially wardrobes. When they throw wardrobes out, they unbolt them, rip off the doors and backing any old how, lean the base, doors and sides against a lamppost and break up the backing into pieces. But I found this one intact. It was a huge double deal that must have stretched the entire width of a room—I've seen Barrio Chino apartments like that: tiny, dark spaces cramped with heavy, varnished ostentation. Impossible to remove whole, it must have stood in the back of a shop. The owners could have just raised the roller door and dragged it out. Some pensioners live in these shop spaces with no natural light because the rent is cheaper. When they die, young people drag their crap into the street so they can renovate the space as a rehearsal studio or bar. This one intact monstrosity loomed like a church altar over all the other broken furniture stacked around it. I immediately ran home, grabbed a screwdriver and unscrewed the back, which came apart in two perfect surfaces of smooth, dark hardboard. These, the backs of wardrobes, or their doors when primed, make the best surface to paint on. On collection nights I restock my studio, scouring the neighbourhood for flat, nail-free sheets.

These panels came from around the Catalan-speaking Gypsy community on Carrer de la Cera, their home since Columbus sailed to America. I lugged them back to our mansion in Carrer Guàrdia and left the rest for the rubbish-men to carry off. Mounted side by side, they measure one metre eighty-five high by two and a half metres long. Huge. If I'm going to paint a real masterpiece, this will be my surface.

I spend an entire session working out the composition—no more studies or drawings, just manhandling my chaise longue into the exact spot in the studio I want it. Studying the background, making sure the shadows fall just right. Then sketching faintly onto the board. I want this composition to mirror Manet's almost, yet add a whole new aspect. A shocking aspect. The original has a slightly off-centre division—a vertical gilt line—which I'll copy through the break between these panels. It draws the eye down towards her groin, which her hand firmly masks. One change I'll make is to move her hand... Mine has to be more uninhibited in an extreme way to achieve the similar shock value that Manet's work would have had a century ago. Another change I want to add is to reveal much more of the chaise longue, make its blood-red presence central, so there's a harsher contrast with Olympia's pale flesh. I'll bring up the green background to a chemical intensity, as if it's lit by turn-of-the-century limelight. Maybe swap the hibiscus flower to her other ear, more prominent. Celia is overt. I'm just trying to reflect who she is.

I use a mirror to place myself in the composition the way I want. In Manet's work, the maid is holding a bouquet of flowers. I go wandering up through the house, looking for something that could work. In the hall, I come across an arrangement of dried sunflowers in a vase. But what do they say? Withered summer. Wilted, blasted fertility. I don't think that's my message. Moving on, the pot plants on the patio won't do either. Bloated aloes, triffid-like, they effuse menace and venom.

Into the kitchen. Álvaro's been cleaning. It's like a bleach-laden hurricane has spun through. The power of the disinfectant has seared walls and floor. All the rust scraps from the antique stove's remains have been swept up, deposited in a tea chest out on the patio. The shallow marble sink is now operational. Running water.

Álvaro's set of kitchen knives are gleaming soft and sure in their greased leather apron on the counter. It's like this tantalising attraction that knives have... Like guns, they seem to throb with their own life. I can't help fingering them... That gives me the idea... I slide the heavy stainless steel cleaver from its hidden position in the apron's back pocket. It's an implement that Álvaro barely uses and unless he specifically looks for it, he won't notice it's gone. My plan is to return it as soon as I've used it as a prop for my painting.

I have to force myself back to thinking about my main problem. Three bags of groceries sit on the floor beside the rusting fridge. It hums smugly in its corner, plugged into a fat transformer fed off two spindly wires that disappear out into the ballroom. There's one whole basketful of vegetables and right on top, staring at me, is the perfect symbol. It represents what it is—working class food—the real meaning of Manet's Olympia. Food in your belly, that's what the class struggle is all about. This perfect, heavy cabbage, just a touch of sooty decay smudging its creaminess, says exactly what I want.

The thing is, this painting, though I'll never show it to anyone—I'll probably give it to Celia as a gift—will have to express what I truly feel about everything: the purple bruise of my *serra*—thrumming in my blood through Dad's clout, Mum's slap, through my absence—the black-night city of Barcelona, soot-stained, velvet-lush, like Narcissus' skin; the neon electricity of San Francisco, of Narcissus' hair, of cocaine and sex; the satin coolness of night breezes off Montjuïc, of Celia's dresses; the jewel-like honey of her perfume bottles, of oily waves rolling under halogen lights down at the port, of Miguel's eyes, of linseed-rich oil paint oozing onto my canvas; the desperation I feel, which must end in... end if I don't find the path, that key to those cultural icons I used to worship—Spender, List, Dalí, Buñuel—before I took on the House, before I began to live in my own right, recreate my own mythic cosmopolis, enact a new, legendary fiction that is mine, uniquely mine, before I realised that every act has its consequence and after so many consequences and acts, events inevitably lead to the cul-de-sac, the white wall waiting for one last splash of paint before you vanish.

So down in the studio again, another aspect bugs me: the black cat. What does that mean to me? I want to include it, but have no ideas. Do I use a real animal? What does it symbolise? It's looking out from the canvas, back arched, warning the viewer away, staking its claim to the sheets. It depresses me. I sit on the chaise longue, now draped imperfectly with a sheet off my bed, and I'm looking and looking at the copy of Manet's work I have taped to the easel. I know his painting is a copy of another. All art is. Yet still the concept of that painting before a painting bothers me. I'm representing a work by Manet, who was versioning his own ideas of a work by Delacroix, Goya or Ingres. But what is more important is that each version is summing up its period, making a declaration about its time. That's what makes it classical, the key to its success. I have to find that reference.

Then a memory: my initial explorations of this soot-clad city, stumbling into one of the few places where I felt justified squandering my meagre savings on an entrance ticket. I'm walking through the gardens in Ciutadella Park, smelling the stink of animal dung, hearing bellowing lions and some kind of howling dingo or wolf from the zoo close by. I walk past the Catalan parliament—a surprisingly humble, pink stucco-and-yellow-stone building, a reconverted arsenal from centuries ago—and enter the Modern Art Museum in the same building. I've always found that weird, that our national gallery, parliament and zoo are shunted into such a cramped space.

I'm here to see an exhibition on the impressionists. Manet's *Olympia* of course, on loan from the Musée d'Orsay in Paris. But what most struck home, impressed me, was the attached educational section on the evolution of each painting. Before you saw *Olympia*, you viewed the paintings that inspired her: Titian's *Venus d'Urbino*; Ingres' *Odalisque with a Slave*; a Giorgione work, *Sleeping Venus*—that was actually finished by Titian himself though it inspired his own piece; and then of course Goya. The two *Majas* everybody knows—clothed and unclothed. But Titian, Titian, Titian. He rings bells. There was an animal, an ermine, or stoat that represented something. It was a dog—a chihuahua?—and it signified fidelity. That's what the black cat means, the witch motif, the enchantment of the female sex. The black cat represents prostitution. Obviously I need to go beyond that; it would be insulting in Celia's case.

But it's time to go to work. I have to leave. I'm walking upstairs, my foot on the first step already. Then I get this shock, like a hallucinogenic flash, feel like I'm tripping—acid-wise. Because the truth is expressed with crystalline clarity in this House, in our layout, why I live and paint in this cupboard under the stairs, why Álvaro could install his studio in the highest light-filled rooms. The epiphanic realisation of such equilibrium surrounds me with this halo-like serenity. The creature on the bed has to be a symbol, the one-eyed carnivore of our time, snapping up the soul we used to enshrine in our artwork.

* * *

Coming home from work, I begin painting furiously, sketching in all the compositional elements around the central figure. It must be after three in the morning. She should be about to arrive home. The magical pull of Celia's room, that delicious sensation—being enclosed in her rose and orange silks, pillowed on scents and essences—it seduces. I love watching her as she removes her makeup, prepares for bed: the anticipated bliss of a goodnight kiss.

I lock up my studio and head up. On the *Principal* floor, everything is in shadow. I can't hear any sound from the stairs leading up to Álvaro's darkroom, and the door to Narcissus and Álvaro's bedroom is open yet dark. They must be out. The house feels suddenly cold, dead or asleep, actively unfriendly. However, there is a welcoming gold bar of light from under Celia's door. As I approach I hear the rumble of voices. It somehow resembles the anger or violence of guns. I'm about to charge in there, throw out the offender, claim my space, when something stops me. I find myself listening from behind the door. It's true there's a kind of violence, yes, but not in the way I was imagining. I hear Celia's voice raised, midway between a grunt and wail, familiar in a way that runs a chill through my body. And I hear a man's voice, the gruff heaviness of his panting exertion, his half-stifled passion, his explosion. It's as if my world tilts and I can't seem to hold to anything stable. I stagger away from the door, move towards my room, but don't go in, am drawn back into the dark doorway of the middle room. Leaving the light off, I stand in shadows, listening to the grunting, the muffled moaning of their sex. Like animals, I think, like pigs! But I'm cold and small, can't put passion behind my outrage. The sex goes on and on. I'm like a fly on the wall of Celia's room, aware of every single thrust and caress on the far side of the thin plaster. It's as if I'm crucified, stabbed through like a rare moth by a pin, splayed against the display cabinet, incapable of any action ever again.

Then hours or nights later, it's over. I stay standing in the shadows, watching that heavy gold bar of light lying on the hallway floor, the golden rod that signifies Celia's passion, my stigmata. The atmosphere transforms. Voices resume their normality. A click, and that bar becomes a spearhead, an axe-head, and then it's just a lighted doorway into a golden world I no longer inhabit. Somebody else is standing there. And I know him.

# Eduardo XV

"'I mean no one will hear about it, will they?'

…

'No,' said Wilson. 'I'm a professional hunter. We never talk about our clients. You can be quite easy on that. It's supposed to be bad form to ask us not to talk though.'"

—Ernest Hemingway, "The Short Happy Life of Francis Macomber" in *The First Forty-Nine Stories*, Jonathon Cape, 1962, p. 14.

Morning. Another hangover. This is becoming dangerously routine. At school, the first two people I run into are José and Dani. They're in the Common Room and Dani is telling José something that has him in stitches and amazed by turns.

"Hi guys."

They go silent as they turn towards me and I get a cold feeling in my stomach. José's mouth even seems to drop open. Dani winks, but there's something supercilious about it:

"Hey Edu! Did you find what you were looking for last night?"

"I told you, it isn't what you think."

"Yeah, yeah, sure. Whatever."

"Anyway, how's your Dad?"

"Oh fine, out of IC… Thanks for asking."

"Didn't I tell you he would be?"

"No thanks to you!"

But a layer's been peeled back from our regular rough joking; it feels naked. I don't say anything else, just head straight to my first tutorial though about fifteen minutes early. I choose a seat on the far side for a change—opposite to where Dani, José and I normally sit—and pretend to be going over my notes. This is bad. I can smell shit boiling and I need to cool it off somehow. But it's all getting beyond me. Dani and José come in just before the lecture starts, sit in their usual place. I think, I should have sat on that side, let them move if they want to ostracise me. At lunchtime I decide to ring Ri. If she'll talk.

"Ri?"

"Edu?"

There's a silence where I don't know what to say and she isn't about to make it easy.

"Edu, what's up? Do you need something?"

"I... ah..." Suddenly my voice goes funny, which is totally unlike me, like it's breaking all over again. "Ah... I don't know... Can...?"

This is crazy. I need to ask.

"What?"

"Um, yeah... let's meet. Can we?"

"Okay. I'll come to yours. What time?"

"No... outside."

"Bar del Pi?"

"Yeah, whenever you want."

"Seven?"

"Right... See you then."

I get off the phone and am afraid to turn around because somebody is behind me waiting to use the cabin and I don't know what my face is doing. In the end I kind of shuffle out sideways, then turn and stride off looking in the other direction. Head for the *ferrocarril* station because I decide that's it for me today. Though I don't have a lecture this afternoon, normally I'd stay and study, maybe use a computer, but I need to get out and away from here fast as. I've always hated this walk—reminds me I ought to buy a car. I decided I don't have much use for one living down by the Plaza del Pino; it would just sit in a parking basement for the rest of its life. If I did have my own wheels though, maybe I wouldn't be quite so deep in this mess... I could have gone searching for Celia myself... and alone... I would never have had to go with her back to her room in the *friquis'* mansion in the first place; we could have just sat in the car and talked... Too late now though.

The Catalan *ferrocarril* trains are old but good, the only passengers a few housewives at this hour of the morning. I get a kid's kind of pleasure at stretching my spine straight on the high-backed, varnished-wood-and-emerald-velvet seats as if I were living fifty years ago, watching the moss-green-on-cream, ceramic-tiled stations slip by like a string of salt-encrusted buoys blown from their historical period to wash ashore here in this fucked-up age.

No-one's at home. I grab a bottle of Vichy from the fridge, a glass, go and lie on my bed. Feel the chilled, sparkling water surge down, scorching my throat. This is not me. Is this me? To have cut and run before a tricky situation. Why did I feel so vulnerable to attack from the guys? I haven't done anything. Why get so choked up to Ri? She's going to think I'm a total moron, a head-case. This is not the kind of person I am.

At some point I crawl under the *nórdico*, still fully clothed, let myself drift into that luxurious zone of daytime slumber, know I'm not awake, but not unconscious enough to lose my self-awareness. And the knowledge of my own fragility hovers, like a swarm of wasps over my comatose body, as if I'm staked in the desert awaiting death from spears of sunlight, from insects with huge mandibles that crawl out of the sand, from fat-coiled snakes that squeeze my breath from ribs and throat... That merges into an image of Zara, about five years old, hair burnished under the sun like a sun-temple goddess, the youngest empress, laughing at Raquel, her part-time nanny, not wanting to eat lunch—knowing she's already too famous for mere mortals to push around, force her to do what she has no inclination of doing; and the faded, Kodacolour print of her dimpled face, which they screwed behind a Perspex plaque onto her coffin and printed—in some revolutionary technique—onto her tombstone.

Dad stands among a group of officers, his green ceremonial uniform covered in braid and decorations... then he is shaking hands in a tailored business suit... but I can't recall a single memory of him in casual clothes, can't imagine him at the beach, or eating a *mar y montaña* paella, his favourite dish with its mix of seafood and game; I remember his moustache, but not his face, no smile—no pseudo-Americano memories of him teaching me to play football, or other schmaltzy B-grade film fodder... Just one—was I about ten?—of Mum ushering me into his cigar-perfumed office of black leather, mahogany and flickering fluorescents to present my report card—all As—and his comment: "Good man, Eduardo. That's how we'll regain the Patria!" And I can't remember ever being congratulated on anything else, though I'm sure I must have been because A-grades were my forte. I knew without being told that a B+ would be a slap-in-the-face to the family, a letting-the-side-down, so made sure I always brought home As. One of my two basic guidelines. The other: protect Zara. Which I didn't... Wasn't there, didn't know, couldn't stop it I know... but still my fault. And I realise in my mind, Dad and Zara inhabit two parallel universes. I can't imagine them together, no memories of Zara in Dad's arms or on his knee... I wonder what relationship they had. But there are no excuses for allowing your family to be decimated. None.

I must have slept properly in the end because when I awake, I have that lost, twilit feeling of wading through limbo, not knowing whether it's morning or evening. Looking at the clock it says a quarter to five. Through the blinds, the sun is slanting golden off the Iglesia del Pino; it's obviously afternoon. I go into the kitchen, drink cold milk, make myself a coffee. Sitting at the table, sipping coffee, munching *magdalenas*—a second breakfast.

Now what am I going to say to Ri? Nothing to say really. Why did I even phone her? I don't think I need to talk to her now... She'll be asking for an apology, for something I'm supposed to have done, for just being me. So I have it all worked out, have my story—well, no story, just my version. The hard thing is explaining it because it's as if somebody has unlawfully taken hold of my life, were writing a different script to all of my actions... actions which are innocent, simple... but somehow I performed them... Now they've been twisted by... in this macabre production... till I'm playing Fu Manchu in a cheap thriller plot. It's as if everybody believes the fictional version because it's so much more exciting than the truth. And my anger rises over the brim like magma from a volcano. Somebody has to pay, somebody will pay for all this that has been done to me.

I finish my coffee—feel as if I'm reclaiming my previous, physical reality—strip, and go take a shower. Hot water pounds my back and shoulders, massages my torso so the heat enters my guts. The rivulets fondle and tickle my genitals, reviving balls and perineum, sluicing down thighs and calves. Stepping out from the torrent, I lather my hair with shampoo, then my body with soap. I luxuriate in the steamy atmosphere, spend time going over my entire body, really scrubbing at my skin—forearms, biceps, chest, armpits—wanting to wash out the dirt and scum that have accumulated over the last few days. I wash my arse, soap my balls and dick, cleaning under the foreskin like a good boy—I toss up whether to have a wank, but decide against it; not really in the mood. Finally plunging back under the hot stream, I let the deluge wash all that shit and past angst away down the plughole.

After I step from the shower, the only slap reality deals me is my damp, cold towel. All the others are in the wash. Life can't be perfect.

***

She's sitting in almost the exact same pose as she sat when she *didn't* tell me she was a lesbian, has let her hair grow in the past year. Instead of the short bob she had for ages, it's now down well past her shoulders. She suits it, doesn't look as tough, more feminine. But when she raises her eyes as I approach, they still have that same fuck-you-arsehole glint as ever.

"So?"

"How's it going?"

"So Edu, lets go back to the beginning because we need to sort out some stuff if we're going to carry on our friendship."

"Like what?"

"Think, because I'm not planning to do all the work here."

"I know, Ri, I think I did something stupid..."

"Now why does that not surprise me?"

"Fuck! Take it easy, will you?"

"Marta calls you the Cock that Shits Golden Eggs. She's mystified why I agreed to meet you."

"That's good. I didn't think Marta was the literary type, thought she came from a fairy-tale-deprived kind of childhood."

"No, she translates from the visual to the textual excellently when stirred enough."

If women generally are touchy, lesbians take the prize for being total firecrackers. But this was not going where I intended...

"I may have got myself into a situation, which could affect things with Fra..."

Ri snorts, stirs her coffee and then clatters her spoon noisily onto her saucer.

"God! Why can't men keep their dicks in their pants!"

"I have!"

"Have you? So what's the situation?"

"It's about Zara and Dad. I needed to talk..."

"No, Edu. You aren't going to pull that one again! That's your excuse for everything. And meanwhile you go around treating people like it's all a cynical game. I'm sick of it. Do you care a toss, Edu? Do you?"

"Of course! You know I do!"

"I don't know that. You're false, smirking and snide about everything. You act like you're superior to everyone when you're the most emotionally cauterised person I've ever met.

"I want some real connection in my life. I don't get it with you. Marta... Marta is the first person in my life who... She means more to me than anyone... She is my life... Okay? I'm going to protect that in any way I have to."

All the things I was thinking about Dad and Zara have just kind of dried up.

"What do you mean I don't connect. I..."

"You don't."

She picks up her spoon again and bangs it back on the table top:

"Edu, we can hook up, do lines and all that stuff, but from where I'm standing that's starting to get boring. I want real connections. I..."

"I connect! I have... What do you think Fra is? We've being going steady for over a year now. If I..."

"What, that's the word, what. Fra's a thing to you: a girlfriend, an object. If she..."

"Slip of the tongue..."

"If she meant anything to you, you..."

"She does mean things, I..."

"Things again! There you go again..."

"She means... I love her, alright? Is that what you want to know?"

Then the silence stretches.

"You wouldn't know... I mean you don't make it obvious..."

"Ri..."

"Don't start talking about Zara, alright Edu? She's gone. You're alive..."

"*FUCK!*"

I stand up from the table. I'm trembling. I want to kill her.

*"DON'T TELL ME WHAT I CAN AND CAN'T THINK! OR TALK ABOUT! FUCK YOU, SABRINA! FUCK YOU!"*

I start to walk, wanting, needing to get away before I do some violence. I don't get far, just as far as the statue of Guimerà—who knew how to write, despite his politics—where I find myself kind of scrunching up against the bronze. How dare she go there, how DARE she? At the same time, part of me knows I'm being totally out of order, absolutely unreasonable, making a massive spectacle of myself... Free show for the shithead tourists in the square... I'm aware of Ri behind me, but she knows enough not to try and touch me.

"Edu... I know... I'm sorry, alright?"

"You don't know, Ri... You just don't."

"Yeah, okay. Accepted. But look, Edu..."

"Hey, we'll talk some other time, Ri. I... I just need to..."

And I'm going, going... gone as I walk out of the square, leave Sabrina behind me. She's got Marta now anyway. Anyway, how would she fucking know if she's never lost anyone close to her? Maybe she should.

# Joaquim XVI

*What effort!*
*What effort for the horse to be a dog!*
*What effort for the dog to be a swallow!*
*What effort for the swallow to be a bee!*
*What effort for the bee to be a horse*

—Frederico García Lorca, "Muerte" [Death], in *Poeta en Nueva York*.

I 'll kill him. There, I've said it. But don't we all swear revenge on the people close to us now and again? It isn't one of the real things. It isn't what's important here. And you shouldn't think it relates to anything that came after. And if it did, I certainly wouldn't admit it here. I might be Joaquim, the Fool, but I'm not a complete idiot. Not so dumb. But you've got to understand, I was in shock. Everything that Celia and I had built up to this point now seemed to have been wrecked by that single act.

The anger takes days. At first I'm just cold for hours. After he leaves, I sneak back into my room, creep under the covers and lie there trembling. For hours. I'm cold, really cold. Can't get warm. I lie all night. Can't sleep. In the dawn—a sky the yellow of the nicotine stains on my fingers—I begin to feel the rage. It starts so slow. Then it just builds and builds. I can't release it. It keeps coming. For days and days, but nobody notices a thing. They're all so used to their little Miró quietly inhabiting the edges of their fabulous world, being so thankful just to exist next to their exalted selves, that I guess they can't conceive I might have anything like real feeling inside me.

My world has been turned upside down and nobody notices a thing. What is most amazing is I went on with my project to paint Celia. When she saw the revamped set I had constructed, her attitude changed. Now she seemed enthusiastic about it, keen to do any number of sittings I needed. It was like she could finally imagine herself into the fantasy. That was important because I needed her enthusiasm, not just a grudging willingness to go along. I managed to unbutton more than her blouse. I succeeded in showing her like she really is, her entire self beaming in a way that can only make the painting work.

So we developed a routine. I would wake her with a demitasse of coffee about eleven. Once more in the land of the living, she would do a perfunctory toilette and apply the minimum amount of makeup she thought she needed to present herself on canvas. I had to remind her to apply the same every day, though I concentrated on getting her face first—after the under-painting—that stark Celia gaze, a kind of staring out into the world, defying it to accept her. She would descend to my studio about twelve, once the sun was squarely hitting the skylight above, when the light was strongest. All those sketching sessions in her room have paid off. She trusts me. We paint for as long as she can stand it, generally about an hour, then while I'm finishing up, she heads upstairs and puts her street makeup on, gets on with choosing an appropriate outfit. Around three, we head out for lunch, generally Romesco's or Mesón David, where I somehow pick up the bill—digging money from out of the cracks of my nails to pay—Celia's fee for agreeing to model.

This might sound perverse, especially after her infidelity. It is. And all the time my anger is growing, boiling up inside me. Yet I have some kind of iron will holding me to task. I can't quite explain. It's like however angry I get, or however I might imagine passionate revenge scenarios, this painting is even more important, more important than my own life. This is true in the end. And the painting is going well. I will have my *obra*.

The other 'masterpiece', the one on canvas. What can I say? After the intense passion of working with Celia, after lunch, if I don't have to work, I return to my studio and concentrate on the other. It's at a stage where I'm more or less happy with it. But they

gloat—*Beauty and Companion*—tucked in a corner, willing me to complete them. And it's they who are the large problem, who remain unresolved.

Yet getting Celia's painting to fall into place also has a beneficial effect on Narcissus'. A common icon even provides a feeling of solid continuity—a series of two. Because this animal should appear here too.

***

Halfway through this period, we're woken up one night. I went to bed early because I was back on a morning shift. But I sleep light. It's like I feel the creaks and sighs of the House around me like a sleeping animal. It's almost like the House—the Beast—and us, the people who live here, have this symbiotic relationship, like we're parasites hooked into its pelt or intestinal wall—like at any moment we could get sluiced away by a dose of worming treatment squirted down the mansion's gullet, the way that we'd do the pigs in Benissola once a year.

So when the front door opens and Celia creeps in—though I don't wake fully because she's an adept at silence—my mind records the fact that she's come home—also the fact that someone strange is with her. I don't know how long they've been there by the time the voices wake me properly. But at a certain point, I'm lying in bed listening to the murmur—the his and the her voice like the wash and ebb of the sea against two separate places: the fine sand (hers) and a baser note, a hollow barge or pylon, the armour plates of a battleship (his)—and with the consciousness, the realisation that all is not right. The voices have a grating quality: she's more admonitory, peace-making, more of a wash like waves on a gravel beach; his, more garrulous, prideful even, then undercutting itself (as if cut down to size), turning querulous, complaining—more similar to the wake from a speed boat as it splashes against the different objects it finds in its path.

Then there's a crash. I'm fully awake now, sitting up in bed. That was glass—vase, mirror, crystal... The voices are silenced abruptly, to be replaced by an urgent hissing: fury and secrecy. Silence for a dozen heartbeats. Then his tones grumble away again. I can tell he's drunk. Is she? Straining my ears in the darkness, but for a while there is little more. I slip on a pair of shorts just in case, but swear I will not get involved. This could almost be what she wants, rubbing my nose in her lack of concern for the relationship of trust and love we'd built up. I pull the sheets up over my head and swear I couldn't give a toss over who she brings back now...

Her scream rips through the mansion's hide like a knife. I'm out the door and down the passage without even time for a thought.

"Celia?"

"Joaquim...! Oh, go back to bed, can you...? I'm okay."

But I've already pushed open the door... and there he is! I want to explode! How *dare* he come into this space! How *dare* she let him in! Lying on the bed, virtually naked except for his leather biker's jacket and his bulging, mosque-like stomach swelling out over

what looks like—is—a worn-out, faded black jockstrap. In front of her commode—mirror and perfume bottles delineating her like a halo—she stands, wrapped in a feathery white robe.

"What are you... Celia! What's he here for? I thought you hated him!"

"Joaquim, listen Sweets, everything's fine... Don't you want to go back to bed, please?"

"How can you? Tell him to leave Celia! Tell him to leave! He's bad for you... You said..."

"I think it's you she's telling to leave, Lad..."

"Shut up! I'm not talking to you!"

"Joaquim! That's enough. Go back to bed. I'm fine. We can deal with this."

"You bitch! You said you were over with him. You were over..."

"Go back to bed, Joaquim. We'll talk in the morning. Just go back to bed!"

But then Narcissus has appeared in the doorway, dressed in a long, pale, cotton nightshirt—something from a century gone by. Álvaro hovering behind.

"WHAT is going ON here? Joaquim, are you moLESTing Celia's guest?"

This is all going pear-shaped... But I am not the guilty one here!

"No, I..."

"Just go back to bed, Joaquim. We'll talk in the morning."

"He was hitting her!"

"Joaquim, don't make accusations you don't know are true!"

"It is true!"

But that's it. I'm shooed back into my room as if I were a six-year-old. I vow I'll never help her with a single thing again as long as I live! I lie awake for hours... fuming, pondering, imagining how I could get my revenge for this latest humiliation. Only a couple of hours remain before my alarm will sound when I finally drop off to sleep, but I don't forget that night. Everything I knew... I'm starting to learn to read below the surface... Starting to see... Yet sleep is oblivion. It rescues me from places where I don't want to delve.

# Eduardo XVI

*...this theatre is a lamentable parody, but, parody or not, it is the truest temple of my race—a parody of a temple for a race of ghosts—*

—Esther Tusquets, *El mismo mar de todos los veranos*, p. 127.

Walking home, I think about my jacket again; then I think about Fra. I should ring her, need to. On an impulse, I go out onto the Rambla de las Flores and buy the biggest bunch of flowers I can see—tacky I know, but the old remedies are the ones that work—then I jump in a taxi.

"Calle Princesa, número veintidós, por favor."

Even if she's out, I'll have made the attempt.

"¿Sí?"

"Fra?"

"What do you want?"

"Can I come up?"

"Why?"

"To talk."

"We can talk like this."

"I want to talk to you, Fra, let me in!"

Finally she relents. I take the six flights of narrow, red-tiled stairs fairly slowly—I need breath and a strategy by the time I reach the top. The door is ajar, but she isn't waiting there—good or a bad? I push it open and step into her space.

"¡Hola, guapa!"

I'd forgotten how tiny her place is, but I can't see any sign of her from the narrow hallway—tiled, like the whole flat, in the same red terracotta. Fra's latest fave boyband Noir Désir are playing softly—another of those here-today-gone-to-morrow, French pop-rock combinations—and the place is thick with incense. Because Françoise doesn't answer, I have the choice of moving left to the living room, or right towards the kitchen and bedroom. I choose left—I doubt she's going to be arrayed in her negligée on the bed—and I'm right.

She's sitting on the sofa with a soundless TV playing (Fra's living room is about the size of a matchbox), a book on her lap and a half-empty bowl of gazpacho before her on the coffee table. She looks up at me and I look at her, knowing she's waiting for me to speak, but I haven't got a clue what to say.

"Hi Fra."

The flowers seem like a cheap conjuror's trick in this atmosphere, so I lay them unceremoniously on the coffee table without offering them.

"Hey, I missed you."

She says nothing for a while, but folds up the book and places it on the coffee table.

"This afternoon I had coffee with Álvaro."

I'm immediately defensive.

"And?"

"You tell me, Edu... the truth."

I realise I need to take this slowly and sit cautiously on the only other seat in the room, a hard-backed wooden dining chair beside the television.

"So you had coffee with Álvaro... And?"

"Tell me what's going on."

"I'm not playing around, Françoise, I can tell you that."

The flickering television beside me is annoying, but I sense that if I turn it off, the sharp focus of her eyes might be too intense.

"You know my Dad and... Zara were murdered..."

She looks at me, suspicious, like I'm trying to change the subject, but says nothing.

"Her... too."

"Her?"

Her tone is sharp, like she's about to get up and slug me.

"Celia. Her boyfriend... a guy she was in love with... was killed... disappeared..."

I can't go on because her laugh shatters the air.

"What do you tell me, that you go down there to *talk*? The two of you, to sit together, holding hands, in commiseration, to share your condolences?"

"Give over, Françoise! Yes, I wanted to talk to her! Is that a problem?"

"So you pay for a night with a whore, just to talk to her?"

"Who told you I paid her?"

"What do you think, that she is protected by the secret of the confessional?"

I am fuming. I feel my blood rushing hot through my veins, but my skin, hands, guts are icy... My ears are buzzing... I need to kill someone! I notice my hands trembling and can't stop them shaking. I clench my fists and clamp them between my knees.

"Nothing happened, Fra. I needed to talk to someone... I thought she might... We just talked!"

"Get out of my flat, Eduardo. You are a fucking liar and a despicable man!"

"Fra...!"

I want to tell her that it isn't true, none of it, however it looks, but I can't control my body, or my feelings. This is too much, it's outrageous... I am not this person! Why doesn't she believe me?

"Françoise, you have to believe me, nothing happened!"

It's no use. I know I've lost. Somehow I stumble to the door and leave. I feel hollow inside. Whose is this fault? Somebody must pay! I have done nothing wrong! Why is this happening to me? Why! Somehow I find myself down in the street and don't know what to do. How could Fra think that! She knows me! What could she... Who...? My brain won't function, but my feet on autopilot lead me along the road towards a bluesy-type bar with a pool table on Comercio and I wander in. A whiskey. I need a drink to sort this out in my head.

The bar is empty—what is today, Thursday? Tuesday? When did I decide to seek Celia out? It was a Tuesday or a Wednesday. Wednesday. Therefore today must be Friday. I ask the barman:

"Where is everyone?"

He looks at his watch.

"It's early."

I look at mine: just before eleven. People won't start coming in till after midnight. I'll have the bar to myself. Good. I've bombed. I've bombed. I've bombed. I order another whiskey, this time with coke. Somebody must pay for this. Somebody must pay. I've been railroaded into this corner where I've actually not done anything and just because of the way I am—because I don't give a fuck what people think—it's assumed that I'm guilty, that I've been fucking around with that *thing* down in the *friquis'* mansion. Somebody must pay!

This is what they're like, the underclass, the criminal class, the arsehole of humanity. Whatever they can take, they'll take; however they can stick in the blade, they will. They are like a sickness that eats into the body of society. The only real way to deal with a disease like that is to cut it out, amputate the gangrened limb. Otherwise it'll just spread, infect every part of the organism.

For some reason Dad comes to mind when I think this. Specifically, when I was about twelve, he took me with him on a trip. Though I hardly remember a thing about it. (Our summers often consisted of Mum, Zara and I staying at the beach with Dad coming and going from Zaragoza or Madrid, depending on whatever business he had going. Occasionally he would take one of us along with him, never both at once. This must have been my turn.)

We visited a famous palace outside Madrid: trudging across an interminable plain of granite flagstones; descending rank upon rank of marble stairs until we reached this circular chamber far underground; tiers of coffins lining the walls, stacked as high as the ceiling, everything in gold and black onyx. Dad had made me dress up—long pants, buttoned shirt—but that dead cold still seeped straight into my bones down there deep among those sleeping kings.

Mostly from that trip I remember lying back in the soft leather of Dad's Mercedes; the smell of his cigar smoke as he drove:

"Remember Edu: we won; they lost. What we have is ours by right. Spain was being eaten away by the cancer of Communism and Freemasonry."

And while he spoke, the hot wind of the Spanish plains pushed in through the window like dragon's breath, harsh and exciting.

"You'll hear lots of Bolshevik ideas in Catalonia. But a famous general once said: 'We have no problem with Catalonia that an army once every hundred years cannot fix.'"

Coming home we stopped at the *Caudillo*'s tomb. I have this vision of that humungous cross, rearing up out of the craggy peaks; but the other recollection is the vast dome of a ceiling soaring high up, showing angels, saints and stuff, plus God on his throne. It was cold in there too.

"A serious operation was needed to cut out the rot. We did so. You can hold your head up high for who you are, Eduardo."

***

Two girls come into the bar: a blond and a brunette. Foreigners, I think.

"Two vodka, lime and sodas."

They are. The barman looks at them uncomprehendingly.

"Try vodka and tonic, or vodka and lemon. Lime and soda are a bit out of his range."

"Okay. Thank you."

They get their drinks, smile and turn away, giving ambiguous signals about whether they want to be left alone. But I'm not in the mood. I need to think, to nut out the Françoise problem... Yet that whole scene I just went through... it brings up a kind of horror in me... especially the... Celia thing—her *accusation*! I could vomit! Do I really care whether people think I've slept with the satin witch? Yes, I do. Do I really care whether Françoise thinks so? Definitely. Do I go back, try and speak to her? Is she so important?

Here I have two long-legged foreigners showing signs of giving out. I could just forget her and go on, choose the cutest of these two babes and take her home for a shag. Then I could forget Fra and that band of *friquis*, make a fresh start and this time stay on my side of the lines, relocate to well north of the Generalísimo's divide, in Sarrià or Pedralbes, concentrate on building the future I know I'm made for.

I pay for my drinks, wave to the girls as I leave. But my legs warn me of my drunkenness. I have to hang on Françoise's buzzer forever until she answers.

"Listen Françoise, let me in… I… love you. Please… can I come up?"

The door unlocks.

# Joaquim XVII

The evening of the party, I have to work. Guests start to arrive while we're still setting up. First to get there are Françoise and Edu. Narcissus, Álvaro and I have been slaving all day to get the house ready—though Narcissus in more of an overseer role. Françoise steps through the portal into the *porte cochère* to find me kneeling on flagstones, surrounded by two hundred brown paper bags.

"Bonsoir, Miró. What are you doing?"

Edu stands gruff, *macho*, behind her. He eyes me with that half-sneer, even slight distaste, he reserves for when he comes around this house visiting.

Hypocrite, I think. I know a few of your secrets now. He is dressed in dark colours to match Françoise: black jeans, a dark Americana jacket and burgundy silk shirt, looking like one of the Rumba catalana crowd.

"They're to light the stairs."

It's my job to get them lit before I rush off to work, but it's taken ages to work out my method. I think I've finally got it, am now advancing fast. The bags are filled with pebbles and sand from the terrace—I've lugged bucketfuls down. The bags now line the *porte cochère* and either side of the main stairs leading up to the *Principal*. Each will contain a tea-light, making it glow like a paper lantern. It's a cheap way of achieving a great effect. But I've burnt both hands a couple of times already, trying to hold a lighter in without setting the bag alight. I tried lighting the candle beforehand, then dropping it in, but it would flip over and go out or fall on its side, burning the bag. Finally I went and bought a couple of tapers at the *estanco* and have managed to get most of them lit in the last twenty minutes, but I'm stressed, late for work and sick of kneeling here on the flagstones to create an effect I won't even be able to appreciate.

"Is Narcissus here?"

"Yeah. He's preparing the fireworks on the terrace. I have to go to work. But I'll be back later. It should all be happening by then."

As if he somehow has a sixth sense, Álvaro appears at the top of the stairs:

"Hola, Françoise! Edu! How's it going? Come up."

But he comes downstairs towards us.

"Joaquim, we need to get your painting set up in the *salon*. You should get it now."

We've taken to calling the ballroom the *salon*. I feel scared but pretty chuffed by the honour. This is pride of place for my work.

"I can't. I've got to be at work. I'm late already. I'll bring it up when I get back."

"That will be too late. Narcissus says he has to see it before people arrive. Otherwise you can forget about showing it. That's what he said."

I'm fine with that. I don't know that I want to show it anyway.

"I don't have time. I've been late too many times for work already..."

"Give me the key. I'll get it."

No! One thing I won't give in to, is Álvaro having the key to my studio. "I don't think so."

"Miró..." Françoise seems to press in towards me with her scent. Eduardo bristles. "I'll get your painting... Do you trust me? And I promise nobody else will enter your studio... or look at anything in there."

Her eyes bore into me, her scent strong, almost crackling like lightning. Something so witchlike about her, akin to the tarot readers down under Plaça Catalunya. I relent, have to leave. I take the key off its ring, entrust it into her warm palm. I'm not so sure about this, but just don't have time to think any more. Edu sneering behind her somehow upsets me too. I've never liked him, but the dominant sexual energy he gives off always leaves me too dizzy to think. I'm going to be late as it is. I step out of the postern gate and sprint off down Guardia for the Liceu metro.

# Eduardo XVII

*¡Por vosotros estamos en línea de combate!*
*Preferiríamos romper todo de un golpe,*
*antes que entregarlo en las manos pegajosas de las*
*senilidades mil veces yertas."*
*[For you, we are in the combat line!*
*We would rather break it all in a single blow,*
*than deliver it into the sticky hands of*
*thousand-times-stiff senilities.]*

—José María Castroviejo, "A vosotros, obreros rojos" [To You, Red Workers],
1936.

Françoise and I were the perfect couple by the time the party came around. I knew I had to show up though it was the last thing I was into—she wanted me there beside her presenting a united front, or something. It was like she had taken Álvaro's lies as a personal insult and was out to quash those rumours with mortal precision. For her that meant riding forth, trumpets blaring. As far as I was concerned, Álvaro and Celia—in fact, all those bloody *friquis*—better make damn sure they didn't end up in a room alone with me at any time that night.

We arrived early because Fra said she wanted to help with "preparations". I wasn't going to argue. Some people might have said she'd got me under her thumb after that whole crisis between us. All I can say—though I think that's a load of bollocks—is that I'd been thinking about priorities. Anyway, we arrive at Guardia and the first person we meet is that little faggot Joaquin. He's scurrying around like a castrated chicken, like they're going to belt the shit out of him if he doesn't keep his eyes crossed and his teeth dotted, and looks at me like I'm the devil, which I kind of enjoy. Apparently he's some kind of painter, has done a portrait of Narcissus which is supposed to be displayed tonight. Can't imagine what it will be like; bad, I assume.

Anyway, he rushes off to work and we head upstairs. Álvaro is preparing a slideshow in his and Narcissus's bedroom, which they have cleared out so it can be a sort of chill-out lounge next to the dance floor. The main ballroom is where the dancing will happen. Morden, a black singer who DJs sometimes at San Francisco, is setting up a turntable there. I can hear Narcissus somewhere at the other end of the house, rising above level ten on his own personal histrionic scale. We'll steer clear.

"Well, we can get Joaquim's painting and hang it for him. After that we will see where we can help."

Fra heads for the cellars and I follow. Joaquin's studio is in the upper basement. You go through a tiny, shoulder-height door outside the ballroom and down a twisting narrow staircase, which after the first landing opens out into a larger stair leading down onto the main space. The kid's studio is at the far end, where the ceiling has a couple of skylights connecting to the terrace above. The smell of compost makes me want to retch as we get close. Fra unlocks the padlock using the key Joaquin had given her and we enter. That stink of vegetable decomposition becomes unbearable. But turning on the light—a sickly, yellowy globe—I'm impressed. It's a real artist's studio. Looks like, even if it doesn't smell that way. An easel, more or less centre stage, faces a chaise longue at the far end under skylights. Trolleys, a rickety table—plus every available floor space—hold piles of drawings, photos, magazine cut-outs, dried palettes, ashtrays brimming with butts, empty coke cans and arrays of objects you mightn't associate with painting (unless you'd met the Tarragona kid): a horseshoe; a graffiti-scrawled LP cover of Nana Mouskouri's *Tierra Viva*; a paint-smeared chef's apron; a half-inflated car-tyre inner tube; a collection of toothpick dispensers liberated from diverse cafes; a stuffed toy cat splattered with red paint; a plastic snake and a valve radio that has been smashed and its pieces wired together into new, odd conformations; in the far corner sits a huge, rotting cabbage—the source of the stench. There are also cassette tapes: the Scorpions, Nirvana, Juan Luis Guerra, Billy Idol, Mike Oldfield. Paintings are stacked around the walls—evidence that the guy has certainly been doing something more than tweaking his foreskin in his spare time.

The portrait of Narcissus—and Álvaro, it turns out—is on the easel; you can't miss it. I want to grab the painting and leave straight away, escape from that nauseating smell, but Fra insists on fussing and pondering how we could hang it to the best effect, where the optimum space would be, and that. I ignore her counting of the ways and start exploring, turning around his other works. I've got natural curiosity.

"Hey Fra, look at this!"

I turn both panels around so she can fully appreciate the faggot's artistic talent. But I can't hide my smile.

"Oh my God! What... No, Edu, leave that alone. Joaquim asked us to take this one painting and hang it. It is the only one he is ready to show."

"But this is art, Fra. Why wouldn't he want to show this? It'll

go down a hoot."

"Edu, you're the last person I would imagine would want to show a painting like that!"

"Hey, I have a clean conscience. I say let everything hang out."

"No, we do what he asked us to and nothing more."

"Just for a minute, forget what has happened over the last few days, forget the subject matter and look at the painting itself. It's good. Is it good, or isn't it?"

"Yes, it is. But he said..."

"Well sometimes friends have to be given a gentle push. Do you want to help him, or not?"

Françoise sighs:

"Edu, I never know whether to trust you anymore."

"Trust me, Fra. I'm not a bastard."

I'm already carrying the panels out of the room, and away from that smell, leaving her to lug the canvas of Narcissus and Álvaro. Let's face it, neither of us were prepared to argue for long in that atmosphere. I know, however, that even though this might not harm Joaquin that much, it will hopefully shake up another piece of lowlife I have in mind.

Upstairs, I leave Fra to organise the hanging of Narcissus's portrait while I go searching out the loftiest, most visible position for the other. Finally I decide on the ballroom and commandeer a spotlight which Álvaro has set up in the bedroom to shine up the wall and provide "mood" lighting. I rip off the red lighting gels he's taped on and fix it on a shelf above the patio door so that, with a single, strong, focussed beam, it shines directly onto the main wall you see as you enter the space, right where my painting will hang.

When she comes back and sees what I've done, she gives me one of those looks, but at the end of the day, I kind of think she feels like digging in the boot too, so doesn't comment.

The key to a good party is the booze supply. I knew I was only going to enjoy myself if I had one—beyond the clutches of the *friquis'* desperate paws. So next up, I set about sorting that out. I'd bought a six-pack and a bottle of bourbon. It turned out the only room in the house with a lock on it was the kid's studio and Françoise had the key. I offered to go down and lock it for her. I gave Fra a beer and took one for myself. Then I locked the rest of our stash out of harm's way.

When I got back upstairs, there was a group gathered around Narcissus in the entrance hall, admiring his portrait. I just wanted to vomit, but I bit the lip of my beer and kept quiet. This was Fra's night and I had promised to be the perfect boyfriend. Álvaro was standing about half a metre behind Narcissus's shoulder as they gazed up at the painting, but slightly outside the group of Narcissus, Fra, Felipe, Ludovico and Paul. I stand beside Álvaro. Narcissus is declaiming:

"Now, you SEE? The MARK of a PAINTer! I knew as soon as I saw, as soon as I met the boy... that's why we took him under our wing. Didn't we, Álvaro?"

Álvaro nods. I murmur to him:

"So did you and Fra have a fun coffee the other day?"

"I have an EYE for talent... NAKed talent!"

Ludovico smirks.

Álvaro looks at me. Those flat, green eyes could be reflecting fear, worry, or uncertainty. Or maybe it's disdain, indifference, masked calculation. If ever a guy was unreadable.

"Yes, we did."

"We SAW... the TALent that young Miró was HARbouring and KNEW it was our CULtural Duty to nurture this young SOUL, help his FLOWer to Open..."

"You took his flower, Narcissus? Cradle-snatcher!" Ludo squeals.

"Well next time just stick with what you've seen, before you start inventing gossip, if you know..."

"I did."

"WHAT?"

"Edu!"

I was ready to slug the guy—the lying, faggot son-of-a-bitch—and if Fra hadn't pulled me away towards the ballroom, I would have.

"You promised! Fuck you, Edu! You promised you would come to this party and behave! So settle down!"

"I am behaving! I'm a veritable leashed Chihuahua. We were just having an urbane conversation. Aren't I allowed to talk to people?"

"Talk, don't fight. Okay?"

I knew then that this party was going to be an absolute, fucking rage.

# Joaquim XVIII

Tota la meva vida es lliga a tu,
Com en la nit les flames a la fosca.
[My whole life is bound to you,
As in the night, the flames to the dark.]

—Bartomeu Rosselló Pòrcel, "A Mallorca, durant la guerra civil" [To Mallorca, during the Civil War], Barcelona, September 1937.

The party is lit up by my candles when I return. Paper bags of glowing light sit out on the narrow footpath like beacons. Both heavy oak doors of the main portal have been flung back and a double row of lights leads in, upstairs to the main entrance. Grouped on the stairs are people I don't know. Also the lower stable entrance grill is unlocked. More tea-lights illuminate the dim labyrinth inside. I hope Françoise has remembered to lock my studio. I am standing there adjusting to this strange sensation of being an alien in my own home when Celia comes in off the street. She is wearing her white satin "Marilyn" dress that leaves her shoulders bare, heels so high she should need a pilot's licence to operate them and a platinum-blond wig bright enough to make Warhol look tawdry.

"Joaquim! Fabulous! You can help a lady make her entrance."

She puts her arm through mine and together we ascend the stairs. We come through the door together and that's where we get our first shock. The entrance hall has been transformed: the mounds of urban flotsam—three-legged tables, chipped and speckled mirrors, borer-infested bed heads, wobbly chairs, broken lamps and hideous chandeliers—all the tossed-out furniture Narcissus regularly brings in off the street has been spirited away. The honey-coloured marble tiles have been swept, scrubbed and polished till they gleam. Two slender stands, as wide and high as bar stools, are staked out at each far corner. A potted plant stands on one—I recognise a wizened monster of a cactus off the patio. The other supports an ornate, Chinese-style vase containing a branch of wattle. But the wall between them is what takes my breath away, or rather what's on it. High up, central, hung to dominate the entire entrance hall, is my portrait, finally resolved: *Barcelona Gothic.*

The colours are deep, brown-tinged and warm—a Romantic yet cathedral ambience that suits these surroundings—I have included woodwork and ceiling details from our salon in a jiggering of perspective that works if you don't look too closely. Narcissus stands centre field, captured from an upward-tilted perspective—emphasised because the picture is hung high—dressed in a tweed, double-breasted suit, white handkerchief in his breast pocket, a red-white carnation in his buttonhole. His hair is bound tightly back behind him, gleaming like metal. The bones in his face are strong, handsome, while a confident smile plays across his features. I remember trying to get that, playing for hours with the highlights, painting and over-painting and over-painting again. He exudes the charm of a winner. Behind him at his shoulder is that other hovering presence. Álvaro stands deathly still, erect, smile-less and focussed on Narcissus, those green eyes boring out from his wide, white forehead towards the other. In contrast to Narcissus, he is dressed in a scratchy, brown shirt—a rural feel. The reference to Grant Wood's *American Gothic*—a mid-western couple standing before a pioneer cottage; sober apparel, stern visages, bible-bashing beliefs; pitchfork in hand—should be apparent. Álvaro, instead of that pitchfork, holds up a camera, likewise gleaming with a dull, metallic precision.

I decided in the end to scrap the 'Beast' concept—far too open to misinterpretation. Still, I'm stunned. I realise the portrait works, am proud to see it on the wall in full view of everybody—there—where everybody, not just me, can also see that it works. And people do. They're looking at up at it. As they drift from one side of the party to the other, they stop and look.

Françoise comes in, her arm linked in Felipe's.

"Ahh, there you are Petit Miró! Your paintings are gorgeous!"

"It's beautiful, Joaquim."

I want to go and find Narcissus, thank him for allowing me to hang the painting.

"Thanks. Umm... I think it works, doesn't it?"

Felipe smiles at Celia.

"Yours is very good. That was very brave."

"What?"

She's gone white through her makeup.

"Joaquim?"

"I... I don't... What painting, Felipe?"

"It's in the salon."

That was where Narcissus' portrait was supposed to hang. The feeling as we walk through the hall, enter the *salon*, is one of floating. But it's eerie, like being pinned on a cold blade that twists in my soft intestines. The ballroom is full. People are dancing. Red bulbs and a broad streak of white light on the far wall, up among the wallpaper creepers. It's suspended there, high above our heads yet it focuses the room, directs people's gaze as they dance. The painting is in two panels, which like I said, makes a virtue of necessity. I don't know whether I'm too keen on that division. Too even, too boxlike, or compartmentalised. Yet maybe that's alright, it structures Celia's essential anarchy. Or reflects that rigid control, the makeup. Her perfect top half is all contained in the left-hand panel. Her ice-queen radiance. Her breasts look quite big. Bare. Huge, in fact. Well, they are. They burst from her torso like two tight teardrops about to explode. Guys are always riveted by them. I was. I've painted them as I've seen them. It's the right-hand panel where things get messy. I sense her stiff with shock beside me. So am I. All the factors that don't quite equal the equation you expect in the left-hand panel are there. I am there. I'm naked too. My white flesh does the service of the maid's crinoline. I'm holding that cabbage in front of me, down at belly level. It's like this huge pale blossom erupting from my stomach, like a malnourished alien.

So I'm "covered" there. I couldn't see the point of doing a full nude. I could have. I don't really care in that sense, but it would have pulled attention from Celia, and she has to be the focus. I'm also staring straight at the viewer. I couldn't work out how to paint my gaze averted, to be focussed on Celia, for example. I could have done it, with a complex system of mirrors, I suppose, but I quite liked the look of our two gazes staring out at the viewer, like a rock band or something.

Sitting on the bed where that animal should be, straps curled serpent-like down at Celia's feet, is a camera. I painted it in a fit of rage. It works. Its lens is focussed upwards, drawing the gaze towards the real centre of that right-hand panel: Celia's sex. Olympia's closing-off hand has been drawn back, up onto her hip, revealing and emphasising. That single object graphically announces its presence over her pale flesh, pale sheets, the pale vegetable, like a live animal independent from her. Across her thigh, the swarthy tube of her phallus lolls heavy and dark.

# Celia I



If ever a girl didn't need fame... Seeing myself up there, my image far away like at the end of a tunnel, spotlighted on the wall—or rather skewered like a dissected frog, pallid legs pinned apart for the voyeurs. My first reaction was to fly, get out of there fast. But life has taught me that survival depends on holding up your head and staring into the cannon mouth. I couldn't believe Joaquim had done that. He shouldn't have. I didn't realise he was so devious. Then almost at once I realised he hadn't. He would never, could never make a decision like that. I don't think he's weak, but his strength lies in such eccentric fortes. Talented, but weird. I should know—I am the Queen of Weird. I knew it wasn't Joaquim. Once I was finally able to draw my gaze away from that image, drop it down onto the swirling, smoky mass—do you call that a party?—let it slither across that crowded room... my line of sight collided with one smirking visage: Eduardo. That's when I could confirm whose idea this had been.

So I turned and left. Not the best defence, but I thought: Fuck it! I was tired, had been working all night. Sometimes you just react—whether it's in your interests or not. I sought the shelter of my room. A room of my own. You might be surprised what these four walls represent to me. They are a haven. For the first time in my life—twenty-eight years—I am living here... have not had to bring my work home... Neither am I at the mercy of my lover, partner or pimp. You cannot imagine what a freedom that represents.

I sat down at my dressing table and looked at myself in the mirror. The painting was payment, the price of my mistake. I shouldn't have jumped on Eduardo the other night. At heart I knew he wasn't one of mine, but I sensed a need and misinterpreted it. And he is quite a sex bomb. It could have been worse.

Look at these eyes—they need redoing. Strength of a man. Still needing a little liner. I was born a boy, but it takes balls to be a fairy as we used to say... God! Years have passed since I last stepped into a gay bar—I'd forgotten about that whole scene. So I've moved up in the world in some ways—toughened—a bit like pasta in the microwave if you like... one of those crusty, curly bits.

I should be inured. People see me—the Queen of Weird—as some sort of *agent provocateur*. Gabi, for example: at the end he was just a mass of accusations, spitting out exactly what had attracted him to me in the first place. So much for happily ever after. A drag queen never gets that. I've used men to get by, taken advantage of their rejection. The same way they've used me. To get their rocks off. They want to maintain the steady balance of their mundane lives. I want to pay the rent. No... There's more... I also want to feel... special... loved... like a woman. Like a real woman. Just like a human being. It's also about sex—not as a cheap thrill, but as one of our basic human needs, a guarantor of sanity.

To make it plain with an example: a friend of mine who calls herself Paloma started life as a suburban boy called Hector. Her journey from H to P in the alphabet of sex laid her flat under several well-paid surgeon's knives before she was satisfied. Knives being the theme of our evening. So Paloma and I were work colleagues for years. Unfortunately for her, her clients stopped Hectoring her as time went on.

If that was one problem, she had a larger one. Paloma spent it all on her sex change. Once done, she found she couldn't come. No orgasm, no ejaculation. Obviously. She knew that, had counted on it. What she didn't know was how tight-wired being a boy was into her deepest parts, not only in her anatomy but her psyche. A boy's need for physical ejaculation. It's sad, but she went a bit loopy.

And the crux—or crotch—of the matter is, while cumming may earn you a little more—the cream on the cookie if you like—it's getting it up that will pay your rent. My clients—all normal married men with wives and kids and prominent positions on sports bodies—pay for me to step into their cars—expensive or otherwise—where they can pull down my panties and gorge themselves on my fat cock. My dick is literally what pays my rent (when young Miró is cruel enough to insist that I do) and for dessert I fuck them up the arse. That's what allows them to return satisfied to their suburban spouses and upstanding sports associations.

I'm getting off-topic. This was about seeing myself painted up there on the wall. And why did I run? I am more or less used to exhibitionism, though never so many at one time. I think it was the coldness of that image, or maybe because I had lost control of who I was. My hard-earned identity was suddenly outside of myself, had become the property of the public domain, as if I was just another plastic copy, a Mickey or Minnie Mouse image.

So, am I a man or a girl inside? Sometimes I feel all woman. Which is why I insist on this elaborate fancy dress even if I know it doesn't fool anyone. I still find it hard to process those diverse reactions, flicked up out of the mud by the fact of a boy living as a woman. It's more than just a boy putting on a dress. It's an entire aura that envelopes me. They might know I'm a guy, and hate the fact, declare they want me dead. Yet they'll step back for me and open the door in spite of themselves.

Joaquim, Eduardo, Narcissus... Álvaro: each examples of such diverse reactions, contrasting cases of the way men display their sexuality, present their persona. I should include myself... which makes us five: five unique case studies, each worthy of hours under the psychiatrist's magnifying glass, the Freudian knife.

I had lulled myself into a false sense of calm. I was going to forego the party and slip into bed. But at that point in my reflections, the door opened and Álvaro walked in. His green eyes are so incredibly disconcerting. You never know what he is thinking.

"Hola, Celia."

I smiled in a kind of neutral way and waited for him to elaborate. We've never really had a close relationship despite living in the same house. It's odd for him to be coming into my room like this, especially with the party going on outside. He sat on the bed, looked at me.

"Hi Hon, how's the party going?"

"Alright."

Silence reigned between us and I concentrated on removing my makeup—always a good ploy when the small talk runs out.

"Do you want something, Álvaro?"

"You should know."

"No, I don't. What do you want?"

"Are you fucking Narcissus?"

"Hello?"

"Answer me."

"Baby, I have enough on my agenda after a nightful of suburban Casanovas. I don't go around stealing people's boyfriends."

"Yeah, I'm sure."

"I'm telling you the truth."

Another pause where I'm thinking that probably I need to find a way to move this scene back into more crowded climes.

"So what have you got that guys find so hot?"

"Are you jealous, Álvaro?"

"Are you afraid to answer my questions?"

"Tits, for one, Honey... And for your information I am not afraid of answering anything."

"It seems to me like you are."

"Well, that will be your personal perspective. Okay, I think I'm done here. Shall we move back to the party?"

"Not so fast."

That's when I realise Álvaro is really drunk, drunker than maybe I've ever seen him. And I thought I'd finished work for the night.

# Eduardo XVIII

One kills without thinking, I have good proof; sometimes without wanting to.

—Camilo José Cela, *La familia de Pascual Duarte*, Ediciones Destino S.A. [2008], 1942. p. 117.

I'm quite drunk now. Fra and I were dancing under the Celia painting. I was right: people thought it was a hoot. I've only glimpsed Celia once during the night—at the doorway, for a moment. She was wearing her white satin, which almost makes her look like a real woman. Her face was pale as the full moon. Then she had gone. I've got the bourbon now, grasped around her crystal neck. Good thinking: the party booze is starting to thin and my glass baby is getting envious looks from everyone. I'm not putting her down or letting her out of my sight for a minute.

So now I'm dancing alone—swaying more like. Françoise has been whisked away somewhere by Ludo. I decide to take a tour through the mansion. Outside, the small terrace is heavily incensed in a haze of hash. The neighbours upstairs must be getting properly fumigated. I see the Tarragona kid through the kitchen doors. He's kissing some other faggot. Yuck. I continue my tour.

Pushing through the jiggling bodies in the ballroom I step through the two double doors into Narcissus's bedroom—dim and red, a pseudo-artistic slideshow flickering away above the bed like a kind of amateur snuff movie. Half a dozen people draped on the big four-poster, others strewn around the floor.

Through more rooms. Where does Álvaro do his photography? I wander through more spaces, but no indication.

I sense the party's reached one of those critical moments, where it either dies or spins into another phase. I'm passing the main door when it opens. Enter: Wulf lugging a carton, grinning like a rosy cherub. Finishing work at his bar, he managed to nab an entire dozen of cheap reds. It looks like we'll be spinning for a while.

I have an urge to find Celia, laugh in her face! Conniving bitch! Filthy faggot! She got hers. What am I doing here? Where did I head off the path? These aren't my types, down among the grovelling artists, shit under their fingernails, stinking of failure. I'm going to be something! I'll be a famous writer when these *friquis* have long since rotted into the gutter. I wish I wasn't so drunk. The party looks like it's getting its second wind. I'll look for somewhere to sit down, have a rest and then go for it through the second half of the night. The night is yet young!

Bloody Celia, the bloody faggot, she bloody drew me in. Like with a lasso, knew what she was doing, drawing me in with Barbie doll, pseudo-bitch charms! That's the thing about faggots, drags, they're copies, like cartoons, so they can be brighter, shinier, almost appealing if you don't watch it. But she didn't have me fooled, the faggot. I knew what she was right from the word go.

Then, like a ghost, she glides by. Shimmering, long, with that metallic elegance. The Silver Ghost, that's what they should call her.

I plan my next move. Strategy, I need a strategy by the time I get up out of this armchair. Take it slowly, so I'll close my eyes, think about the move.

***

*Zara and I on the beach at Calafranca, down close to the water's edge. I'm holding a donut filled with cream in my hand. Zara wants it, but I'm laughing, keeping it out of her reach, licking off the cream, devouring it in small bites, which makes her livid.*

*"Mine! That's mine! Give it to me, Edu!"*

*"I don't think so. Possession is nine tenths of the law, Zara. I've got it and I think I'll keep it... Mmm... Yum, this is delicious!"*

*"Edduuu....! Give me some!"*

*But I don't and we're dancing into the waves. Surf breaks around our calves and knees. Tears stream down Zara's red face. She looks so ugly like that. Who would ever want her on TV? And it feels right and just that I should have the bun, since it was her who got to go on TV and I was the one who had to stand around and be grown up about it. Now this is for me. I'm going to have it and Zara can scream all she wants; she's not going to get any.*

*The water is swirling about my waist—up to Zara's chest—and she's blubbering so hard she can't see the waves coming, takes a mouthful of water right down into her lungs. She just screams louder. I laugh. Waves are breaking high over both of us now. We're both swimming, dog-paddling around in the waves. No idea where the cream bun went, whether I've eaten it all, or the sea washed it away. Zara's screaming, scared, far out over her depth. I'm worried too, can't see the land anywhere, no idea in which direction it might lie.*

*"You'll just have to swim harder, Zara. I can't help you. You're on your own."*

*And I turn and start swimming off. No idea where I am, but I know—because the world is round—if I just start swimming, I must come upon land soon. If I reach land, maybe I can get help; then they'll come back and save Zara. But I know I won't: won't reach land; won't find help; won't save Zara. I'm leaving her on her own to drown out of my own cowardice... because I don't want to die.*

*I keep swimming on and on. Eventually her cries and gurgling become fainter till I can no longer hear. And the sea turns calmer. It stretches out, shrugs away its rough waves, becomes flatter until it's a broad, smooth expanse of silver-grey on which I lie, limbs adrift, floating face-down, deadly still.*

# Joaquim XIX

*As the poet whispers, startled among the pines,*
*Or where the loose waterfall sings compact, or upright*
*On the crag by the leaning tower:*
*'O my vision. O send me the luck of the sailor.'*

—WH Auden, "Spain", lines 25–28, 1937.

I had sworn to her never to show this painting to anyone.

"Celia..."

I'm aware people are watching us. Not obviously, but they are aware we are the models for the work above their heads and I can feel that curious attention honing in on the two of us. Celia is absolutely still, breathlessly still.

"Celia... I didn't know... They weren't supposed to..."

But she has turned and gone. Fast and silently. I want to follow, but don't know what I could say, or do. I've betrayed her, that's clear. I gave her a promise to keep that work of ours secret and here it is displayed before everyone. Across the room someone catches my eye. They are looking at me. It's Álvaro. He smiles, then he's before me. He raises his glass.

"Congratulations, Miró. Your paintings are a success."

I hate him.

"You did this on purpose!"

"Joaquim, you can't have an exhibition of just one work. Relax. Enjoy it. People love them."

"Right."

I head through the *salon*, red lights, thumping music, jumping bodies, find myself in the kitchen. Among the clutter on the bench is a half-bottle of whiskey, the cheap, no-brand stuff. I pick an olive jar to use as a glass, pour, no ice, gulp it down, feel the fire-water burn my throat, the way it kicks up into my head, my gut wants to throw it straight back out of there. Eyes, ears roar. I take another swig, feel that floating feeling, but warm now. Miguel comes in from the patio, guns me with his honeyed eyes.

"Cool paintings, baby."

He's kissing me on the lips. I respond, kiss him back, wonder where Celia's gone. Should I look for her in her room?

"I've got a joint."

Like he ever doesn't. Miguel pulls me out of the kitchen. Outside. Next door is a tiny laundry space. We go in, scrape the door closed. He lights, tokes, passes it to me. Then we are undressing, tugging off shirts, unbuckling jeans, feeling the delicious heat of bare flesh on warm skin. Someone half-opens the door. We pull it shut, carry on. Painting stresses and the worry of having betrayed Celia fly away. We are just in the moment, licking sweat and whiskey from each other's bodies. Miguel pushes me on the shoulder, urging me down, wanting me to do what I've now done so many times before. I start to descend, feeling the lust, temptation pulling, beginnings of humiliation, guilt at giving in to what I passionately want to do. Yet it's as if at that moment I disgust myself. I can almost see Dad standing in the shadows, sneering at his anaemic son. And I'm suddenly sick of being Joaquim the push-over, the one who passively just does exactly what everyone else wants, pays their rent, lets them do whatever they want... and Dad laughs at me...

"Bastard!"

"What?"

"Nothing."

But the rage has taken hold and I push myself into Miguel, grab him by the neck and am kissing him violently. Now it's me who is forcing him down and to my shock, he relents, drops to his knees. The first time in my life, I feel his lips around me. I couldn't believe the sensation was so hot... soft, moist... And yet the strangeness of it begins to creep over me and I feel myself soften, even as Miguel seems to become obsessed, insistent with the act which, second by second I am finding increasingly embarrassing.

"Miguel..."

"Ughh. I..."

Then it's over, he's clinging to my thighs, jaggedly panting. A damp smell of almonds rising from the concrete floor. No release, I'm thrown heavily back into my own self-consciousness. I take a slug of whiskey, pass him the last of the jar.

"When are you going to paint me?"

I look at him. How would I do him? Just like that. Squatting on the concrete, one knee drawn up, the other flat against the cool floor. Naked but for that forelock. And those eyes like hives, humming into your soul like a summer meadow. Almost a kind of male Bernhardt.

"Soon as you want."

I feel frustrated, like holding on for hours to go to the toilet and then finding I'm constipated once I'm sitting on the bowl. And Dad is still unforgivingly wedged in one corner of the laundry. Dad or no Dad, the smoke picks me up.

"Come on."

I get some of my clothes on, but leave other rags there. I can get them tomorrow. Seeing, feeling, my hand on the door handle—the rusted, rattling, tin knob—I grab Miguel's hand, hear the door scrape. Smoke sends me floating out through the party, pulling Miguel behind me. We dance for a while in the salon. I can't help gazing up at Celia laying there on her chaise longue—in the Land of the Gods. I'm proud. I mean it's good! I don't care who doesn't want to believe me, it's enough to see that canvas up on the wall in front of people, know I painted it—kind of a magical impossibility because I really can't believe I'm capable of that. But I did it! I keep moving to the music and studying her. I've never really known her, still don't. As the music pumps, her phallus seems to grow, become more majestic in its dominating slackness, more threatening. It's like it's bearing down on my infidelity and broken promises, hissing:

"Yes, it's you, Joaquim, you the Fool; you, the untrustworthy one!"

I walk off the dance floor, push through bodies—Felipe runs his fingers down my chest, suggestive. I head through the sliding doors into the relative darkness of Narcissus and Álvaro's room. For the night we've converted this into a kind of *after*, a lounge space. It's lit by a couple of dim red bulbs and by Álvaro's slide show projected onto the wall. Shadowy figures sprawl across the wide double bed. The floor is empty. I stand there watching the slides. They're good, some unbelievably profound. That might be the hash, but no, I think they *are* good. The bastard.

Then one of those slides comes on and I freeze. It's like I'm caught in the freeze-frame, some kind of *Soft Cell* moment. I am. This lasts forever. The slide is of a boy, slight and adolescent-looking, with a flop of dark-hair, seated at an old-style café table. The pale, naked lines of his neck and shoulder seem to express yearning yet at the same time intense vulnerability. His face is raised in profile, large liquid eyes brimming with adoration. He could be one of El Greco's young saints if it wasn't for the impoverished thirties atmosphere of the surroundings. The next thing I see is that the object of his worship is that familiar print, *Boy and Dalmatian*. Herbert List. I realise with a shock, the worshipping boy is me. This was the first time I met them, Narcissus and Álvaro, in that café—our bar. Here I am, enlarged into grainy black and white myth across the wall above their bed.

I become aware that Álvaro is in the doorway, surrounded by a group of friends, watching the slides too. My eyes meet his and his friends turn to look at me. I feel special again, like that night. I smile, know that I'm part of a myth too, however small. People smile. I feel talented. I have *duende*.

# Eduardo XIX



—Charles Madge, "The Times" 1933.

Damn the *friquis*! I'm awake. Someone's stolen my whiskey, but I don't think I could drink anymore anyway. The party has dimmed. I get up out of the armchair and find I'm seriously unstable. I need to piss. I wonder where Françoise got to? I stumble along a darkened hallway with a vague intuition I'll find a bog at the end. Yeah. And it deserves its name. The cataracts exploding from my bladder haul me closer into reality. I can still hear music going in the ballroom. I walk back and realise I'm near Celia's room. There's a light on and the door's ajar. Does she still have my jacket? I might as well get it, no need for subterfuge now.

# Joaquim XX

*"Why does someone have to die?"*

*"Leonard..."*

*"In your book, you said someone had to die. Why?"*

*...*

*"Someone has to die in order that the rest of us
should value life more—for the contrast."*

*"And who will die?"*

*"The poet will die. The visionary."*

—Michael Cunningham/David Hare, *The Hours* [Screenplay], Universal Pictures International Ltd.

Most of the tea lights have gone out, the party is just embers. Drink bottles, plastic cups, jars, ashtrays and dirty plates cover every available surface. The projector blew its bulb. Large patches of the floor all over the house are sticky with alcohol. The dance floor looks like a battle was fought there, black scuff-marks crisscrossing the parquet. A couple I don't know are sleeping in my bed. I wander through the house. I'm drunk, stoned, tired. I want to tell the people, those few who remain, just to go away, I need to sleep. Then I remember my studio. Maybe I can sleep on the chaise longue. I head downstairs. This basement is empty. Approaching, I remember I don't have the key, but hear sounds: a kind of rhythmic grunting. This has the unreality of a cheap TV drama.

The door is unlocked, the light on. I don't want to, but I'm going to confront them. They can't use me like this! I push the door open and enter.

Paintings, studies and sketches of mine are scattered and displayed around the room. It's obvious people have come in here, turning around all the paintings, delving into my folders of drawings and leaving them scattered across the surfaces. The chaise longue is turned away, facing the wall. This is where the sounds are coming from. I am furious: people screwing in my studio! I march across the room:

"What the fuck are you doing? Get out!"

But instead of the two forms I expect, there's just one. It's Juanjo's huge bulk. Stretched out on his back, snoring like an orgiastic pig. My shout half-wakes him:

"Huh! Joaquin... Very good... paintings... some of those sketches... You should continue..."

He coughs, swallows phlegm thickly, shudders his kilos into a fresh position, not quite turning on the chaise longue. In a few minutes he is snoring again, oblivious to my indignation. I sigh. Where can I sleep? The cleaver is lying in the middle of my worktable. I'd forgotten I brought it down here. An idea for the Barcelona Gothic painting which didn't go anywhere. I painted Álvaro holding his camera instead, providing that iconic link to Celia's. I should return it to the kitchen, or Álvaro will be livid. Too big to slip in my pocket, I hold its heavy weight in my hand as I retrace my steps to the top of the house, approach Celia's door. Reconciliation. Time to make up, explain. And if things go well, maybe I can sleep with her.

Her door is slightly ajar, that rose-gold light filtering into the passageway. I hear the heavy rhythm of her sleep, that deep rise and fall of her breath—like a steam train pulling slowly out of its station. I won't wake her, just slip in beside her, hope she'll understand. I push the door, step in. Celia is half-standing, facing her bed, back to the door. Her dress is hitched around her waist, revealing curved white buttocks. She turns just her head to look at me, mid-thrust. Panting. He is lying on the bed, on his back. She is gripping his ankles, holding his legs wide as she thrusts in. She doesn't change her rhythm, just continues with that long, slow panting thrust-and-withdraw, which I mistook for her sleeping breath. Her eyes keep a fix on me. Then she half-sneers:

"What do you want, Joaquim? Do you want to watch?"

I see red.

# Eduardo XX

Mother Courage: Don't tell me peace has broken out just after I
laid in new stock?

—Bertolt Brecht, *Mother Courage and her Children*, Methuen, 1983. p. 61.

In Celia's room again. I was mad. Mad drunk. I was ready to slaughter her. I could have. Now I'm past hating her even slightly. Her problem is she's an insecure young poof who thinks his makeup makes him invincible. It doesn't. Her life is an illusion. Even I got sucked in, treating her—*him*—like a girl. We all know that now. But he couldn't play that nutcase from Tarragona. He thought Joaquin was harmless, just a good source of free drinks, a nerd who would let him off large chunks of rent, immortalise him in paint... Paint him! Who would want to paint a mouldering old tranny like that? There are some true weirdos in the world.

I was there at the doorway, deciding whether I'd step in and ask Celia—or whoever was there—for my jacket.

The light was on so I pushed the door. Inside, were three people: Celia, the Tarragona kid and Álvaro. Celia looked like he'd been in a bar brawl—his dress was kind of scrunched up around his thighs and he was panting like he'd been in a slugging match with someone. Álvaro was no better, shirtless and his belt unbuckled. No secrets here. All three turned to look at me when I pushed the door.

"What is this, the after-party?" Celia's a bitch with the tongue when he wants to be.

Joaquin turns and screams: "So you've been fucking her too?"

Instead of demonstrating the better part of valour, or whatever—only my personal opinion—Celia has to go and spell it out for him, which was his big mistake:

"Sweetie, in case you haven't figured it out, that's what they pay me for: my clients are straight men who like to suck dick and get fucked up the arse."

Then the Tarragona Kid went into action. I should have let him go for it because that bitch's last comment was so untrue! I swear, I've never seen a real loco in action before. This was priceless, an absolute lack of control. It must be fun to be mad. You can just let go, forget about the consequences.

He did this kind of magician's flourish and there he was brandishing a meat cleaver. None of us had seen it. Things got serious very fast at that point. He took a swipe at Álvaro (and I thought it was me that he hated!), then one at Celia. Missed Álvaro, but a spray of red shot out from Celia's wrist, streaking a wide, crimson arc across the wall. As he pulled his arm back for a third swipe, I lifted it from his grasp. Children should not play with matches and this was getting a bit too heated.

He turned around and shrieked, attacking me, claws scratching at my face. I was so shocked I didn't even defend myself. Before I knew it I couldn't see—just red—blood streaming into my eyes. I had only one clear thought thumping in my brain: *Don't let go of the chopper! This is your life!* But he had me on the floor and we were slipping and sliding all over the place. Celia the Trannie was screaming his silicon tits off. It was chaos. Joaquin and I were writhing on the floor, everything was slimy with blood like in some lesbian mud-wrestling contest and then... I don't know how it happened: the chopper slithered from my grasp. Or rather, more like it was *whipped* out. I swear the survival instinct is the most basic urge of the human animal. I was lying on the floor and I jumped about two metres back, to a standing position—I still have no idea how I did that. The Tarragona nutter came after me swinging. Something cool and fresh like a silk scarf whished across my thigh before I got hold of his wrists again. After that, all I was interested in doing was controlling that fuckhead, not giving him any kind of a chance for another clean sweep. But he was strong. I would never have guessed. And blood was gushing from my thigh by this time—though still no pain, strangely.

Then an odd hiatus: I'm facing the door and Narcissus appears before us in the doorway. He's gripping his silver-handled cane. It's like we're all caught in this freeze-frame, except that blood continues to pour from my leg at a rate of several pints a second. Celia is plastered flat against the wall, as pale as plaster, as pale as white satin against the blood stains. Álvaro stands still as a statue, in an almost beatific calm, his green eyes fixed on the struggle but not making a single gesture to help anyone. Then, like an apparition, Narcissus steps through the doorway; he brings his cane up in an imperious gesture and—*crack!*—whacks it down onto Joaquin's skull. The boy collapses. Narcissus steps back and exits. That's when I faint.

I woke up in the ambulance, Françoise practically growing from my side, the way she's been ever since. I've managed totally to redeem myself in her eyes. It turned out the psycho severed the femoral artery in my thigh so I had to spend several days in hospital. When I collapsed it was Celia who had the presence of mind to slap a scarf over the flow and clamp it hard until the ambulance arrived—despite blood streaming from her own arm. So I recognise I owe her my life.

Narcissus's saving act there in Celia's room was the last time anybody saw him—even Álvaro. He's gone, disappeared into the Barcelona night. Álvaro keeps waiting for him, alone in that big house, but the mansion's days are numbered. Celia got her wrist seen to at hospital, collected her stuff and moved straight into a pensión with a working friend of hers, one of the mulatas from the strip, maybe the bitch who knocked me down. With over three months' rent owing, Álvaro's facing eviction any day now. Fra says he won't talk about anything: not Narcissus leaving; or what happened in Celia's room; his future plans; or even—especially not—his feelings.

Ri came to see me. Her and Marta are still going strong:

"Marta sends her love."

"I bet."

"She says she's finally figured you out—so she can forgive you."

"I'm interested. What's her diagnosis?"

"You're a closet case."

"Sorry?"

"You are repressing subconscious urges which you came nearest to expressing through your relationship with Celia. The transvestite's pseudo-feminine aspect constituted an acceptable channel for you to empathise with another gay male in an action that was simultaneous to your attempt to exorcise the guilt you felt at not being there when your father and Zara died, through your shared communion with her."

"Right. Okay, I'll think about that."

"Yeah, I think she might be shooting a bit high too."

"It doesn't explain why things are rocking along between Fra and I, but..."

"If you're happy...?"

"We aren't crying."

"Good."

What more is there? The Psycho. I'm not going into that. Go read it in the papers. Sorry if this wasn't the tale you were expecting, but I'm sworn to stick to the truth. Once I'm over this I'm going to write that novel though. I'm going to do it. I will.

# Joaquim XXI



The end. I've been in here since soon after the party. I got the worst end of the deal. I always do. I didn't see the way the night ended obviously, but Fra says the house was swarming with cops within an hour. Ambulances came. They took Eduardo and Celia to hospital. I got taken to the police station, though I was hurt too, they didn't care. You see? I get the worst deal.

My parents came down to Barcelona, Mum looking repentant, Dad seeming more scared than anything else, a look of real affliction on his face. What had his faggot son done now? What'll they be saying at the Marc de Set? Actually, if I could change anything, I would take back the shame that I seem to have brought on my parents. In a weird way, I was just trying to make them proud, but typical Joaquim, it's all gone the wrong way. This is the influence of my number, the Fool's number, Number one.

Dad paid out more money and they finally released me on bail. I was told not to leave town. Well, I was allowed to return to Benissola, as long as I stayed with my parents. I didn't. I took a pack and went to the *bauma*, my cave. I know that was stupid. I thought nobody would find me because no one knew that place, I could live alone, away from people, forever.

I lasted three days. I got sick even before my food ran out. I think it was not being able to wash or cook properly. I literally had to crawl out of there, vomiting and with diarrhoea all the way. No one even came looking for me—which shows exactly how much they care.

But when I got back, Dad suggested we go for a drive. He brought me here. Just for a visit, he said. I'm a legal adult, they can't make me stay. But actually I quite liked it. It isn't a mental hospital, more of a rest home, though I probably should be locked up after what I did. I need a rest anyway.

My doctor's called Claudia. Claudia Gensmeier, though she's Catalan. Her Dad is Bavarian, like Jürgen, so I talk to her about separatism. We get on okay. One of the first things she asked me to do was record my entire story, all the stuff I couldn't tell anybody. She said just to let go, just go for it; it could help my trial too. That was when we thought I was going to trial, which I'm not because Celia is out of the picture and Fra convinced Eduardo to drop it. He said if I stayed in here and got help, he would leave it alone. Bastard. Things are alright for him.

I don't know if you can ever say everything that's in your mind even to a tape recorder or on paper, but, you know, I've got to say it somewhere. I imagine myself leaving this story, these records, in my *bauma*, buried in a watertight chest. Maybe someday in the

future, a hermit will find them, maybe thousands of years from now, like in Manuel de Pedrolo's *Typescript of the Second Dawn*. It could be the start of a whole new era. Yeah, right.

The other day Claudia gave me a gift. It was a tarot card: number one, the Magician. The Fool is numbered as zero or twenty-two, according to her, so I was wrong. My card is really that of the esoteric guide who helps the Fool grow up. The Magician personifies Apollo, the sun, and Thoth, and is the link between the divine and earthbound, helping us unleash our creative potential.

I can't say I believe all that, but it gives me something to go on. It's better than being a Fool, anyway.

Narcissus disappeared. That's odd, stupid even. It incriminates him when he wasn't even incriminated because nobody's going to charge him for whacking *me* over the head. Disappearing didn't change anything for me. For him, maybe it was survival. Fra wasn't quite sure what the situation with his papers was.

Celia. I know she used me. I don't care. The truth is I think I loved her, but I don't know now. I don't know anything. I want to get out of here and go back down to Barcelona and find her. But I know that would be stupid; I know she doesn't want to see me, despises me even.

Claudia says I should paint. She has no idea—I can't! Not yet. I spent hours painting Celia's room, going over the walls, the grey and gold highlights on the doorframes, making it perfect. Then there was her presence, that rose light and the rose scent with which she managed to permeate the whole space. The delicacy, the femininity, of her makeup, her perfume bottles and creams. The thousand and one details a woman surrounds herself with. But though all that is clear in my mind's eye, the strongest image that remains is that final violent one, of the blood, her blood slashing wide, scythe-like arcs across her walls—my walls. Celia's room was my best painting ever.

# Historical Note

Wherever possible I have aimed for maximum historical accuracy in this fictional narrative. Nevertheless, a couple of events require commentary.

A terrorist attack took place at the Zaragoza Civil Guard barracks, at 6.00 AM on 11 December, 1987, killing twelve people, including three women and five young girls. The attack I describe in the summer of 1981, while bearing similarities to the aforementioned event, is purely fictional. None of the characters portrayed in this book are based on real persons, living or dead, and any resemblance is coincidental. It is not my intention to show any lack of respect towards the victims or their family members, infer political blame on any political party, or distort history. My aims are purely literary.

Secondly, the International Congress of Intellectuals and Artists, which Gabriel Sabater attends in 1981, in fact took place in Valencia in June 1987—exactly 50 years after the 1937 Congreso de Escritores Antifascistas, held in Valencia during the Spanish Civil War. I made this change for literary reasons.

# Feedback

T hank you for reading *Celia's Room*. I would love to get your feedback and spread the word about my author publishing website . So if you enjoyed this book, please go right now to the site where you purchased it and post a review. Reviews are hugely helpful in allowing independent authors to earn an income. Thank you so much!

Click <u>here</u> to go to the *Celia's Room* book page at most major retailers.

# Acknowledgements

Many people have read *Celia's Room* in its progressive stages and given me valuable feedback, both supportive and critical. My first reader was Tim M., and for his enthusiastic comments, I am grateful. He succeeded in making *Celia's Room* feel like a real book for the first time. I also want to thank Evan Woodruffe and Jeanne Clayton for their effusive, thoroughly biased praise. Steve Norris's opinion has been constructive and considered while pushing me mercilessly to take a leap off the publishing cliff. Estrella Ramon, who I appreciate as a friend and admire as a writer, made incisive contributions. Thanks to my mother, Ria Booth, who took the time to go over the manuscript carefully, picking up many significant errors. Andreu León has been fantastic, providing ongoing technical and design support. I am also indebted to the many anonymous peer readers on youwriteon.com, whose frank and constructive if sometimes harsh criticism greatly improved Celia's Room. Lastly, I owe a great deal to one of Elmore Leonard's rules for writing: "Try to leave out the part that readers tend to skip."

Thanks are also due for a brilliant new cover design by Jessica Bell at Jessica Bell Design, and to Maria Friel for proofreading the entire text and offering valuable input. Finally, I am grateful to Sara Calviño Cerdeira for our enjoyable, eleventh-hour photo shoot, out of which came many amazing shots!

I want to acknowledge Manel Rives, at Unesco, as the source of the metaphor for a decapitated Spain that Felipe expresses on pages 155–6, extracted from an interview he gave in Barcelona in 2005. The Lena Boldfoot excerpt, that heads Joaquim VIII, contains valuable ideas from Nicholas Perry & Loreto Echeverría's

*Under the Heel of Mary* (Routledge: London, New York, 1998), which outlines the role of Marian Catholicism within Mola's attempted coup and Franco's ensuing military campaign and dictatorship.

Over the years my friends have had enormous patience with the daily frustration and monotonous obsession that go with writing a novel, so in addition to the above, I thank everyone unmentioned who has endured this process.

# About Kevin Booth

I began writing professionally while working in the theatre, penning English language learning plays including *100 Meters*. Nowadays I write contemporary and gay fiction, sometimes humorous, often about Barcelona and its history, such as my first novel, *Celia's Room*. I also write about the city's art and architecture in the BCN Free Art guides, such as *BCN Free Art 01: The Port and Barceloneta*. Writing as K. Eastkott I created "Seeking the Jewel Fish", an environmentally focussed ocean fantasy exploring non-Eurocentric worlds. It currently comprises *Through the Whirlpool*, *Twilight Crosser* and *Lake of Stone*. I combine writing with work as a translator and editor.

Also a keen visual artist, I work in oils and mixed media. Born in Aotearoa New Zealand, I have lived in Auckland, Sydney, Melbourne, Madrid and London, though since 1988, Barcelona is the city I call home.

If you buy my books directly from my website www.kevinboothart.com, it truly helps me to earn an income as an artist. However, you will also find links there to your favourite retailer.

Thank you for reading *Celia's Room!*

www.ingramcontent.com/pod-product-compliance
Lightning Source LLC
Chambersburg PA
CBHW020107310726
48970CB00002B/523